Cherry blossom Headshot

C S Dows

An Amesbury Press Publication

First published in 2021
This edition published in Great Britain by Amesbury Press,
Grimsby, United Kingdom

10 9 8 7 6 5 4 3 2 1

Cover illustration by KDS
Edited by Hugh Riches

ISBN: 978-1-9164738-2-9

Also by the same author from Amesbury Press:

Lokomotive

Panthea: The Darkness and the Light

Cherry blossom Headshot

Contents

Introduction to this collection   4

Cherry blossom Headshot   7

The suffering of angels   45

Negative Span Discrepancy   61

The War on Trevor   109

Computational Error   161

The World Above   179

Introduction to this collection

Short stories are hard to write. Ask any author what they think and, regardless of whether they've found success with or avoid them like the plague, they'll likely agree with the sentiment at the very least. The shorter they are in fact, the harder they are to get right; one wrong move and you've got a sequence of events at best, a vignette or isolated scene at worst. They might be self-contained, but what do they ultimately offer? I can think of a lot of ways to insult a writer, but a cry of 'so what?' as the last sentence is digested has got to be one of the worst.

Getting the balance, shape and combination of characters, events and story-space correct stretches every technical and creative muscle but, like all good exercise, needs several sessions to get the best results and makes you feel better after you've done it. I'm not for one second suggesting this collection contains stories that will improve your health – some of them are intended to do quite the opposite to be honest – but I'm hopeful at least one of them will challenge your way of looking at the world, or consider what's important in your life. Lofty aspirations I know, but it's among the reasons I've written these in the first place. That being the case, I thought I'd give you a quick historical overview of this anthology, with relevant warnings about content at the same time. I might want to shock and surprise, but I don't want to upset.

'Cherry blossom Headshot' came from an idea thrown around when I was a comic book writer in the noughties. Its basic premise of a Japanese industrialist wanting to fight back against what he sees as an erosion of his culture isn't entirely new, and we – my writing partner at the time Colin Clayton and I – never quite got the ending figured out. We had a title – 'Floating butterfly Headshot' – but not much else. The rest of it came when I revisited the idea last year, the story as finally written emerging from the introduction of the other major character Genko. Writing it from his perspective instead of the industrialist Nobunaga unlocked the story and led to its present form. I hope the solution proves entertaining.

'The suffering of angels' was one of those 'what if…' simple ideas and went from concept to final draft in two weeks. If I tell you what the 'what if…' is, it'd give the end away, so I'll keep it to myself. Originally 3000 words long, a second viewing of HBO's staggering 'Chernobyl' series expanded it to its present 5K and I'll warn you now – there's some pretty dark stuff in there, so if you're feeling a bit squeamish, I'd steer clear of that one to start with.

'Negative Span Discrepancy' is the culmination of several loosely worked up concepts that suddenly coalesced into a single, deceptively simple idea. There's quite a bit of 'hard' SF in the story but, once again, working on the central character's motivations and failings helped me enormously. She's not a terribly likeable person, I'll give you that, and her view of the world isn't one I share – but you'll hopefully understand why she does what she does, even if you don't agree with the morality of it (which happens to be non-existent).

'The War on Trevor' is by far the oldest story in this collection. Originally a standalone graphic novel written by me and Colin in the late 1990s, we got as far as commissioning an artist friend of ours to pencil, letter and ink it, and were looking to get it published with a couple of independent presses in the States we were working with at the time. Unfortunately, we got side-tracked into other (paying) projects so abandoned it. Years later, I reworked it as a radio play and sent it to the BBC Writers Room. They liked it, suggested some changes which I duly did, and resubmitted it – to be told they didn't take resubmissions which, to this day, confuses me. I always liked the idea and wanted to reformat it as a prose story, but it's only fair to give Colin credit for its original version, although there are a few changes here and there from what we created.

'Computational Error' started life as I watched a 'How

do they do that?' documentary on the manufacture of car batteries. During the ads, I got to thinking what would happen to all the old ones once we went entirely electric, then drifted into the realms of just how dangerous a disposal facility might be – particularly if it was being run entirely for personal gain (and the latest luxury car) with scant concern for health and safety. As an aside, my wife is a H&S officer, so I've overheard an awful lot about the hideous things that can go wrong within an industrial setting. I also liked the idea of calling a robot M-5 in a nod to Star Trek. It's only a short read and is intended to be science fiction comedy, so I hope it makes you laugh if that's your kind of thing. I tend to gravitate towards 'slipstream' writing, which either pleases no-one or has enough to amuse both ends of the intended spectrum, so I'm hoping for the latter rather than the former.

This brings us to the final story in the collection, the novella sized 'The World Above'. I've written fantasy before ('Panthea') but it was a YA novel and I wanted to do something a little more adult. Not that it's full of gore, sex or horror, but the basic premise is pretty grim and, fun fact, uses a concept I came up with for a Star Trek: Deep Space Nine story a long, long time ago, very early in my comic book writing career. It just goes to show you should never throw anything away when it comes to writing – notes, ideas, thoughts, characters – because they might just come in handy 26 years later. 'The World Above' is the longest text in this anthology, and while you may not be a fantasy fan, I'd urge you to read it because I think it hangs together quite well and has a cool ending. But then I would say that, because I wrote it.

Anyway, enough of this preamble. I very much hope you enjoy this collection of stories. Granted, some might appeal more than others, but if there's at least one that makes you laugh, shudder or, fingers crossed, *think* once you put it down, and don't shout 'so what?' at the front cover, then I'll be a very happy author.

Cherry blossom Headshot

Shushima Genko blinked in astonishment at the images before him. Movement, colour and drama filled his vision. Lights popped and flashed, pictures zoomed and panned then swapped from one part of his view to the other in a mesmerizing pattern. To anyone outside the room, they may have appeared wildly random and disconnected but Genko knew the truth of it. He was one of only two men in the world capable of decoding the link between the constantly shifting visual tsunami before him.

Despite his great knowledge of what had - and what was - to come, Genko still did not entirely understand how all the puzzle pieces were going to fit together. This was partly because of deliberate concealment, but mostly because the great majority of these interlocking actions would be shaped by events yet to unfold. He had learned to his cost that no plan could address every potential external influence. The smallest thing could have the biggest impact, regardless of how brilliantly the plan had been conceived and executed.

To Genko, the images were a realisation of the years he had worked for and on behalf of his employer, sitting tranquilly only a handful of metres away. The great man's dedication to the conclusion now unfolding had been absolute, powered for decades by a fathomless depth of feeling. Given his privileged position, Genko had been witness to and an integral part of the majority of the preparations but had, of course, understood there were some details that did not involve him. Regrettably, Genko was too young to have participated in this most extraordinary venture from the very start, but he prided himself on being a crucial part of the scheme, his importance rising over the last twelve years when he had been involved in virtually every step.

At first Genko had not fully understood the magnitude of the mantle inherited from his late parents. Like their son after them, they had dedicated their lives to this most honourable of men, existing only to further his glory and influence in the world. And just the same as his beloved parents, Genko had shared the passions of his employer without fully understanding the sophistication of his emotions. To do so would have been to compare himself with the mighty industrialist, an action that was as insulting as it was absurd.

The pictures on the sixty identical flat screens swapped and changed in a dazzling ballet of cuts and wipes. Under normal circumstances, Nobunaga-san would have occasionally looked up from his seiza style position and peered over the low black, heavily lacquered tenchaban table he used for his beloved tea ceremonies. From his central position in the technology-packed yet beautifully simple media room, the view of the ten-screen wide and six-screen high bank of rectangles was unrivalled, close enough for detail yet far enough away for a peripheral view of the entire wall. Under normal circumstances, the great man would have channelled his concentration into his impeccably crafted freehand comments and thoughts in his notebook, rather than dictate into a machine. But these were not normal circumstances. These were exceptional circumstances, made reality by the will of this great man.

The notebook had been dispensed with, left for posterity in the adjoining room on his specific instructions. Genko knew within its worn leather was a vital treasure of dates, times and costings, payments and receipts, names and actions. He also knew that, because of the nature and latitude of the information it contained, its true role was yet to be fulfilled. The words and numbers would be a part of that future Genko knew was yet to be written, their function changed by time from recording that which had been, to shaping that which was yet to come.

Kneeling with ramrod-straight back despite his seventy-eight years, his employer watched the expansive screen, his gaze flicking from one side to the other, from the lowest row to the top, his grey-flecked, bespectacled eyes in constant motion. Not once did he look down to the large tablet resting on his lap, nor to his perfectly manicured fingernails which tapped constantly on the control app glowing beneath the device's smooth glass surface. This ability to control so much with such little effort was, like so many things to Genko, impressive.

The electronic images on the screens danced to the tune created by the venerated man, a sweep of a fingertip freezing certain captions here, the flick of a thumb enlarging others there, before sending them to a cluster of screens to provide greater detail or sweep them aside entirely. Had the sound been active, the cacophony of reporters' voices, anchor-persons' analyses and interviewees' excitable opinions would have been unbearable in the perfectly square, low-ceilinged room. Other than the whisper of the air conditioning set into the pure white ceiling tiles and the faint rumble of traffic and honking horns from the congested Kyoto streets, all Genko could hear was the steady breathing of his beloved employer, and the rhythmic thumping of his own pulse inside his ears.

With a flick of his index finger, the white-haired man sent the image of an immaculately presented NHK reporter over to the central three by two monitors. Unusually, the young woman looked flustered. Genko found it surprising, distasteful even, from this most trusted of broadcasters. NHK had fallen in his opinion, and that of Nobunaga-san. The previous year their idiot Prime Minister had made the crass attempt to influence this once revered institution's reporting by removing several highly respected - and much older - journalists. Genko had nothing personal against the youthful influx of reporters. They had tried their best to uphold the traditions of the network, though he was surprised the institution was still held in such regard by most of the country.

The youth audience, of course, had rejected what they saw as a crass attempt to appeal to them. They had turned their back on what they saw as yet another stuffy Japanese establishment clumsily attempting to modernise, choosing instead to flood their empty minds with all manner of imported social media. Nobunaga-san had stated on several occasions that both the lost audience and the broadcaster were ignorant of a culture they did not deserve or wish to embrace. Some might have said it unfair to include the new NHK staffers in this group but, despite their efforts to maintain standards, Genko agreed that most of the new reporters were yet another aspect of their society's continual erosion. This present display of on-screen emotion by the investigative reporter - or, to be more accurate, this display of trying not to be emotional - was a clearer sign of decline than her chattering words.

Finishing her remarks to camera, the dark-haired woman respectfully offered her microphone to the ageing Chief of Kyoto Prefectural Police who, even more surprisingly, looked shaken at the information rapidly emerging into the feeble light of that January morning. Genko had met the Chief several times, and knew the situation unravelling before him and the rest of the Prefecture would be extremely difficult for him to comprehend.

With the harassed-looking Chief speaking to the off-camera reporter, Genko scrutinised the graphics, statistics, dates and photographs disappearing then reappearing across the central block of monitor screens. While he was standing a respectful distance behind Nobunaga-san and against the door leading into the living area, he could still see everything in perfect detail thanks to the high resolution of the screens and the quality of the broadcast image, now NHK's only saving grace. A series of arrows exploded out from animated maps of Kyoto, then Honshu, into the rest of the world, terminating in glowing red dots settling mostly on the West and East Coasts of the United States. The brown bamboo of the viewing room's wall panels did their best to soak up the burst of scarlet colour from the television wall, and the softly rear-lit squares of white paper tiles set into the panels pulsed in time with the on-screen animations.

Genko nodded as he digested the torrent of information. Much of what was being reported was based on fact, some of it on conjecture, but the overall story being told was deeply disturbing - and that to a man who knew much of the detail of it. Now the graphics and statistics were replaced by something quite different, images that, when they had first flashed across the world two years previously, had been as unexpected and unnerving as they were fascinating and dreadful. Images of women and men that, unbeknown to them, had become the living embodiment of what the motionless, impassive white-haired man had willed into existence, the first stage in proving a point that so desperately had to be made.

Hurriedly recalled from fresh archives, the studio-based pristine anchor-persons looked earnestly to their teleprompts, reminding the masses of what they could not have forgotten; photographs of Western women and men, mostly American, showing how they looked before - and after - their radical transformations. With polite warnings that some viewers may find the following scenes unsettling, the photographs changed to footage of pre- and post-operative patients, their normal features now distorted beyond recognition. Eyes made huge and oval, mouths reduced to a tiny slit, the jaw line hewn into a triangle, the heights of foreheads, noses and chins disproportionate to nature.

And then there was the hair; it seemed to float, to have a life of its own which indeed it did thanks to the revolutionary DNA treatment and enhanced surgical techniques developed on the precise directions of the great man. The procedure had first been embraced by Western women, girls mostly, old enough legally to do what they wanted with their bodies yet young enough not fully to comprehend the long-term implications of their actions. If anything, the speed at which the surgery had been adopted had surprised both Genko and his esteemed employer; Nobunaga-san had planned for a relatively limited but influential interest, such was the radical effect it had on the body, and had often said that only a handful of key 'influencers' and 'celebrities' were needed to make his point. What happened next was beyond the man's greatest expectations. The popularity caused enormous extra costs, but he was happy to meet them.

In the first year, demand for the transformative operations quadrupled. In addition to women, an increasing number of men, straight and gay and transgender, drawn to the asexual appeal of the bodies and personae they could adopt, undertook the excruciatingly painful procedure. And what did they get for their agony? The opportunity to become living embodiments of Manga characters, a cross between the young teenage shojo style and older josei styles, their altered features capable only of the expressions available to those created by the brushes and pens of Manga-ka.

Not blind to potentially crippling lawsuits, Genko had developed considerable pre-operative counselling and discussion, with every agreement legally binding and entirely attributed to the free will of the patient. The various surgical teams continuously pressed home the facts, that while the healing process would be accelerated by experimental drugs to promote their miraculous recovery, their range of movements would be changed forever by bone lengthening, bone shortening and skin grafts. Some reconsidered but, astonishingly to Genko at least, most continued with even greater enthusiasm.

The news of these transformations first broke across social media, exactly as the great man had planned, with the traditional world news networks typically following behind. At first the original batch of Manga o jitsugen - 'Manga made into reality' - would not give details of how they had become what they had become. They had signed punitive non-disclosure agreements which the great man knew would create an air of mystery and generate much greater interest than had the early adopters been allowed to discuss their grotesque new look. For several weeks the world thought it was a joke, some coordinated effort by second-rate bloggers trying to improve their ratings, but then the news of the Geka-tekihenka clinics in major Western cities was revealed to be the source of these months-long surgeries and the story took on the momentum of a juggernaut. Rarely had Genko seen Nobunaga-san smile so often when, in this very same room, he would catch up with reports of the phenomenon before breakfast.

Confirmation the surgery was real led to reaction in the West splitting into three camps. There were those who thought it obscene, immoral and little more than exploitation of weak-minded or mentally unstable individuals desperate to make some form of statement about their characters (or lack of). A significant number of academics and scientists pressed for the extraordinary medical advances behind the procedures to be made public to benefit surgery across the world. And then, gloriously, there were those who wanted to join the freak show.

Perhaps the deciding factor for those wishing to undertake the surgery was the fact that, while it was incalculably expensive, it had been offered for free. Nobunaga-san's masterstroke avoided a raft of consumer and client law, although many other legal minefields had been traversed by Genko as part of his part in the great scheme. Despite several injunctions and attempts to block the clinics' operations across the world, other than a handful vandalised or destroyed by local vigilantes, most were reluctantly allowed to operate within various Western clinical and ethical frameworks. The only aspect of his involvement Genko regretted were the anguished pleas of horrified parents publicly trying to stop their offspring from joining the worldwide circus. As for their misguided children intent on reshaping themselves, he had no sympathy at all.

Images of grossly distorted faces and figures blended into each other in a series of ghoulish montages. Library footage and statistics continued the narrative across the screens, showing how the early adopters were all die-hard lovers of Manga. Genko knew the type; they would dress up at comic conventions and wear painful prosthetic teeth and sclera lenses, ignoring potential damage to their eyesight so they could play out their fantasies for a weekend. Psychologists queued to give their opinions on the phenomenon; some of the more respected were wheeled out once again, their archived interviews stating the various reasons they felt that individuals might do such a drastic thing to themselves. The theories ranged from extreme expressions of body dysmorphia to Munchausen syndrome. Some therapists suggested the surgery offered a lifetime of others looking at them, the freedom of expression to stand out in a crowd they craved above all else.

To Genko at least, this seemed an unconvincing argument. The original MoJees - a name that had quickly surfaced on social media and subsequently been adopted with great affection by the transformed - had jumped at the chance of looking like their favourite heroic figures and immediately banded together to share their experiences and generate even greater impact and shock on their millions of subscribers. This did not suggest to Genko a desire to be different, but to belong to something, to be a part of an exclusive group.

However, as he continued to watch the screens, Genko tired of guessing their motivations. They were all stupid and weak-minded. How else could one explain why they disregarded the unseen, drastic biological changes that accompanied the exterior modifications; stomachs so small they would barely take one tenth of a normal person's food, a lifetime of drugs to boost the immune system, all things that, written down for most rational people and clearly presented during the pre-op counselling, would be reason enough not to commit. Genko shook his head. He still could not believe someone would be so stupid, regardless of how poorly they might view themselves.

The information on the screens changed. Dates advanced on captions, showing how the second wave of interest had broken, much bigger this time thanks to an unexpectedly large ripple effect. Those who saw the attention the MoJees were getting wanted some of the action and the waiting lists had only just begun to subside from the original patients when Westerners who wanted 'the look' for themselves pushed the clinics to their operational limits. And then, despite the comic book proportions, an undeniably beautiful MoJee appeared on the screen, sending Genko's thoughts in an unwelcome direction.

Watching her laugh in her limited way and the sparkling light in her grossly distorted eyes, he fleetingly wondered what his fashion-conscious sister would have made of it all. Angrily, he dismissed the question with a shake of the head and focused on the information before him.

The reaction to the MoJees in Japan had been one of astonishment followed by officially expressed embarrassment and a deep mistrust of whichever malignant organisation was responsible for it. After enormous global payoffs and 'convincing' of certain people, Nobunaga-san's mighty industrial empire's link with the phenomena had been hidden. Even so, and entirely by his devising, some information had to be leaked out. Once vague details began to emerge of Japanese involvement, parliament urgently debated the situation and demanded further inquiry. Even Nobunaga-san's influence did not extend to the entire Japanese Diet, which quickly voted to block any clinic in any part of the country; an irony because it had never been the great man's plan to provide this service in Japan. Most importantly, Nobunaga-san's identity as chief orchestrator of the repellent scheme had remained hidden, and those who suspected his involvement were dealt with in a variety of ways. The world would learn the truth soon enough, but only on his terms.

If the rumours surrounding the Emperor's support for the Diet's decision had disappointed Nobunaga-san, the steady stream of Japanese nationals who had left their country to seek the surgery abroad had enraged him. Why, the great man had once railed, would Japanese nationals, Japanese, blessed to be born in the greatest country on Earth, want to distort those gifts bestowed upon them by the gods? What fundamental flaw in their character would lead to that? And yet, after calming his rage, both he and Genko had concluded it only reinforced Nobunaga-san's beliefs. Talk about a culture that had lost its identity.

Genko watched as such an individual talked animatedly on several of the television screens. This character had become quite the outspoken critic of the government and, even now, as her recorded interview complained of everything from human rights violations to preventing the natural development of Japanese culture, Genko observed a change in the great man's posture. Of all the unpleasantness that had been shown in the last few minutes, this was clearly the most unwelcome image broadcast before him. With a flick of the finger, the girl - who had died in an unexplained accident shortly after her five minutes of fame - was sent to a solitary corner and replaced by a dreadfully disfigured young man who had attempted to get the same MoJee look in a Moscow backstreet surgery. The results had not been pleasant.

Of course, the activist had been murdered, like so many others who threatened this great statement. There was no question Nobunaga-san could be callous, even to those who devoted their lives to him, but this was to be expected from such a great man. Of the very few colleagues Genko worked closely with, a couple had tentatively ventured how hard he was worked, even by Japanese standards. This meant nothing to Genko and he had dismissed it with harsh words, making it clear it was of nobody else's concern, no matter how good their intentions. With all his family gone, all Genko had in life was work. In fact, with the death of his parents, Nobunaga-san had increased his workload and his station in the conglomerate. The elevated duties and additional pressure had kept his mind occupied and focussed. Yes, they had and continued to be exhausting, particularly over the last year, but his toil had been of peculiar comfort, too. It had not been without variety or, to him at least, fascination.

Following his legal role, much of his recent time had been devoted to examining media trends, tracking the growth of the MoJees' influence and pursuing the more resourceful and inventive journalists in their quest to discover who was responsible for the clinics. One individual, linked to a known detractor of Nobunaga-san, had got very close on a couple of occasions, but those reports had been based far more on conjecture than fact. Genko and his team had successfully boxed in and contained their accusations. Along with the pressure his esteemed employer was able to bear on many media outlets, the sanitised reports had amounted to little more than carefully suggesting the creation of the MoJees was 'some kind of hideous, immoral and unethical protest against the West's erosion of Japanese culture' without giving any names. Genko knew if the accusations had been more precise, the copy would never have made it to the public, either in print or digitally, and the reporter would not have made it to work the following day. Or any other day after that.

Genko's eyes were drawn back to the kneeling figure, resplendent in pure white silk. Within the next few hours, Nobunaga-san would be confirmed as the creator of this counterattack on the West. In fact, the endgame of the great man's audacious plan depended entirely on the revelation. Despite Nobunaga-san's xenophobia, there was no denying he understood the gaijin deeply, their psyche, their shallowness. He often referred to Westerners as 'the magpies' in that they were always drawn to something shiny and new, but their attention span was short. This was why so many Westerners had little or no cultural foundation on which to maintain and truly develop their societies. Some of the older European countries clung to past glories, masquerading them as rich heritages and ancient history. It was ironic that the erosion of such once-great empires as the British and French were all the warning signs Japan needed to see how might and influence could so easily slip into weakness and irrelevance.

The West, particularly the Americans, had no claim or right to permanence. The damage they had caused to the Japanese way of life since the war was, to Nobunaga-san, humiliation by inferiors. Genko knew his esteemed employer was infuriated by the suggestion that Westernisation was natural. Nobunuga-san was intractably convinced that everything had been calculated to bring their beloved nation down and was a deliberate crime. His offensive had begun with his first laboratory in the late 1980's. It had been a long, secret counterattack, and Genko felt tremendous excitement in knowing the killing blow – quite literally - was near. As his eyes were drawn back to the grossly distorted features of a thousand MoJees smiling painfully to camera in a hideous group photograph, he allowed himself a smile.

"Excellent."

The word hung in the quietly recycled air. Sitting back on his haunches with a rustle of heavy silk, Nobunaga-san's head snapped to the screen at the very top left and, with a flurry of hand movements over the tablet, the Chief of Police was replaced by breaking news from Kyoto University's Innovation Hub. Harsh lights shone into the face of a lab-coated, middle-aged woman as she attempted to answer questions being hurled at her from several unseen reporters, their microphones surrounding her in a row of bobbing black foam cones. While the security doors behind her were firmly closed, it was obvious there was considerable activity going on in the unseen laboratory. Silhouettes moved rapidly behind the heavily frosted windowpanes, a suggestion of urgency bordering on panic. Genko recognised the names flashing up on the caption strip beneath the irritated scientist. As she pushed back silver-grey hair from her eyes and attempted to keep her patience, Japan's leading biomedical companies were named one after another, all owned by the man watching the drama unfold as avidly as Genko.

"Is everything in order, kaishakunin?"

Genko started despite himself. The voice was low and calm, as direct and clear as the thinking that had made him such an enormous success in so many different fields. Genko had seen some of the greatest industrialists, economists, scientists all reduced to emotional rubble by Nobunaga-san's precise arguments. The man was a master of the spoken and written word, wielding it as expertly as he did the ancient weapons he revered. Genko had accompanied him on many oversees visits over the last couple of decades, gently reminding him - as instructed, of course - discretely to indicate when his usually impassive face betrayed the disgust he felt travelling outside his beloved homeland. Nobunaga-san had given Genko's family an excellent education, allowing all of them to speak on behalf of their employer in a dozen languages, thus allowing a buffer to protect him from distasteful interaction with the inferior.

Part of the early 'divine mission', the precursor to Nobunaga-san's current great plan to combat the destruction of Japanese society, had been the location and repatriation of items of great cultural and historical value. Some had been modest, mere scraps of parchment or cloth, others of inestimable value that had somehow 'made their way' abroad, an insulting euphemism for 'stolen'.

Genko's part in the mission had grown with his confidence and competence and, on several occasions, his honoured parents had pointed out their master was grooming him for greater things. For the endless hours he had dedicated to study and work, Genko had indeed been rewarded handsomely, but that was not the most important consideration. He was far prouder that, at the relatively young age of forty-seven, he had developed diplomatic and legal skills that would put any senior government advisor to shame. In the coming days and weeks, these abilities would be called upon as never before. Little wonder he was on edge.

Despite the heightened expectations, it had not been the tone of Nobunaga-san's voice that made him jump. Hearing himself referred to as kaishakunin was thrilling, despite the enormous accountability that came with the title. To be nominated was an honour in itself, but there was more to it than that. To Genko, it suggested their relationship had transcended servitude into something approaching friendship. If only his father and mother were alive to see how their son had risen in the eyes of the House they had so proudly served. Looking down to the intricately woven Mon on his Kuro Mon-tsuki Haori, the pounding in his ears increased yet further with excitement. This crest on his ceremonial kimono jacket meant far more to him than a symbol of the great man's station in Japanese society; it had become a part Genko's identity, more so since he and his sister had secretly been tattooed with the exact same design when they were teenagers.

Being the wayward spirit she was, Cho had defiantly shown it to their mother after a day of constant arguing between the two headstrong women over his sister's commitment to the House of Nobunaga. Outspoken and wilful she may have been, but Genko knew that, in her own way, she would do anything for the old man who she looked upon as the grandfather she had never known. On seeing the Mon proudly displayed on her upper shoulder, their parents had been furious. To diffuse the situation Genko had revealed his, pulling back his shirt to reveal the still-covered design above his heart. The tactic only made things worse; both parents accused their children of becoming Yakuza. Cho had laughed at the suggestion of criminality and the feud had bubbled along for days until, in an act of unusual contrition by his sister, she had agreed to keep it covered rather than removed.

The whole episode had worried Genko so much he had hidden the tattoo from his employer lest he react the same way. For years he succeeded until the fateful occasion when they had travelled to the West Coast of America to investigate an alleged eighth century Amakuni sword, suggested to be older than the legendary Kogarasu Maru weapon held in the Japanese Imperial Collection. Genko had been injured during an abortive kidnap attempt on Nobunaga-san, his naked chest briefly revealed when the emergency services had stitched the wounds caused during the defence of his employer. If the great man had seen the symbol, he had made no comment to this very day.

Instead, Nobunaga-san had remained stony-faced while the detectives questioned him, his fury simmering at the affront and for falling for such a ridiculously simple trap. On their silent journey back to Japan, both he and Genko knew that, had the weapon existed and had Genko been wielding it, the attackers would have been slain in seconds.

Genko's heart sank again. If only his beloved sister had been here to witness her brother's nomination of kaishakunin. Despite her embracing many Western fads and traits, she would have quietly understood the significance. Fighting against rising emotion, he stiffened his back and set his jaw firm. With everything happening literally before his eyes, and with the final act for his master yet to be performed, thoughts of Cho were an emotional weight he could not afford. He had a job to do and could not be distracted from it. Clearing his throat gently, Genko took a step forward and bowed, unseen.

"I have but one final preparation to make, Nobunaga-san. I shall return with pen and parchment for your jisei."

The white-haired man nodded once, his eyes still fixed to the screens as the captions and images continued to flash before him. The news story was developing apace; while the scientist frantically responded as best she could to the bustling reporters, she glanced back at the sound of muffled bangs from behind the laboratory doors. Seconds later, several television screens cut to various exteriors of Kyoto's busy streets. One agitated male reporter from a lesser network pointed behind him into the near distance, past the high-rise blocks flanking the unusually still traffic towards a line of flashing police lights. A series of roadblocks was being constructed at the main intersections of Gojo dori Street and Onmaedori Street, with others to follow to the south of the Kyoto Research Park.

Given the locations of the other outside reports, the entire KRP was being encircled by a rapidly developing cordon, with no vehicles or pedestrians allowed in or out of the West and East campuses of the sprawling facility. If this disturbance to the normal order of city life was not unusual enough, the familiar Kyoto Municipal Subway map started to appear behind anchor persons on other screens. They announced that, without any explanation from the authorities, all subway trains running south from Karasuma Oike Station had been suspended until further notice.

This enormous disruption had, of course, been predicted by Nobunaga-san.

Turning, Genko slid the narrow bamboo door on which he had been leaning to the side and strolled from the viewing room into the adjoining private living room, his sandaled feet rustling over the straw mats on the floor. Despite its spartan furnishings, the gently lit apartment had a feeling of homeliness, reinforced by the faint smell of the motsunabe stew his esteemed employer had eaten less than an hour before. Only the odour lingered; Genko had removed the single pot from the top of the sunken table set in the centre of the room, along with the bowl that had contained Nobunaga-san's favourite, last meal. It would have been uncouth to leave the remains of food exposed in such a way, so Genko had taken the cast iron pot and simple wooden bowl into the small kitchen behind a sliding panel set into the far wall. He was unconcerned about the smell from the food. The unseen air extraction system hidden in the traditional wooden beams above his head had dissipated it to little more than a hint, and was busily doing its normal job of removing the smoke from the fire beneath the central irori table. Untended, its flames would soon be extinguished, along with the life of his venerated master.

Something seized Genko's chest, unseen and powerful. He stared for long seconds at the black lacquered writing desk tucked into the far corner of the room, its glossy surfaces reflecting the orange and yellow of the low fire. Taking a breath, he turned and walked over to the huge, heavily tinted triple-glazed picture window and tried to regain control of his ragged breath. Inhaling deeply, he looked out over the roofs atop the boxy glass and steel buildings of the KRP and regarded the sprawling Kyoto conurbation to the North. He needed to get things into perspective, to understand how vital it was he retained his composure and, for that matter, nerve. The view before him was a perfect reminder of the man he served, the rain-heavy black clouds forming over the cityscape a perfect visual analogy of his all-encompassing power. Beneath them, everyone could get on with their lives thanks to his benevolence, and Genko was reminded of his place in the universe.

Genko considered the enormous influence Nobunaga-san held over the city. Spread out before him, from the Park below to various municipal buildings in the distance, were living embodiments of the man's will, perfect examples of thoughts becoming things. Of course,

Nobunaga-san had not built it all with his own hands. Much of it had been achieved via the myriad favours owed him by officials whose positions did not match their ability to act discretely, along with the great man's colossal business acumen and ruthlessness. The headquarters of NKC, in which Genko stood, were also a powerful reminder of the enormous honour that had been bestowed upon him. Much like the reputation and influence of Nobunaga-san, it towered over every building in the Kyoto Research Park and almost every other structure for several miles around.

Genko's father had once confided in his son that, had it not been for the massive financial backing Nobunaga-san had provided, entirely secretly, to the Kyoto Prefecture in the mid 1980's, the high-tech business incubation park would never have been built, or at least not to the scale it currently enjoyed. Nobunaga-san's headquarters had been one of the last to be constructed - and not without considerable controversy at the time.

The building looked to most like a homage to one of the greatest exporters and ambassadors for all that was Japanese. In fact, it was an early, uncharacteristically subtle protest against the dangers facing Japanese culture. It had been provocatively and deliberately designed to mirror the brutalist concrete cube of the Nintendo Development Office less than an hour's walk to the south, but on a much bigger scale. According to Genko's late father, as far as Nobunaga-san was concerned, old man Yamauchi had betrayed his heritage when he incorporated Disney characters on his playing cards - and that was in the fifties. Many admired Yamauchi's shrewd business move, by one of Nintendo's most honoured founding fathers, because it effectively built the cornerstones for the global entertainment titan the company had become. Nobunaga-san was not one of those devotees.

Eschewing an enlarged version of Kyoto's famous Nanzen-ji Temple because it was perhaps too obvious a statement of cultural promotion at a time when 'all things modern' were appearing all over Japan, Nobunaga-san's structure, at three times the size of the truly ugly Nintendo building, featured deliberately ornate Toji-styled towers at each roof corner. This was his way of infuriating many of his critics by smashing together the utilitarian with tourist postcard nonsense. Nobunaga-san detested his own creation but, as he once calmly explained to a nervous architectural journalist, the great man could not actually see the dreadful façade when he was inside looking out.

Genko also appreciated the huge pleasure Nobunaga-san derived from knowing every aspect of the gaudy towers that faced the Nintendo building were painted black. While he could not care less whether anyone actually noticed this insult, had the colour scheme been queried, Nobunaga-san would have happily repeated the mantra that had made him so detested by the youth of Japan and those looking to embrace cultures outside their own - that Westernisation of the Japanese culture was a choice, not an inevitability. Hence, black walls faced Nintendo's building to wish upon it nothing but bad luck for the deliberate asset stripping and bastardisation of their precious cultural legacy.

Breathing in deeply, Genko's resolve returned. Turning towards the desk, Genko paused, his eye drawn to a burst of red flashing lights through the huge window at street level a couple of blocks away to the right. Knowing Kyoto as he did, he realised it would be the same police cars he had just seen on the news report, taking up position at the busy intersections leading to the KRP. The scarlet lights bounced off the roads, now slick from the rain that had begun to fall, and reflected in the windows of the emptying streets. Small black dots were now running away from the Park towards the cordons, probably having watched the unfolding events on their own devices and wishing to be far away from whatever dreadful disaster was about to unfold. This was not without good reason; many conspiracy theories surrounded some of the more avant-garde businesses that had taken residence on the business park. Most of them were nonsense, but Genko knew several low-key companies set up by Nobunaga-san had been dedicated to a variety of unusual and highly experimental pursuits.

Had the truth about their work been known, it would have surpassed the wildest guesswork and excused the rapid exodus taking place on the streets before him. As it happened, in line with the plan, some information would become public. The harassed scientist on the television screens, for instance, worked for a key subsidiary of NKC, the link between Nobunaga-san and the nearby Kyoto University Innovation Hub now besieged by the media. Genko wondered if she had any knowledge of the part she may have played - knowingly or otherwise - in Nobunaga-san's rapidly maturing strategy. Either way, it did not matter.

Genko sighed and stepped back from the window. Partially backlit by the fire dying quietly beneath the irori table, he caught his reflection, made brighter by the granite clouds lying low over Kyoto's cityscape. He stared into his own ghostly reflection, past the neatly trimmed beard and high forehead into his deep brown eyes. He had thought himself prepared for this moment. But was he? Yes. He was ready. He would not succumb to feelings of regret and sadness. Thoughts of Cho had nearly broken his resolve, but his fortitude and focus were, he assumed, the main reasons the great man had chosen him as his deputy and, ultimately, executioner.

With that realisation, pride in his newly promoted function swept through him. He hooked his thumbs into his hakama waistband and stood proudly admiring his clothing. More red lights blinked on the junction to the far left, more dots fled towards them. The sheer scale of the plan in glorious, cinematic motion threatened to overwhelm him, but he dragged his thoughts back to the here and now, into this penthouse atop the enormous building. Whoever eventually arrived to witness the aftermath of what was to come might find his attire preposterously old-fashioned but, within the confines of Nobunaga-san's penthouse, this most formal of kimonos was the measure of the day. Genko never had any issue with it. Admittedly, he had a sneaking admiration for the tailored Paul Smith suits he and his esteemed employer would, at a push, wear to visit other parts of the Kyoto Research Park or to venture oversees, but the sheer luxury and comfort of the heavy silk was, to Genko, entirely appropriate. The same might not be said of the great plan's conclusion.

Some might claim the event to come was no more than a theatrical stunt, an anachronistic embarrassment not seen since the suicide of the once-respected Japanese author Yukio Mishima in 1970. However the authorities dealt with Genko after he killed Nobunaga-san, it would be down to him to ensure the great man's funshi, the version of seppuku that expresses indignation, was not written off as the same misguided attempt to achieve a futile goal. Despite his great artistry, Mishima and his Tatenokai group had always been idealistic and unrealistic.

It was true both the writer and Nobunaga-san lamented the Westernisation of their cultures and erosion of their traditions, but the author's ultra-right-wing thinking had distorted his understanding of what could reasonably be accomplished. Storming the Japanese Self-Defense Force's Tokyo headquarters with a handful of men, taking a senior General hostage then spouting nationalistic drivel to a thousand hastily assembled - and understandably hostile - troops was always doomed to failure, not because of Mishima's method, but because of the message he tried to convey. This included the author's ritual suicide, which entirely failed to suggest nobility. Nobunaga-san's death, while on the face of it identical, would be entirely different.

The great man did not want a return to the old ways of

bushido, of feudal lords and in-fighting; there were some Japanese traditions he had little time for. No. Nobunaga-san wanted to show Japan - and the world - what he, and his beloved country, were truly capable of.

Others would question the ridiculous drama of Nobunaga-san's death and revile him for escaping his guilt over the unbelievable crimes that were yet to be perpetrated. Genko hoped that, in the fullness of time, many would at least understand Nobunaga-san's actions and appreciate they were not borne from a desire for drama or an expression of cowardice. He hoped they would see, just as he did, the absolute truth of conviction secured to a simple act of logic. To protect his colossal fortune and be able to unleash it to its full effect, Nobunaga-san had tied the great majority of his assets into various trusts around the world, trusts that would only become liquid on his death.

Seppuku had been abandoned since the 1870s so anyone involved in the act – those who wished to die and those they nominated to assist in the killing - were equally criminal under Japanese law. The suicide ritual would be incomplete without an assistant, a second, to wield the final blow and ensure the head was completely severed. Besides, without a second, the great man would be guilty of suicide and the trusts would not pay out. However, if Genko delivered the killing blow, he would be found guilty of murder by request.

The precedent for his sentence was slim. One of the survivors of Mishima's Tatenokai, Koga, had received a four-year sentence of penal servitude, a relatively light sentence considering the crime, but if even this tentative guide was accurate, Genko was perfectly willing to serve this time. Indeed, Koga had been released early due to his good behaviour. While Genko had no desire to spend the rest of his life behind bars, the longer he stayed in prison, the better. After all, enough time had to pass for the various genetic 'hidden surprises' built into the MoJee biotechnological methods to infiltrate mainstream medicine. Genko's connection with these future catastrophic events would never be proven; he would be a free man, able to blame it entirely on his long-dead employer, whose 'murder' had triggered the financing of his post-mortem devastation. If questioned, Genko would refer to the words he knew formed the epilogue to Nobunuga-san's notebook; interfere with our society at your peril. We are far, far cleverer than you.

The time for reflection was over. Nobunaga-san was awaiting him in the viewing room, changed and ready in the all-white kimono he would wear for the upcoming ritual. Turning from the window, Genko strode over to the area that had been cleared for the ceremony. Crouching, he inspected the small wooden table on which rested the tantō short sword, the flat of its gleaming blade laid across the diagonal width of the podium. There was no need to check its readiness; Genko's expertise with traditional Japanese weapons included their honing and preparation, so he knew its medieval blade, cleaned and sharpened to a white-silver brilliance, was razor sharp. The white linen cloth wrapped around it was more for show than function. Genko felt certain Nobunaga-san's grip would remain firm as he thrust the blade into his abdomen, just as he was sure he would fully complete the left to right horizontal cut across his belly.

Genko glanced at the three-tier sword rack resting against the nearest wall. The top level was empty, having held the tantō until an hour ago. Below it was the larger wakizashi sword, still in its scarlet sword bag. Underneath this sat Genko's ancient katana, bag removed, its perfectly curved form protected by its simple wooden shirasaya scabbard. It would be unsheathed only at the moment the tantō blade penetrated his esteemed employer's body. Nobunaga-san would not feel the incandescent burn of the steel slicing through his stomach, nor see his blood spread over his kimono like the opening of blossoms on a cherry tree. Genko would ensure the great man did not suffer. Nobunaga-san might have protested a few seconds of agony meant nothing compared to the importance of his death in triggering the final stage of his revenge on the Western world, but his rapid and painless demise was Genko's single most important objective.

Rising from his inspection of the short blade, Genko walked past the perfectly arranged low cushions surrounding the sunken table, stood before the writing desk and opened the large drawer set beneath the highly polished ebony surface on which Nobunaga-san's notebook rested. From the draw he took a single sheet of hand-made washi paper and a yatate writing set. Dismissing more time-consuming reminiscence over the conversations he would miss in this serene room, he slid the draw shut and adjusted the notebook so its lowest edge lined up perfectly with the desk. Then he walked back over to the viewing room.

Sliding the door to the living area closed, he tucked the writing set into the folds of his Haori jacket, approached Nobunaga-san with silent steps, bowed, then gently placed the rectangle of parchment onto the low table before him. Genko then withdrew the long, bronze pipe-shaped writing set, placed it to the left of the parchment so as not to obscure the view of the screens and flipped open the lid covering the ink bowl. He would leave his esteemed employer to withdraw the brush within the handle and add water from a small pitcher on the table to the ready-ground ink within the bowl. It was not proper for Genko to witness the writing of his master's death poem.

Walking backwards with head bowed, Genko's deference went unseen as his master continued to absorb all that was happening on the screen wall, his hands palm-down either side of the parchment that was awaiting his final words. Genko was still looking to the polished wooden floor when a gentle, insistent beep issued from a glass panel set into one of the wall panels to his right. He turned to it with a swish of his kimono tails, touching the screen lightly to activate it. The NKC logo was immediately replaced by an immaculately presented young woman, her pale face creased with a look of concern. Genko thumbed the speaker icon and nodded to the woman, giving her permission to continue.

"Shushima-san, I have the Chief of Kyoto Prefectural Police on the landline for Nobunaga-san."

The woman's voice was laden with urgency and fear. Clearly, she had been watching some of the broadcasts absorbed with such fascination by their esteemed employer. Equally clearly, she knew something was very, very wrong.

"Please inform the Chief Nobunaga-san is unable to talk with him at this time."

The woman's rosebud mouth opened slightly, then closed when she considered her response might not have been appropriate. Even down to the staff working on the reception desk, Nobunaga-san insisted on exactly the right kind of person, enforced by an HR department with rigorous rules. It selected only staff who were engaged with and devoted to Japanese tradition. Years past, a couple of junior administrators had been found drinking in Western-style bars and eating in McDonald's. Despite being highly promising, they had been dismissed immediately.

Word soon got around the headquarters that their employer was serious about his requirements, with the added side-effect of attracting a small but dedicated number of applicants who found the company's strictly traditional attitudes to their tastes. True, Nobunaga-san had passed up the opportunity to employ many brilliant minds over the years, and these very same people had helped the infiltration of Western influences yet more into their country. However, the backlash planned and executed by Nobunaga-san was now well and truly underway. Anyone who had opposed or offended them was looking at a day of reckoning like none other.

"May I ask when Nobunaga-san might be available to communicate with the Chief? His calls are becoming… insistent."

Genko stopped himself from brusquely replying "Never", instead breathing in slowly then exhaling in an effort to control his response.

"I shall talk directly with the Chief when he arrives here."

The young woman looked confused. The faint wail of multiple police sirens could be heard approaching. Genko waited for the realisation to dawn in the young woman that the Chief would not take 'no' for an answer. He was coming to confront the great man in person.

"Is that understood?"

Blinking vacantly for a second, she recovered enough to bow then deactivate the intercom. Turning, he saw the great man had finished writing, the brush having been placed back into the long stem of the set's container. Ignoring the screens, which were now showing detailed maps of the Kyoto Research Park and various NKC company logos, Genko walked over to Nobunaga-san, bowed and took the writing set away. The short poem was left where it had been written, its four perfect columns facing upwards on the table, ready to be discovered by the authorities. Genko would not read it until after he had killed Nobunaga-san. To do so would be inexcusable.

Genko returned within seconds, having carefully repositioned the yatate set on the top of the bureau in the living quarters. He had no doubt the authenticity of the great man's poem would need to be ratified, the perfect curves and sweeps of Nobunaga-san's handwriting scrutinized for legitimacy, so they would need the ink and brush from which it was born. Re-entering the viewing room, Genko could see the ink still glistening in the light cast by the wall of screens. The detail of the words eluded him, which was right and proper, but to resist temptation he focussed his attention on the central square of monitors which now showed an animated representation of the police cordon. By the time he had quietly slid the door closed behind him, a final pulsing dot confirmed the authorities now surrounded the Kyoto Research Park entirely.

More sirens sounded, closer now. Genko's eyes flicked over to the full-height windows and expected Nobunaga-san to acknowledge the approaching show of force, but instead he craned forwards, scrutinising the female scientist who had now been joined by an insistent female reporter who had somehow muscled her way past the forest of her fellow journalists. The scientist's discomfort was obvious. She ignored most of the questions and kept looking behind her. Slender fingers moved over Nobunaga-san's tablet device and, in a blink, every one of the sixty screens turned into a single image, the quality degraded by the enlargement despite it being a high resolution 4K transmission.

Still capable of showing telling detail, Genko's eyes were drawn to the sparking lights through the windows in the double doors to the laboratory which, without warning, burst open. Clearly taken by surprise, the reporter looked from the scientist to the camera operator, unsure what was going on. A breath later, three figures dressed in full chemical warfare protective suits rushed into the narrow corridor, knocking the scientist to one side and the reporter to the other before colliding with the other news crews. As the camera crashed to the floor, the image on the screens shook violently before tipping to one side, blacking out momentarily then flickering back to life. Enlarged to such a massive extent, the movement made Genko's stomach lurch, but he quickly recovered his senses, mesmerised at what was presented before him.

Somehow, the lens remained angled upwards, and even though it was slanted at forty-five degrees it was still possible to see the chaos unfolding. Two of the mysterious, gas-masked figures loomed over the near-hysterical scientist, pinning her to the shiny green wall on the right. They were both pointing furiously through the open doors, through which several similarly protected operatives could be seen dragging large objects across the floor, their rubber suits reflecting a set of harsh strip lights running into the distance.

While the image was gradually obscured by the closing doors, it was clear the previously hidden room was not a laboratory but a mortuary with several large drawers opened from opposing racks on both walls of the rectangular room. To the left of shot, the third masked figure who had appeared seconds earlier could only be seen from the waist down, as could the slim yellow pencil skirt of the reporter whose heel had comically snapped off her shoe, making it difficult for her to stand correctly as she was confronted by the unknown assailant. A second pair of trousered legs, possibly belonging to the camera operator or director of the reporting crew, suddenly ran into shot, presumably to protect their colleague. They quickly backed away as the suited person unholstered a pistol and brought it to bear out of shot.

As the arguments continued to the left and right, the doors burst open once again, this time knocked back by a fourth hazmat-suited figure. Looking between the two groups, this one unstrapped an assault rifle, touched a small button located below the oversized circular filter at the bottom of the respirator and began to shout instructions. Despite being held back by her assailants, the scientist yelled something back, clearly furious at those instructions. Behind the shouting figure, through the open doorway, the objects being dragged on the floor became recognisable as body bags. A couple of figures stooped to unzip one of them, but the view was obscured by the rifleman, who was making it very clear with the muzzle of his weapon he wanted everybody out of the area immediately. Genko noticed Nobunaga-san staring intently at the scientist on the right, whose expression was now one of terror. With a single nod, his slender fingers started their tattoo on the tablet device, but this time the view did not change on the screens. Instead, the harsh strip lights illuminating the mortuary beyond the doors switched to a deep red.

This change in circumstances clearly confused the hazmat figures in the room who, at first, looked to the wall of metal drawers on either side, from which they had retrieved the occupied body bags, then back to each other. In the corridor closer to the camera, the scientist looked back in horror at the lights and turned to run, only to be roughly grabbed by one of her assailants and pinned back to the wall by the other. The woman kicked and lashed out and all three disappeared off-camera to the right in a furious struggle.

To the left of the bank of screens, Genko watched as the legs of the reporting crew backed off slowly out of shot, followed menacingly by the heavy boots and heavy protective trousers of their antagonist whose weapon was presumably still trained on them. This left the fourth black-suited rifle-toting figure who turned his back to the still-broadcasting camera and advanced on the dozen or so men crowded into the mortuary. Shocked into action by some unheard order from their commander, they grabbed at the body bags lying on the floor and began dragging them across the glossy tiles through the open doorway, the red light beating like a heartbeat.

Looking to his left, the commander threw his rifle over his shoulder and reached down for a long, thick strap attached to a smaller bag and began dragging it forwards, back through the doors towards the still-transmitting camera. Unaware of the fact his actions and those of his troops were being broadcast all over Japan, as the commander disappeared frame left, the bag caught a steel security pin holding one of the doors in position. The strap went tight, slack, then tight again as he attempted to tug it free, the bag's plastic at first tearing and, with one final yank, splitting apart completely.

Despite the flashing red lights and degraded image stretched across the sixty screens, what spilled from the bag's innards were unmistakeably body parts. A leg severed from the knee fell onto the boot print-marked floor of the corridor, the petite foot resting on its side, daintily painted toenails suggesting the limb's owner had taken pride in themselves during life. Realising what had happened off-camera, the commander let go of the strap, which fell limply to floor level, partly obscuring the view in the bottom left corner. The figure re-entered the image and, crouching down, frantically attempted to repair the tear, only making it worse. Another body part flopped onto the floor.

At first it was difficult for Genko to make out what it was because of the strange shape, but as it slid across the floor towards the camera, its true horrific form was revealed. A hand lay palm-upwards, clawing lifelessly at the empty air, and beyond it an arm all the way up to and past the shoulder, which was still attached to a diagonally sliced section of the torso. From the obscenely exposed breast, it had clearly belonged to a woman.

Genko watched, transfixed, as the appalling scene continued to unravel. The commander grabbed the leg and thrust it back into the darkness of the split bag, pushing the half torso of the woman even closer to the lens. In the background, members of his team returned to gather more body bags while, in the foreground, their commander continued his desperate attempt to stuff the limb back into the ruined sack. Reaching now for the arm connected to the torso, the figure froze directly in the middle of the shot, the blinking 'recording' light reflecting in the twin circular lenses set into his respirator.

Three things then happened in rapid succession. First, the commander lunged forwards towards the still active camera in a desperate attempt to switch the thing off.

Second, the torso section attached to the arm fell directly in front of the lens, revealing something that Genko only just had time to register before, thirdly, a brilliant flash of light within the mortuary obliterated the suited figures and the broadcast disappeared.

Genko stared at the sixty static-filled monitors for some seconds before Nobunaga-san manipulated the tablet device, re-assigning the screens to alternative broadcasters. Many showed the stunned faces of anchor persons sitting in front of monitors that had shown the same transmission, now hastily replaced with logos or 'signal lost' messages as the presenters tried to recover from the shock of what had just happened live on air.

Slowly, exterior shots of the Kyoto University's Innovation Hub, much of it now on fire, confirmed the obvious - the mortuary before which the scientist had been talking and the body parts discovered had exploded. Flames licked upwards into the brooding January sky, thick black smoke pouring from several locations. Dazed workers staggered from the nearby main entrance, others rushing towards them to help, as the on-location journalists tried to make sense of the situation.

Silently, Nobunaga-san rose to his feet, placed the tablet controller gently onto the surface of the low table next to his poem and turned to Genko with a look of serene satisfaction.

"It is time."

Genko did not move. He felt disconnected, as if he was not occupying his own body. Looking to the screens, he searched them for the image he had seen just before the brilliant flash of light but could not see it. Panic began to build in his chest. His mouth felt cotton-dry and his stomach lurched.

"Kaishakunin!"

Genko's gaze flicked back to Nobunaga-san. Standing less than a metre away, the great man's snow-white eyebrows were lowered in a look of reprimand, his eyes burning like coals. Genko opened his mouth to speak but could not find the words. The wail of police sirens rose and fell in the background, louder still. With the barest turn of the head, Nobunaga-san acknowledged their approach for the first time, his fierce gaze never leaving Genko's face.

"Let us be about our business."

The voice had a flint edge to it, one that Genko had heard countless times during meetings and committees. It was not an invitation for discourse or debate, but insistent and commanding. Genko nodded once, turned, and slid open the door to the living room, struggling to mask the raging confusion within him. Nobunaga-san swept past and headed straight for the mat on which the tantō laid waiting as Genko tried to call upon his years of diplomatic training to maintain his resolve. Hundreds of small questions swelled in his thoughts and joined in their demand for answers.

Barely able to keep his balance, Genko turned like a marionette, ignoring the beeping from the wall intercom that had started just as the police sirens stopped directly outside the building. A small area of clarity within Genko's head concluded the police were here, and while the receptionist could stall for time if requested, it would take them at least two minutes to find their way to these rooms.

Time was the one thing Genko suddenly, desperately needed, and time was the one thing that was running out.

Nobunaga-san was already kneeling on the mat next to the low table and facing the windows, regarding the sprawling Kyoto district before him. Genko could barely put one foot in front of the other. The thunder of blood in his ears was deafening. No amount of effort would fashion a mask of determination to continue with this task. The great man would see through it like gossamer, just as he had done at the funerals of his parents and the simple memorial service they had held to commemorate the death of his sister.

Oh God. Cho.

It had been three years since her disappearance and would be another four - hopefully in time for Genko to be released from prison - until she could be officially declared dead due to the lack of a body. It had been widely reported Cho's adventurous nature had contributed to her vanishing, a conclusion Genko had accepted as a truth despite his misgivings. When there were particularly difficult research jobs to undertake on behalf of NKC, Nobunaga-san had always favoured her because she had extraordinary mental and physical strength, despite her slight frame and graceful demeanour, to think and fight her way out of potentially lethal situations.

One of the most painfully ironic factors in Cho's presumed death was that she had not been in the service of the great man when she disappeared, but instead on a long-deserved walking holiday to Shikoku. Despite the best efforts of the locals, alerted when she had failed to return from a three-day exploration of the Ishizuchi mountain range, her body had not been found. The presumption she had fallen and been too injured to get to safety had been a very tough one for Genko to accept but, with the quiet persuasion of his employer, he had finally abandoned his attempts to look for her, urged to celebrate her life and rededicate himself to their cause.

Genko walked over to the sword rack like an automaton. The only sound in the room was Nobunaga-san's gentle breathing. Reaching for the katana, he felt a searing rush of fury build in his chest.

Had his eyes deceived him? Did he actually see what he thought he did?

Taking the neck of the wooden sheath with his right hand, he flipped it upwards with a flick of the wrist so it lay across both outstretched hands. Bowing deeply to respect the weapon, he then swapped his grip of the tsuka to the right hand, grasping the scabbard with his left and gently withdrawing the sword a few centimetres by its beautifully bound handles. He then swept the full length of the sword free of its wooden sheath. Despite being a movement he had practised a thousand times, never had the blade rattled against the sheath as it did this time.

"You will need a steadier hand for your task than that, kaishakunin."

Genko carefully replaced the shirasaya onto the bottom of the sword rack then turned to see the great man looking up at him. He expected concern, perhaps even the suggestion of pity for the enormous responsibility he had bestowed upon his most trusted servant. But neither of these could be read on the great man's face. Instead, there was contempt. It was an expression he had seen many times before in many circumstances, but never directed towards him or his family. This only acted to unnerve Genko more.

"Have I chosen poorly? Is the role too much for you to honour?"

Genko took a step forward towards the kneeling man. Outside, rain spattered noisily on the huge window.

"Nobunaga-san. What is the truth behind my sister's disappearance?"

Furrowed brows, a pause.

"We do not have time for irrelevancies. See to your duties."

The words were devoid of compassion or interest. Genko moved closer and looked down. The sword was now a natural extension of his right hand. He pointed its gleaming tip towards the head of the glaring man as he would an accusatory finger. Words flashed through his head.

Parents. Devotion. Sister. Employer. Honour. Sister.

Liar.

Grabbing at the white under-garment under his black mon-tsuki kimono and Haori jacket, Genko yanked angrily at the material with his left hand to expose his upper left shoulder. The old man did not break eye contact to look.

"This is your ancient family crest, Nobunaga-san. I have worn it proudly on my clothing and on my body for decades, as did one other person. I just saw it on the screen wall, barely recognisable on that desecrated flesh."

Genko was experiencing emotions he had never felt. He was in freefall, desperately clawing at the remains of his collapsing reality. He was enduring a terrifying shift in his perception of the world and his place in it. If the old man realised this, he did not show it. Not a flicker of concern could be seen on his emotionless face. Genko silently willed a response but none came, so he continued, bitterness tainting his every word.

"I know something of that laboratory in the University. I know it was set up many years ago in preparation for the great plan. I also know you had personal control of every activity there, including the selection process for the unfortunates who endured the experimental procedures that would lead to the clinics. So I ask again. What is the truth behind my sister's disappearance?"

Muffled shouts could be heard from the floors below. It would be the private security guards, hand-picked and fiercely loyal, demanding to know on what grounds the police were heading upstairs to seize their employer. Their efforts would only buy a few extra seconds, but Genko was grateful for Nobunaga's typical back-up plan, and he desperately hoped it would be all he needed to have the truth about Cho confirmed to him. With a sigh, the old man rose. His eyes burned with rage and jaw was set as he hissed through gritted teeth, the bony knuckles of his right hand white as he gripped the smooth wooden handle of the short sword.

"The truth is she served. That is all you need to know."

The hateful old man took a step forward, his eyes narrowing. Genko instinctively positioned himself into the Jōdan-no-kamae stance, sword raised above his head with both hands, weight distributed equally between his feet. The aggressive posture seemed to please Nobunaga who stopped his advance, lowered his own shorter weapon, and spoke in a low whisper.

"So now you must fulfil your duty, just as she did. Prove to me you have the honour I thought within you."

Genko's hands tightened on the long handle. From this position he could decapitate the old man with a single blow, take off the arm holding the weapon, remove the hand that grasped it... the choice of wound he could inflict, fatal or otherwise, was great. With every second he hesitated, the look of disdain on Nobunaga's face increased.

"You used my sister like you did the street trash recruited from every slum and ghetto in Japan. How could you do that? How could you treat her the way you would those undesirable strangers?"

Nobunaga puffed out his chest, tilted his nose back and assumed a haughty posture.

"You forget your station. I have no need to explain my actions to you. As for your sister, I needed her for a very special experiment, one that suited her particular body chemistry."

Genko's arms shook with rage. The old man glared, his face transformed into a mask of scorn.

"And be in no doubt. In common with all the assets in my laboratories, she suffered greatly."

Genko let out a tremendous roar and sprang forwards, the sword raised higher in readiness for the killing blow. As he brought it across and down to cleave the man's head from his shoulders, he twisted his wrists and body to the right, transferring the momentum of the blow so the curved blade arced away from the vile man, the tip slicing into and through the tatami mats on the floor by his forward foot. Recovering his balance, Genko allowed his sword to hang at his side and regarded Nobunaga, eyes closed in readiness at his fate, a smile of contentment across his lips.

The provocation about his sister's suffering had been

deliberate; the old man wanted Genko to kill him and, for the fraction of a second as the blade had descended, Genko had every intention of taking his revenge for Cho. But, he realised just in time, this would have given Nobunaga exactly that which he had intended and once again, Genko's family would have sacrificed everything and been rewarded with nothing - not even the respect Genko had mistakenly thought accorded to him.

Nobunaga opened his eyes and stared with disbelief at Genko, who shook with the exertion of self-control. For the first time, a shadow of panic danced across the old man's wrinkled face. Looking down at the short tanto blade, he arced it upwards and inwards towards his abdomen but Genko was ready for the move. With a swift upwards swish of his sword, Nobunaga's weapon spun through the air and clattered to the floor some metres away. Shouting came from the corridor outside the viewing room followed by a couple of gunshots, spurring Nobunaga to turn in an effort to retrieve his weapon. Genko hit him with the hilt of his sword in the back of the neck and he fell to the matted floor like a sack of rice.

Genko looked down at the shuddering figure at his feet as the splintering of wood and thundering feet could be heard from the adjoining room. He would not let the old bastard die. He would live, and Genko would ensure the last, dreadful stage of the old man's plan would be revealed then disabled. Both would face the charges they so rightly deserved and perhaps, somehow, Cho would forgive him for his blind devotion. Only now, as the Chief of Kyoto Prefecture threw open the door and shouted for him to drop his weapon, did Genko understand the ugly, immoral truth of the man he had once revered, and his own unforgiveable role.

The sword slipped from his grasp, and the rain fell harder on the windows.

The suffering of angels

"You don't look at all well."

Barnard scrutinised the woman propped up on the rusting bed directly opposite. Thanks to the broken blinds at the draughty window to his right, light slanted in at crazy angles from the afternoon sun, illuminating Tara's deeply lined and troubled face. Her eyes, once bright blue and sparkling, were cloudy from the cataracts that had spread across her corneas over the last few months, robbing her of sight and defiling her best feature. Her skin, pale and dry, looked as if it had been taken from a much thinner person and stretched across her high-cheeked, elegant face.

Barely turning her head to acknowledge his voice, the only noise she could muster through her thin lips was a sigh. She didn't even have the energy to speak, her feeble reply accompanied by a barely raised hand and bony finger pointing to nowhere in particular. After a few shaky seconds, she sank back into the oversized blue pillow behind her, heavily stained from its previous occupant, who had fared even worse a few days previously.

Barnard blinked a couple of times and watched her slip back into a fitful sleep. The green line on the ancient cardiograph to her right leapt up for three or four beats and then returned to its steady upward nudges, the beeps having been turned off or stopped working months ago. Tara must be the seventh… no, eighth occupant of that bed since he'd been admitted. He'd managed to see them all off, watching them come in screaming and go out silent, while his own torture had reached new heights - or should that be depths? - of monstrous suffering.

This was, if he was thinking straight, the third time Tara had been admitted during his time here. Whatever was wrong with her on this occasion was really kicking her arse. As if to confirm his hypothesis, her jaw suddenly clenched with a ghastly snap, fingers clawing at the frayed bed sheets in response to her sudden paroxysm. After a few seconds of ghoulish entertainment it was all over, and

Tara slipped that bit further towards the inevitable.

Losing interest, Barnard turned his head and squinted at the brilliance of the day. It was pointless asking for shade as the nursing staff, such as they were, couldn't care less. He'd not seen a doctor since he'd been admitted what... nineteen weeks ago? Even then it'd been a cursory discussion in a cramped office of what to expect from his condition, with both agreeing he wouldn't be leaving the place alive. As an added bonus, because of the nature of what he'd contracted, it was going to be lingering, slow and excruciating, so trying to stop a sunlight-induced headache by fixing the blinds was like putting a sticking plaster on the stump of an amputation. Despite himself, Barnard chuckled at the thought. Now that would be interesting.

Tara gurgled, bringing Barnard back to the present. Looking to the three vacant beds on his left and past the room's partly glazed boundary, he considered shouting for assistance but thought better of it. There had been a particularly messy departure that morning, resulting in the Matron herself having to muck in and clean the spattered walls and frothy brown mess that had crept across the perpetually filthy linoleum floor. She had not been at all happy having to get her hands dirty and had soon disappeared back to the comfort of her station past the frosted wall panels to the atrium beyond, muttering darkly about not being paid enough for this shit - literally.

Despite the nurse's station outside being dimly lit, shadows occasionally flitting past Ward Four could still be made out, masked heads briefly seen in focus as they glided across the two plain square windows set high in the double entrance doors. Glancing down the length of the firmly shut barrier below the windows, Barnard noted that no-one had bothered to wipe off the wide streak of blood that slashed across the corroded steel push plates. Nope. He wouldn't be thanked for demanding anyone's presence in this truly dreadful room. So he wouldn't bother.

With a sigh, Barnard's gaze drifted back towards the shafts of light forcing their way in through the horizontal blinds. Dust motes floated in and out between the brilliant streaks, pushed around by the ill-fitting window and Tara's fidgeting in the bed opposite. Following the glistening particles around the low-ceilinged room, Barnard lost sight as they drifted towards the three identical beds lined against Tara's wall. Two occupants in a room designed for eight. The hospital wasn't doing well these days. Barnard was used to pain and suffering, but a truly dreadful thought sliced through him. What if they shut this place? What if it stopped being viable? Where would everyone go?

"Jesus CHRIST!"

The pain swept through his body like an electric current, starting in his abdomen and tearing up through his chest to burn incandescent behind his eyes. His insides felt as if they were on fire, broiling what was left of his organs that hadn't been ravaged by the cancer rapidly overwhelming him. Barnard grabbed a hold of the cold, pitted rails either side of his cot and shook with the intensity of the pain. His own cardiograph, which he had angled towards his field of vision so he could record these increasingly frequent assaults, flashed and zig-zagged upwards, the number going from 79 to 98 to 136 in three furious bursts of insanely painful energy.

A low throbbing began in the back of his mouth, burning spear tips levering beneath his teeth which felt as if they were tearing from his jaw. Sweat beaded on his forehead, dribbling down into his eyes. The stinging was insignificant compared to the rest of his agony and, somewhere in the distance, Barnard heard a tremendous rattling. The onslaught held its peak for several unbearable seconds and, as the misery began to subside, he realised the noise had been caused by him convulsing violently on the rickety bed.

For long seconds, Barnard lay in his own moist film,

attempting to catch his breath while he watched the numbers slowly return to normal on the readout. The stinging sweat returned, so he tried to wipe it from his brow. It didn't work; like Tara's feeble attempt to raise her hand earlier, he didn't have the energy to lift his withered arm. If the once beautiful woman's skin was stretched and thin, his was little more than parchment. Gasping for air, he looked down at the back of his hands and watched the spider network of veins feebly pulsing beneath their translucent sheath. Twinges from the roaring pain attack hit his joints and muscles in a random drumbeat, aftershocks of his very own earthquake of agony. Slowly they reduced in speed and intensity until, finally, he relaxed into his previous laboured breathing and watched the flashes and dots floating across his vision as they blinked away to nothing.

He could, of course, have asked for pain relief, but it would have been as futile as asking for any other kind of help. Drugs, gases, medications of any and all kinds were only available as a very last resort and were prohibitively expensive, on top of the cost of actually being there in the first place. Routine medication did not seem to be in the spirit of suffering actively and enthusiastically encouraged by this hospital.

Even if they did pump him full of something, feed bags of fluids through a cannula into the back of his wizened hand, there was still the question of their efficacy. Barnard was so far gone, so entirely riddled with cancer, there wasn't anything in existence that would touch the pain other than doses so high of anaesthetic he'd be rendered unconscious. Regardless of how ferocious and towering the pain was, he knew the inevitable darkness was quickly approaching. Why waste his few remaining hours with sleep?

For some reason, Barnard found that funny. He laughed loudly, then coughed for two minutes straight.

Barnard awoke with a start, disoriented and unsure of where he was. The last thing he remembered seeing was a black, pulsing sphere, wet and slick, hanging in the air like a vile balloon of darkness. It faded quickly from his memory as most dream-images do, replaced by the familiar view of the ceiling directly above his head, a patchwork of brown on white where water had seeped through from the corroded pipework. His still sharp eyesight picked out the pits and holes of the ceiling tiles illuminated by the single strip light that still worked, its incessant buzz reminding everyone it was doing its best to fulfil its job despite years of neglect. Familiar smells returned to Barnard, a mixture of decay, cleaning fluids and bodily gases. All of these, while unsettling in their own ways, had not brought him back to consciousness so abruptly. It had to be something unexpected.

The answer came with the clattering of a trolley from beyond the double doors to the ward, followed by indistinct voices raised above the unseen squealing casters and rattling metal frame. One of the voices belonged to the Matron; as was the norm, she sounded pissed off about something, but not as aggrieved as the booming low-frequency rumble that answered her. Barnard felt the man's voice more than heard it, and it didn't surprise him in the least that Tara let out a pitiful cry.

Barnard's gaze flicked over to see her move her head weakly from side to side, cheeks ghastly and sunken in the harsh light cast from above. As she groaned herself back to sleep, he turned sharply as the double doors burst open with absolutely no consideration to the delicate condition of Barnard or his fellow sufferer.

With an explosion of noise and movement, a burly orderly, well over seven feet tall, launched the gurney into the room, shaking its unfortunate occupant between the safety rails as the rickety frame collided with the slowly closing double doors. Cursing and muttering under his breath, the huge, shabbily dressed porter abruptly stopped, propping the doors open with the trolley as he leaned forwards and yanked off the high retaining rail on the right and throwing it behind him with a clatter towards the nurse's station. Barnard heard the Matron scream a string of obscenities at the man, who smirked with satisfaction before putting his considerable weight behind the trolley and lunging directly towards Barnard and Tara's beds. Unmasked and unkempt, Barnard could see streaks of blood up the man's massive, hairy arms, still wet and glistening in the overhead light. Knowing the hospital's staff as he did, Barnard would have betted good money it wasn't the porter's blood smeared all over his skin.

Just before the head of the gurney reached Barnard's position, the giant blue-clad being huffed and swung the trolley to the right, sending the contraption in a shaky arc between Barnard's bed and the vacant one to his left. Metal clashed on metal as the side of the trolley collided with the bed. In a spectacular demonstration of zero patient consideration, with the safety rail removed, the occupant barrel-rolled off the gurney onto the grubby sheets of the bed, face-down and panting. Pulling the trolley back towards him, the ogre threw a warning 'say a word and I'll throw you through that window' glance at Barnard then smashed the trolley back out through the doors. Barnard didn't hear the orderly's retort to the Matron's animated abuse as the doors swung shut once again.

Any movement was an effort for Barnard, so turning himself over on his side took considerable preparation and planning. Taking a deep breath, he forced his right shoulder off the filthy mattress, transferring his pitiful weight to his left arm which started to burn with the additional pressure. Too late, Barnard felt a fierce tugging on his exposed chest as the heart monitor pads pulled away. It was unlikely the flatline showing on the nurse's station would provoke the slightest reaction from the Matron, or whoever else might be out there. He'd seen fellow occupants lie dead for a couple of days before they'd been removed from the ward. Despite being quite the long-term resident, Barnard had never witnessed such a spectacular arrival and was curious to see who had landed next to him and, ever-morbidly fascinated, what was wrong with them.

"I'm Barnard. Pleased to meet you."

The figure breathed shallowly, bony spine poking through his carelessly laced operating gown. Barnard assumed from the shape and size of its backside the unfortunate was male, but that was all the clue he got. Other than the disgusting condition of the robe that had been thrown around him, what was most alarming in the harsh glare of the ceiling light was the almost translucent appearance of his skin, not thin and papery like Tara's, but oily and suppurating. The backs of his legs were a patchwork of black, red and blue sores, some so large the skin had torn open, exposing dark tissue that glistened within. If it was painful for Barnard to be lying in his filthy pit, it must be agony for this poor soul.

"Melkogh."

The voice was a low rasp, the words indistinct and poorly formed.

"Ish I ould shay a shane."

The man's shoulders shook a few times with laughter before he fell still.

Barnard puzzled over the words for a few seconds then concluded it was something along the lines of 'wish I could say the same'. Fair enough. At least his new neighbour had a sense of humour. After a few seconds to recover from the exertion of talking, the man began to turn, every movement accompanied by a whimper until he came to rest, exhausted, facing Barnard. Now, Barnard thought he'd experienced pretty much everything this place had to offer, but the sight before him was on an elevated level of horror.

Where there would normally be hair, there wasn't even

a scalp. Skin had rucked and stuck onto the pillow as the man had turned, forming an appalling fleshy bridge to the bedding. The eyes stared as if they were being pushed out from his skull, unblinking because the eyelids had disappeared, and the tip of his nose was missing, exposing a triangle of cartilage and gristle. Barnard's curiosity over the man's strange speech was immediately answered by the lack of lips. Blistered skin stretched around exposed, bleeding gums, the tongue flicking in and out of the broken tombstone teeth like a fish pulled from the water. In short, the man, or what was left of him, was a spectacular, offensive mess of hideous decline.

"If you don't mind me asking, what's wrong with you?"

Barnard's question was laughable. It would have been easier to ask Melkov - which he assumed was the correct pronunciation but might be wrong - what was right with him.

"A oot adiashun indro… indro… icknech."

It was unsettling to watch the man attempt to speak. Every time his jaw moved, another part of his skin would rupture. Despite it being warm in the ward, he had begun to shake violently, creating blooms of blood where his suppurating flesh touched the material along the full length of his already stained gown. If Barnard had been able, he would have got out of bed and pulled some covers over Melkov but he simply didn't have the strength. Thinking on his strained words, Barnard concluded the man had acute radiation syndrome, something he'd heard of and was intrigued by.

Nuclear power had, of course, been replaced by fusion energy decades before, meaning there were no more active reactors and all the atomic weapons had been dismantled and disposed of. Wherever Melkov had received his obviously massive radiation exposure, it must have been somewhere very secret for Barnard not to have known about it.

Across the room, Tara began to groan. Barnard looked

over to her, as did Melkov. Tara's eyes flickered open and swivelled over to the new arrival. There was just enough time for her mouth to fall open and for her to issue a strangled scream of horror before she passed out with the shock of seeing him. Barnard sighed then returned to his questioning.

"I'm presuming your condition is untreatable? You must be in agony."

To an outsider, such a question might seem as blunt as it was impertinent. For those who had spent a long time in this hospital, such a brutal approach wasn't a problem. Most patients admitted to Ward Four were in the last few weeks of their lives; even a lengthy conversation might never be completed as one of the participants expired mid-sentence. Barnard was amazed he'd lasted this long. He'd survived several newcomers whose condition had, surprisingly, been even more advanced than his own. But then in this hospital, patients were only ever moved to suit the needs of the so-called nursing staff, not for their comfort or to receive better care.

"Yech... oo othe eshtuns."

Assuming the strangulated answer was 'yes to both questions', Barnard nodded. And then, something occurred to him. If Melkov's dose had been that large, surely he would be radioactive? No. If there had been any chance of cross-contamination whatsoever, the orderly would have been garbed head to foot in protective gear. 'Carer first' was very much the motto in this institution. Similarly, turning Melkov into a human projectile to get him off the trolley wasn't anything out of the ordinary; he'd seen it done as part of a competition between the orderlies on more than one occasion. If the staff had their way, they'd not be inconvenienced with physical patient contact at all.

Shaking more than ever, Melkov began to sweat. Combining with the blood oozing from his torn scalp, scarlet rivulets ran diagonally across the front of his ruined face and into his staring eyes. The rickety bed frame began to rattle with Melkov's convulsions so, with a supreme effort, Barnard threw back his grubby bedspread, propped himself up then swung his skeletal legs over the side of his bed.

The second he felt the cold linoleum on his feet, Barnard knew he'd made a mistake. Melkov's bed was less than two metres away but it might as well have been a thousand kilometres. Barnard hadn't been out of bed for seven weeks, had barely eaten and couldn't support the weight of a half cup of water in his hand, let alone his own pitiful body. Every joint from his ankles to his shoulders burned as he moved, wafer-thin muscles doing their best to pull and push against gravity. Willing his diseased bones forwards, Barnard staggered a step, then another until, miraculously, he made it to the side of Melkov's bed.

Up close, the remains of the man's face were even more horrific so, not wishing to dwell on the view or lose the momentum he'd painfully built, Barnard reached for the rumpled filthy blanket at the foot of the bed, grabbed it with bony fingers then put the last of his strength into pulling the threadbare rag over the man's shuddering body. Acknowledging Melkov's imperceptible nod of gratitude, Barnard focussed on the part of his hasty plan he'd not fully thought out - getting back to his own bed.

Ignoring Melkov's trembling behind him and Tara's pitiful mewling across the way, Barnard launched himself towards his filthy cot. One step, then two, but then he pushed his luck and immediately knew he was going to fall. As he toppled forwards he tried not to reach out to steady himself, knowing his brittle hands and arms wouldn't be able to take any form of impact, so the sickening crack that came from his wrist as it connected with the side of his bed came as no surprise. What did was the excruciating belt of heat that shot up his arm and seized his chest as he threw himself over his own shattered hand, falling face-first onto the covers, his ruined limb pinned below him.

Tears ran freely from his eyes with the shock. He'd endured pain so many, many times, but the unexpected nature of this accident caught him unaware. Feeling his heart thump erratically in his bony chest, Barnard shuffled his feet forwards, putting extra pressure onto his hand as he did so, ramping up the temperature of misery from red to white hot. If he didn't continue forwards, there was every chance he would slump onto the blood and shit-stained floor and stay there until he died. While his bed wasn't exactly the most comfortable place in the world, it sure as hell beat that option.

Hamstrings burning from the tension upon them, Barnard took a breath, rotated himself to the right and pushed himself forwards in an attempt to lever himself onto the bed. This transferred his entire weight onto his arm and hand, making him shout in pain, but he had to keep going. Slowly, his weight transferred onto his right side and he felt his legs lifting off the ground. All he had to do now was to swing his legs onto the bed and rotate himself onto his back at the same time. Bathed in sweat from the exertion, his wrist throbbing pulses of flame up his arm, Barnard gritted his teeth, screwed his eyes shut, rotated on his bony backside then heaved and shunted until, finally, he was resting on his back.

When he opened his eyes, the view of the ceiling was blurry with tears. With one final shove from his freezing feet, he pushed himself back up on his pillow, never more grateful for its dubious comfort. Panting for breath, he looked down at the black and purple balloon forming around his snapped hand. He didn't even bother trying to move his fingers; he'd had just about enough for one day and took the opportunity to pass out.

Barnard awoke with a moan. He wasn't sure if it was the pulsing sphere that had visited him in his fever-dream again or the throbbing needles of pain from his comically swollen wrist. Probably a bit of both, given that the sphere had taken on a dark purple hue along with the black, mirroring the colour of his useless wrist. The room was filled with a deep orange light, heralding the dawn and another day of abject misery and despair - if he was lucky. For a few seconds he considered calling out to whoever might be beyond the double doors of the ward, but this early in the morning any staff that might be around would be tucked up in their cots in the small room behind the counter, oblivious to and uncaring of their charges. He'd just have to bear the pain in his arm, along with the burning sensation in the rest of his joints and his increased difficulty breathing.

Turning to face the left, the back of Barnard's head slowly peeled away from the pillow thanks to the membrane of sweat connecting him to it. He could see Melkov lying on his back, his parody of a face peeping out above the blanket that had caused Barnard so much pain. Barnard squinted away the tears in his eyes and tried to make out whether the wretched man was still breathing. His mouth, a black, gaping maw, was open, and the glistening lustre of his oozing skin had gone.

Barnard could see there was no movement from beneath his covering, and concluded Melkov had died while he had slept. He may have screamed and shouted; Barnard hadn't heard a thing and felt disappointed he hadn't been witness to the man's final moments. After a few seconds of consideration, Barnard decided to shift position once more and see how Tara was getting on. Despite the stabbing pain from his wrist and slowly building agony from his condition, he had just enough room to feel sorry for neglecting her when someone new and novel had appeared.

Unlike Melkov, there was plenty of movement from behind Tara's blanket. Her chest was heaving up and down rapidly, her mouth wide open as she gasped for breath. Barnard recalled seeing an old recording of a fish, back when there were such things, taken out of the water by an angler. While he'd fussed around for whichever long-dead person had been filming it, showing off his prize with puzzling pride, the fish's mouth had done exactly the same as Tara's. Barnard remembered thinking it comical, but the comparison with Tara's struggle towards the end of her life didn't amuse him now. With a loud grunt, her near-sightless eyes snapped open and she gaped, panic and terror competing on her face in a grim last stand until, with a throaty crackle and a long, wheezing sigh, she died.

The line went flat on her cardiograph, the numbers quickly counted down to zero, and Barnard found himself sharing a room with two corpses. With the full expectation it would be hours until the staff discovered Melkov and Tara's lifeless bodies, Barnard turned his head towards the window and watched the sun inch its way across the skyline. Right now it was quiet, peaceful even, but it wouldn't be long until red-hot knives of agony returned to carve their way through his body once again.

"You can't keep away from the place, can you?"

Barnard tugged at the sleeve of his jacket and smoothed imaginary creases from his lapel as Tara glided into the hospital waiting room, nodding to a couple of people she recognised before taking a deep, luxurious seat next to him. Barnard waited for her to rearrange her dress and rummage through her bag before he replied. She had a habit of taking calls from people the second she sat down, so starting a conversation was always a risk. However, with no bleeps or flashes from her phone, Barnard replied.

"I could say the same to you."

Tara laughed, her teeth perfect, eyes flashing brilliant blue, reminding him they were, indeed, her best feature.

"What are you in for this time?"

Barnard looked around the animated visualisations built into the sleek, immaculately clean plastic walls. One showed a young woman in the last stages of bubonic plague, writhing in pain and clawing at the blackened skin surrounding a huge bite on her neck. Another showed a man with yellow skin, thrashing and wailing on a hospital gurney as cirrhosis rampaged through his liver. Both looked equally excruciating and enticing.

"I fancy something a little less long-term. You've had three nasty ones to my one."

Tara looked at Barnard and frowned.

"Ah yes, but you were in far more pain for much longer."

Barnard nodded. That much was true. What he'd endured on Ward Four, he could still remember, which was always the hallmark of a good, grim illness. Tara looked down at her phone and thumb-scrolled through a series of images on her screen.

"You know what? I think I might go for what you had. Cancer wasn't it?"

Barnard nodded again, this time with a grin.

"With a couple of extras thrown in by the doc for good measure. You weren't around to see my broken wrist, were you?"

Tara looked up from her phone, intrigued. Slipping the sleek silver device back into her bag, the side of her mouth turned up in a smile.

"A broken wrist? Are you kidding?"

Barnard laughed.

"Take it from me, on top of everything else, it really, really hurt like hell."

Tara frowned, looking less than convinced. On the other side of the airy waiting room, someone exited out of the row of flush-fit consultation room doors looking excited and terrified in equal measure.

"What about you?"

Barnard sighed and looked around. The doubt that had crept up on him shortly before his last life's end crawled back and made itself an unsettled bed at the back of his mind. It didn't seem as busy here as it used to, and that worried him. It might be prudent to go for something really, really bad.

"Well, I'm thinking something along the lines of Melkov."

Tara raised an eyebrow.

"Who?"

"You probably don't remember. He came in just as you were checking out."

A low chime sounded twice, and Tara's name glowed on one of the opposing waiting room doors. Standing up with a sigh, she gave him a 'that's settled then' look and walked over towards the gleaming wall. The two people Tara had greeted had gone, leaving him on his own. For aeons, this hospital had been providing sick care of the very highest quality in delightful, authentic squalor, offering the chance to experience pain so profound and distress so complete it transcended into the exquisite. If this was to disappear, despite having exhausted just about everything that was available, Barnard felt a fear that went far beyond any physical pain he'd endured in the past. Futility and boredom were far deadlier than a broken limb or failed organ. He decided he had to make the most of it while it was here.

The chime sounded again, and Barnard's name glowed on the slowly forming doorway next to the one through which Tara had disappeared. Standing, he straightened his back and strode over, muttering 'acute radiation syndrome' under his breath. Given its obvious, terrifying pain, that would be the next ailment of choice. It might be costly, it might be difficult to arrange, but if it felt as horrific as it looked, he'd 'die' a happy man - again. He'd also try to find out just how viable the hospital was, long-term.

After all, without the opportunity to suffer, what point was there in being immortal?

Negative Span Discrepancy

Karol Shybeck watched the sun rise over the mountains and sighed. Down between the frozen trees in the valley below, the occasional flash of amber lights from the barely visible road suggested the local authorities were failing to honour their promise of keeping it clear of snow, regardless of conditions. Living at such an altitude was, she acknowledged, problematic. As hers was the only property to which the road led, this maintenance cost her an extortionate amount of money to ensure she and, more importantly, her clients could travel to her facility without interruption.

Helios were all well and good for seven or eight months, but the windshear caused by the nearby mountain range and the volume of snow that could quickly fall meant air transport was unreliable at this time of the year. The road had to be open but, with increasing irritation, she could tell from the stop-start movement of the ploughs the single carriageway was close to becoming impassable again.

This simply wasn't good enough.

"Auberon. Holocall Schiller."

Clicks issued from the speakers built into the low ceiling.

"Holocalls are being refused."

The AI's unhurried, soft voice only ramped up Shybeck's annoyance further.

"Audio call Schiller."

More clicks, then the old-fashioned burr-burr of a dial tone. A few seconds later, a man's voice answered, coarse and croaky from being woken at 6.30 in the morning.

"Yes, Fraulein Shybeck."

Schiller's voice was heavy with the anticipation of an unpleasant call. She wasn't going to disappoint him.

"My road is blocked again, Schiller. You assured me you would keep access to my property at all times. What are you going to do about it?"

The interior of Karol's room began to brighten with a deep orange glow, strengthening her reflection in the enormous glass panel before her. Outside it was minus twenty degrees, but the triple glazing and state of the art heating system built into her extravagant penthouse ensured she could stand in her bedroom entirely naked without the suggestion of a chill. Unless the plough drivers had very powerful binoculars and a clear field of vision through the dense pines between them, they wouldn't see her athletic silhouette, arms folded beneath her uneven breasts (she had to get around to fixing them), breath misting up the inner pane through her sneering lips.

"Fraulein, as I have explained before, you are not our sole priority when the weather is particularly bad. May I remind you I was on the committee that strongly suggested you did not build your facility in that location because of the micro-climate this time of the year. You were fully appraised of the issues that might – "

"I don't need a history lesson Schiller. You weren't so stuck in your beliefs you turned down the ridiculous amount of money I offered you to service the road, nor did you press your concerns when you agreed the price I was willing to pay for this location."

The complex had been built into the solid granite of the hillside opposite to the mountain range, stupidly challenging terrain in which to construct so large a property. The difficulty of construction and isolated location had, of course, been the reason to choose it in the first place, along with the breath-taking view that met her every morning. She had no neighbours, nor would she ever have because no-one else in their right minds would build here or have the wealth to do so. And she'd simply not allow it.

"Fraulein, I ensured last night that all available crews would be dispatched to your location. I have just had a message from the Chief the road will be clear within the next three hours. Surely you will not be planning to travel so early in the morning?"

Karol's face turned to thunder, her eyes darkening and

jaw line firming at the man's insolence.

"What I do and when I do it is no fucking concern of yours, Schiller. Do your job or I'll make it my business to ensure you're replaced before the sun goes down. Understood?"

There was a pause as Schiller processed the threat. If she'd had her way, which she'd attempted to get on several occasions, she would have bought the entire regional department out, sacked all the local government officials and put in her own staff to run the place as it would have been far cheaper, if not necessarily any more successful. Unfortunately, local government was not for sale, but her wealth and influence extended to Schiller's immediate boss and one level above. She could do what she threatened, and the man knew it – although there was no guarantee his replacement would be any more reliable than he had proven to be. She could also take ten, twenty or even more years off his life if she wanted to – but that would just be petulant, if hugely enjoyable.

"Understood."

"Auberon. Terminate call."

Frustrated with the struggle unfolding against the heavily falling snow, Karol turned and walked back towards her emperor-sized bed, toes gripping into the deep-pile cream carpet that covered the entire third floor of the penthouse. As she walked, she cast a diminishing shadow over the untidy silk bedding strewn across the enormous mattress and deep pillows propped against the jewel-encrusted headboard.

By the time she reached the entrance to her glittering wet room, their gentle twinkling had changed to a dull ochre as the early morning sun was obliterated by snow clouds. The maids would soon be in to make the bedroom pristine, better than the most luxurious hotel. They'd even clean the interior of the massive picture windows overlooking the valley and mountains, now shrouded in a low, grey mist, wiping away the evidence of her angry words.

"Auberon. Activate shower."

Feet warmed by the under-tile heating, she stepped into the pristine bathing area and ran her perfectly manicured fingers through her short blonde hair. Putting the exchange with Schiller to the back of her mind, she gloried in the steaming water from the dozen high-powered jets, indulging herself in the pressure on her well-toned body. She'd not bathe fully because, within ten minutes, she would be in her gymnasium on the floor below, being put through her paces by Giselle, one of the few people she could rely on to speak her mind. Blowing out a fine spray of water through her mouth, she turned to allow some jets to pummel her back, buttocks and thighs then stepped out.

"Auberon. Deactivate shower."

The water stopped immediately, dribbles running for a few seconds from the chrome nozzles as Karol dried herself off with a warm, fluffy towel. Tossing the soaking cloth into a corner of the white-tiled room, she strolled back into her bedroom, opened the mirrored door to her dressing area and entered the rows of designer clothing and accessories.

There was no need to choose her outfit for the morning; pulling on compression leggings, a tight top that exposed her muscular midriff and a pair of Salomon trainers, she exited the wardrobe, left her bedroom then skipped over to the sweeping oak staircase down to the second floor. Turning to the right, she headed straight for her office at the bottom of the softly illuminated corridor and entered a room lined with banks of metallic flat-panelled servers to her right and a wall of glass-thin monitors to her left.

Dropping onto the high-backed soft white leather office chair with a sigh, she activated the touch-sensitive membrane on the surface of the glass desk directly beneath the monitors with a sweep of her hand. Her fingers danced over the keys, some familiar to any computer user, most sporting symbols known only to Karol, activating three of the screens at eye level and a few others in her peripheral vision. As lines of code and various login instructions flooded onto the displays, she glanced through the picture window overlooking the main sweep of the wide Electric Vehicle parking area reception two floors below. Her staff were already busying themselves with clearing equipment, heaping piles of fresh snow over the low wall surrounding the circular parking area onto the frozen grounds rolling away to the tree line. With a 'humph' and a nod, her anger subsided further. With the access road cleared and the parking area ready she would be able to leave and her clients arrive.

"Auberon. Any new business detected for today?"

Karol could have typed the instruction, but since she'd recently upgraded her scratch-built AI, she'd increasingly used voice commands so it could improve its stress analysis routines. It was old technology, granted, and she'd reduced its audio reply ability as the last thing she wanted was lengthy conversations with a computer. Come to that, she really didn't care about talking with anybody – apart from her accountant.

"No new business has been detected."

It didn't really matter; with her newest client coming in tomorrow, she'd already exceeded her target for the year. Even so, it left her feeling disappointed. Nothing quite matched the thrill of the game she'd refined to an art form over the last ten years.

"Very well. Auberon. Run algorithm selector."

Behind her, the gleaming banks of decryption units began to whine as their massively powerful processors shifted the trillions of terabytes they'd need to access the inaccessible. It was a point of pride to Karol that the racks of equipment in this room alone would put most government departments to shame, particularly after the shitty way several of them had treated her when she was quite a different person. This was the smaller of the two quantum server rooms she owned; housed on the floor below, next to her laboratory and clean room, was where the majority of the data crunching took place. She'd considered putting her office down there, but this well-ventilated and carefully filtered room meant she had to walk only a few steps if she chose not to start the day with gruelling physical punishment. With a shudder, she took her mind off the pounding Giselle was bound to give her, followed by far more pleasurable activities - if Karol was in the mood for it.

After a few seconds the words 'algorithm selected' blinked on the monitor, light green letters on a dark green background. Karol enjoyed the retro look to her data representation; yes, it was nearly a hundred years since the first cathode ray monitors and she could so easily have had the full wall as a reconfigurable series of screens, but she always thought the look of separate monitors was cool – and easier to adjust and read.

"Auberon. Initiate selected algorithm."

The room-high banks burst into action again, a flurry of blinking white and orange lights reflecting on the screens before her. The whole process would take around ten seconds, such was the sheer brute force of the computing power unleashed. Any longer, and it would attract attention from the ever-changing detection and prevention systems she so carefully evaded. Any shorter, and she'd not be able to get in.

Foreseeing her normal success, she pushed herself back on her chair, the soft leather hissing as she sank into it, and idly inspected her nails before checking again through the narrow window on the staff outside. They'd made good progress on the parking area despite the snowfall increasing, and were now steaming off the circular, beacon lined Helio landing pad. With a smile, she returned her gaze to the large main screen. It was now presenting the information that only twelve people in the world could access – legally, at least.

Welcome to Server 1441- Secure Connection Open
User authorisation level 12
*Confirmation code *******-****
Gateway security timeout 30s

Keyboard option selected – press back for virtual comms channel

Press 1 to search CDC database
Press 2 to communicate with DCDC support
Press 3 to report an error message
Press 4 to Exit

She leant forwards and stabbed at the number '1' on her keyboard.

Press 1 to submit CDC ID tag
Press 2 to interrogate open search fields
Press 3 to communicate with DCDC support
Press 4 to report an error message
Press 5 to Exit to previous level

Karol glanced at the countdown clock that had started on the smaller screen to the left. The over-sized numerals showed plenty of time remained before the access portal she had smashed open would close. Again, she pressed '1', typed

Shybeck, Karol ID KS-P-044F132E-34

then pressed return. The screen froze for a couple of seconds, and while she had seen this hundreds of times before, the pause – while the system hunted through every person in the world for the right identity – always made her uneasy.

A few blinks later, and the screen refreshed.

Shybeck, Karol ID KS-P-044F132E-34
DOB 12/21/2034 Kracow, Poland

Press 1 for CDC breakdown
Press 2 to facilitate span discrepancy
Press 3 to communicate with DCDC support
Press 4 to report an error message
Press 5 to Exit to previous level

A final press of '1' and she sat back with a smile.

Shybeck, Karol ID KS-P-044F132E-34
DOB 12/21/2034 Kracow, Poland
CDC 03/11/2129
Current date 03/13/2075
Time elapsed since birth: 40y 2m 20 days
Time from birth to CDC: 93y 6m 17 days +/- .5 days
Time remaining to CDC: 54y 3m 25 days+/- .5 days

Press 1 to submit blood sample update
Press 2 to communicate with CDCD support
Press 3 to Exit to previous level

And there it was. Her birth, her life, her death, before her very eyes.

The following morning, Karol rose early because it was a client day. Even though she could see the tops of the mountains, which meant the weather was improving and Helio flight might be possible, arrival times could be unpredictable. While she insisted on punctuality (strict time constraints were a major part of her sales shtick), she had to be realistic, particularly with her visitors coming from all over the world. There might be a plus or minus four-hour window of them turning up, so being up earlier meant she would be prepared regardless of their arrival by road or air.

Strolling into the bathroom, she toileted then activated the shower, enjoying the steam heat and allowing her mind to drift as she worked shampoo deep into her scalp. Yesterday's fitness class – and the sex afterwards – had been exceptional. Her smile faded as she once again realised she could rely on people more to clean after her and maintain her fitness than provide real friendship and company. If that was the truth of her existence, then so be it. It was her choice to live in the shadows and skulk around the underbelly of society, lest her talents be discovered by those who would not bestow the enormous rewards she had become accustomed to demanding.

Drying off brusquely and discarding her towels for the maids, she marched over to her dressing room. After a few moments of shuffling hangers and sighing to herself, she chose a dark blue cat suit, white Napa leather trainers and matching belt. Gone were the days of her 'power dressing' to impress. Given the unique service she offered, her clients couldn't care less about her clothes, fixated on their survival as they inevitably would be.

Two floors below, the automated laboratory systems would be running through their checks, the robot arms swinging and flexing behind the air-tight viewing windows, mixing their fake chemicals and creating a snake-oil elixir in a show of impossible technology that never failed to convince. Damn, thought Karol as she made her way down the spiral staircase. I am clever.

Reaching the second floor living area, Karol turned left and walked down the corridor to the expansive kitchen, nodding to her chef as she entered. Whether Karol had a client or a rest day from physical exercise , her staff always started work at 5am; Marco was already whisking up egg whites and getting her omelette ready, the coffee having been ground and brewed when he'd heard the shower. Upstairs, Karol could hear the maids sorting out her private rooms. Grabbing an oversized coffee mug, Karol poured herself a drink and left Marco to get on with it. He would serve it to her in the living room when she called for it.

Strolling back up the corridor, Karol retraced her steps and headed towards her office at the far end of the corridor. As she neared the staircase she glanced to her left over the expansive, minimalist living room. With an identical floor to ceiling uninterrupted view of the mountain range as her bedroom, she saw her own reflection as it was far too early for the sun to appear. For a second she considered taking her drink on one of the two L-shaped twelve-seat white leather sofas arranged around the Japanese-style sunken fire pit in the centre of the room but thought better of it. The furniture was more of a statement than a practical decision; she'd rarely had more than three people in this room, the great majority of her daily business conducted on the floor below. Sitting there watching just how alone she was in her reflection wouldn't do her any good.

When she had first moved in nearly four years ago, she had decided to throw a party of sorts in this very room. From a social perspective, it had been a disaster. However, it had facilitated a ruthless cull of those she once viewed as friends who insisted on trying to convince her she could do so much for so many people in the world if she turned her mind to it.

Despite the obvious trappings of her success - this complex (including the third of four homes she now owned), the astonishing views over the mountains, the solitude - those former 'friends' couldn't understand it all existed because of her bloody-mindedness and focus away from the very people they urged her to help. Furthermore, none of them had known her long enough to realise that, once, she had attempted to use her enormous intellect and engineering abilities for the betterment of humanity. It had led to nothing but frustration, humiliation and resentment.

The resulting blazing arguments with her guests had left her with slammed doors, tears and accusations of no moral compass. The only people left were sycophants and 'advisers' whose counsel was entirely aligned with her world view, self-serving marionettes who she utterly despised. Acquaintances at best, they were useful to her at this moment in time. The second they became anything less than that, they too would be gone.

Karol felt the muscles in her jaw contract. Now wasn't the time to get angry with things she could not change. She needed a clear head and absolute focus for her performance later in the day. A few purposeful strides later, she entered her office, put down her coffee, sat in her chair and activated the keyboard.

"Auberon. Any new business detected for today?"

A hum and a few clicks issued from the decryption stacks behind her.

"Affirmative. New candidate selected."

Karol's heart thumped. Sitting upright, she felt every sense heighten as adrenaline pumped through her fit, muscular body. The screens were already alive with information, some resorting to limited three-dimensional projections of still and moving images while others presented green on green text. Pictures of an ageing man of colour, craggy faced and big in stature, showed him in several places and scenarios. For a few seconds Karol couldn't place him; just as his name flashed up on the screen, she realised who it was.

"Jesus Christ. That's Enzo Randall."

Karol pushed herself back on her chair, the castors gliding slowly towards the humming machinery behind her. In addition to flat and holo-footage of the man were streams of news and police reports, all freshly cracked and hacked by her ever-prying software. Of the top twenty criminals she'd been looking to catch in the last few years, he was the top of the list. One particular document caught her eye, detailing the murders he was suspected of having committed in the last six months alone. It was real, deep FBI and Homeland 'Eyes Only' material from the States;

they knew he was an utterly ruthless villain. They'd likely been trying to get incriminating information from his own files for decades. Karol knew masses of data would already be downloaded into her system but had no interest in blackmailing so dangerous a man – what she was interested in was his CDC identity tag. That would be the key to earning far more than she could with some mundane lists or dates and addresses. It would also carry significantly less risk, given the nature of the man.

"Auberon. Display candidate CDC ID tag. Run algorithm selector."

One thing Karol had learned very quickly in her business was to work as fast as possible when it came to discovering new candidates. While she'd dispensed with real-time alerts when her systems had broken into individuals' protected files, leaving Auberon to dump as much information as possible as quickly as possible then compile the data for Karol's attention, there was no telling whether the target's hacked systems might be able to track where the information was being sent. It hadn't happened yet, but a couple of her old competitors from back in the day, she was convinced, were trying to discover what she was up to with their own snooping systems. One of them co-designed the DCDC system. If the idiot knew he had allowed Karol to formulate her infiltration strategy, the embarrassment would probably kill him.

'Algorithm selected' appeared, so she instructed Auberon to initiate the code chain that would find a route into the CDC's impregnable system, jar it open wide enough for her to get in undetected, then seal it back up after she had done what she needed to do. There were no guarantees all her risky efforts might be rewarded; in the early years, with the CDC only just having gone live and the world shakily adjusting to the concept of knowing the day on which they were going to die, it had been very lean pickings. For the first eighteen months she had spent sleepless days casting her net wide to build her business, living on caffeine and much worse. But, spurred on by her fury of being treated so badly by so many individuals and companies and her absolute, total belief in her intellectual superiority, she had refined her approach to a razor's edge, with no way of anyone ever finding out what she was doing – other than her dark and shady clientele sharing her name in hushed tones.

"Madame, shall I serve now, or do you wish to wait?"

Marco's voice drifted down the long hallway outside. He knew better than to approach the office. Karol barked an irritated 'Wait' without turning her head. A skipped breakfast to make the biggest catch of her life was a small price to pay. If she was right, Randall would take the bait. All her targets shared the same instinct for self-preservation. Greed for life surpassed wealth and power.

Welcome to Server 3776 - Secure Connection Open
User authorisation level 12
Confirmation code *******_****
Gateway security timeout 30s

Keyboard option selected – press back for virtual comms channel

Press 1 to search CDC database
Press 2 to communicate with DCDC support
Press 3 to report an error message
Press 4 to Exit

Karol pressed '1' with a shaking finger. This was her absolute favourite part of the process.

Press 1 to submit CDC ID tag
Press 2 to interrogate open search fields
Press 3 to communicate with DCDC support
Press 4 to report an error message
Press 5 to Exit to previous level

Engrossed in the moment, Karol barely noted the countdown clock ticking patiently down to her left. Pressing '1', she deftly pasted the information she had copied moments earlier and waited for the screen to refresh.

Randall, Enzokuhle Algernon ID RR-F-931K804L-13
DOB 03/03/2013Capetown, RSA

Press 1 for CDC breakdown
Press 2 to facilitate span discrepancy
Press 3 to communicate with DCDC support
Press 4 to report an error message
Press 5 to Exit to previous level

Karol leaned forward in her chair and stabbed at the touch-sensitive keyboard with unnecessary force. Looking down to her hands, she smiled at her shaking fingers. It was nice to know there was still something that excited her, thrilled her.

Randall, Enzokuhle Algernon ID RR-F-931K804L-13
DOB 03/03/1998 Capetown, RSA

CDC 09/26/2079
Current date 03/14/2075
Time elapsed since birth: 77y 0m 11 days
Time of exact CDC: 81y 6m 23 days +/- .5 days

Time remaining to CDC: 4y 6m 12 days +/- .5 days

Press 1 to submit blood sample update
Press 2 to communicate with CDCD support
Press 3 to Exit to previous level

She stared at the numbers for several seconds without blinking, running various calculations through her head.

This was roughly the same screen any subscriber of the CDC database could see, presenting them with a countdown clock to their demise, the ability to update their information with a relatively simple blood analysis, and link to contact the database bots if they had a query. What differed between her view and normal users was the third option. Subscribers could only exit out of the system completely, not work back up the various administration levels Karol's hacking system allowed her to interrogate.

Sitting back in her chair, Karol swept back some rogue hair from her eyes and considered. The bad news was Randall only had four and a half years of natural life left, probably reduced significantly by his lifestyle. Wheeling herself closer to the desk, Karol's fingers danced over the keyboard, calling up sub-menus and drilling down into Randall's upload history. Sure enough, the number of submitted blood samples had increased in the last fifteen years as he had realised the effect of all the narcotics and stress on his longevity.

Karol smiled. That confirmed he was as hooked on how long he'd have to live as all the other murderers, extortionists and worse she had chosen to target over her career. Unless he was murdered or had an accident (which some claimed could be foreseen by miraculous intervention – certainly not by her), his time was up on Tuesday 26th September 2079, plus or minus half a day, regardless of any transfusions or other quack medical procedure.

Many 'miracle cures' and 'guaranteed extension treatments' had appeared since Cell Death Calculation had been unveiled, their effects either marginal or actually detrimental to DNA, RNA, whatever they claimed their procedures manipulated. All of them had, at one point or another, been disproved. The transfusion Karol offered, however, had a one hundred percent success rate - even though it was, just like the others, a total fabrication. There was not a scrap of biological science to her procedure, but a manipulation of numbers thanks to her unbridled and completely illegal access to the CDC database. Like all great plans, her con was extremely simple; first, she took the time away from a victim and then, having approached them with her 'cure', simply restore the time she stole with the stroke of a finger. The greatest irony she could never share with the despots and murderers she courted was the inescapable fact she was a bigger crook than all of them combined.

To her left, the numbers on the countdown screen turned from green to red. Shocked back into action, she returned to Randall's Cell Death Calculation breakdown screen. Her fingers paused over the keyboard as she considered just how much time she should take from him. Too little, and it wouldn't be financially worth her while. Too much, and the margin for things to go wrong, such as accidental death or worse, increased. Calling up a time and date calculator on the smaller screen to her right, she ran a few numbers and finally decided on eighteen months as a good figure. That was enticing enough an extension to offer.

She would, however, have to tread very carefully with this man. Given what Karol knew of him from previous research, if he wasn't entirely certain she could deliver what she promised, it could all go very badly very quickly for her - not to mention if he thought he was being tricked. Offset against that was the potential of this being the biggest payroll of her life.

Taking a deep breath, Karol pressed '3' to return to the previous screen, taking her to the levels no subscribers ever saw or anyone outside the database's minimal supervisory team. To her left, the countdown clock began to flash its red numerals, showing she only had one minute left to press '2' and cast her bait for Randall to hopefully swallow. Within thirty seconds, she had written and triggered the eighteen-month negative span discrepancy, pressed 'send' to inform the hapless gangster of the bad news, shut down her terminal and gone to eat breakfast.

The sleek black Helio glided gently down onto the freezing landing pad, the sun disappearing behind the massive granite rock housing Karol's facility and deepening the shadows cast over the freezing grounds. As its two circular fans spun down and retracted towards its cylindrical body, the side door slid open behind the oversized pilot's blister and a dainty figure stepped out, supported by an absolute giant of a bodyguard. Karol watched her front-of-house staff greet the tiny woman and huge man, pulled the zip on her catsuit up to her neck then marched over to the spiral staircase. One full revolution later she was on the ground floor, through the security lock into the main corridor and heading for the client and staff entrance.

The large glass doors swished open and Wang Xiu Ying entered, shaking away the supporting arm of her monstrous security guard before striding towards Karol, right hand extended, left hand clutching a high-quality laptop case. While she appeared relaxed, Karol knew this was just a façade. Like all the other clients before her, she was trying to hide how desperately hopeful she was that Karol could restore the time that had inexplicably disappeared from her forecast life several months ago.

"Miss Ying. I am so very pleased to meet you at last. I trust your journey was not too difficult?"

Ying stared directly into Karol's eyes. If she was surprised at the Polish woman's lack of accent in her near-perfect Mandarin, she did not show it.

"It was challenging at times. I find it surprising you would base your facility in such a remote location."

Karol had heard this challenge many times before, rarely couched so politely. Given this woman was one of the greatest criminal kingpins in the west of China, she had an eloquence and understated charm that, had Karol not known quite so much about her, would have been disarming. Ying didn't look anything like her eighty-four years due to a series of eye-wateringly expensive cosmetic treatments. Her skin was smooth, and her soft brown eyes twinkled like those of a woman a quarter of her age. Had it not been for the slight stoop, exaggerated by the expensive two-piece dark blue suit she now wore, she could have passed for fifty at the oldest. Not that any of that mattered when a person seemingly had three years of their life taken from them.

"It's the light here that's important, Miss Ying. It works extremely well with the panels I use to power my facility. It's difficult to find such air quality in most parts of the world these days."

Karol's explanation was partially true. The higher altitude did allow for stronger, wider spectrum light, below the trapped smog which now covered a good part of the world. Yes, it would eventually be dissipated across the globe by the latest generation of carbon scrubbers and yes, climate change reversal was finally bearing fruits, but right now this was the best place to be. The dramatic spectacle of glass walls and lines of steel protruding from the slick black rock went a long way to convince her clients the complex was a legitimate venture.

Karol did not need to point out the money others had paid - and they were about to forego - to get back the life she had secretly stolen from them was being continuously and obviously invested. The whole thing was a massive, elaborate con, but it sure looked good. Ying looked around the brightly lit corridor and nodded.

"Indeed."

Ying's gaze returned to Karol then past her to the high security door behind her.

"How are we to proceed, Miss Shybeck?"

Karol smiled warmly.

"Please follow me into the laboratory. There is no need for your bodyguard. You are quite safe here."

Ying waved a dismissive hand to the security man, who

scowled at Karol's two passive-looking, identically dark-suited women that had met him and his charge at the Helio pad. Karol nodded to them both. They would accommodate the bodyguard or leave him to his own devices. Either way, he would not be entering the processing area. Karol had made it absolutely clear that, due to the highly secretive nature of her (fraud) treatment, only her (dupes) clients would be allowed to enter. Ying had not questioned it, suggesting to Karol she had made enquiries into what to expect from her underworld contacts. Karol never asked for references. Everyone realised the need for discretion.

"Auberon. Open secure area. Access code Alpha Zero Four Nine."

"Access granted. Stand back please."

The voice-activated security door was pure theatre, but it was a good way to interrupt any awkward conversations. The less she had to talk with them the better she liked it, but many clients were nervous and garrulous, uncomfortable with having to rely on someone they didn't know and had to trust. Ying was quite different, and Karol was glad of it.

She walked serenely past the thick metal door into the brilliant white room, glanced through the large window to her right that showed myriad robotic arms transferring various vials and fluids from one gleaming stainless-steel container to another, then sat, unbidden, on the single chair next to the various syringes and the applicator unit laid waiting on the pristine square white table. If Ying was curious about the function of the sealed hatch built into the wall directly above the gleaming table surface, she did not let on.

"You have brought your own laptop to access your CDC information I see. Please feel free to interrogate it while I prepare your treatment, Miss Ying."

In addition to narcissism, paranoia was a trait shared by the great majority of Karol's shady clientele. She learned early in her venture that providing electronic equipment for them to use was met with suspicion, so she insisted all clients brought their own laptops, holo-screens or other devices to access their personal account on the CDC database. This was absolutely key to her conning them out of their brutally earned money, and it was the time of greatest anxiety to Karol. From this point on, everything had to work properly. There had only been a single breakdown with the dummy machinery in the hermetically sealed lab.

It happened shortly after installation, and while it could have been a major problem, she quickly persuaded the client to enjoy a meal quickly thrown together by Marco while the equipment was being repaired. The second they had left the building, she had sacked one of her then three technicians on the spot and threatened the other two with extinction if it ever happened again.

"I have access to my information, Miss Shybeck. Do you need to see it?"

Karol busied herself with the syringe bodies lined up on the table, making a show of looking through the clear plastic tubes into the brilliant lights set into the treatment room's ceiling and gently swirling the single cylinder that was half-filled with a dark brown fluid.

"No need. I trust the span discrepancy you have reported is accurate. If you were to request any longer time than this, it would be futile as I cannot extend your life beyond what was originally forecast. My treatment will restore the time lost to your original Cell Death Calculation, nothing more."

Miss Ying's gaze flicked from her laptop screen to meet Karol's eyes. There was real hope there now.

"And that is all anyone could ask. Despite my constant requests, no explanation of the discrepancy has been forthcoming. My physicians could find no indications in my body chemistry to explain the difference. Several new blood cultures were analysed and uploaded, but to no avail.

And yet you claim you can restore that which was lost? I do wonder how so."

This was the most dangerous part of all. Karol had to be in total control of her body and face, lest any 'tells' might be revealed. Years training in the gym allowed her to reduce her breathing, relax her facial muscles and control the timbre of her voice. Lying convincingly to professional liars was closer to art than science.

"Suffice to say it is a process that has taken me the best part of my life to perfect, Miss Ying. And one that extracts a significant toll on my own longevity."

This was, of course, absolute nonsense, but Karol had accidentally discovered that hinting she used her own time allotted on this earth as a trade-off to help her clients had a curiously convincing effect. That, and the charade that was to occur over the next few minutes.

"Yes. And, of course, you can give no guarantees for the time granted being cut short by… unnatural causes."

Another question she had heard so many times. Karol carefully placed the empty syringes back down on the tray, gently clasped her hands behind her back and faced Ying directly. Body language, NLP training, carefully rehearsed explanations with just the right stresses and tonality, everything came into play within the confines of this room.

"While some may claim accidental death, murder or other unattributable causality can somehow influence the CDC result and trigger a negative span discrepancy report, as a scientist I completely rebut this. Disregarding the ongoing philosophical discussions around the merits of knowing one's own demise, the side-show antics of spiritualists and other charlatans have never impacted or influenced any of the treatments I have provided. Nor have I seen any convincing evidence to support changes to an individual's Cell Death Calculation other than illness or previous trauma."

Like all good lies, Karol's rehearsed speech had a

strong element of truth within it. There had been some peculiar cases over the years where a sudden change to a person's Cell Death Calculation had coincided with their accidental death or murder, but she had chosen to include them with a variety of other fringe theories and not given them any credence. The best way around this shaky topic was to employ the kind of language all of her clients understood – money.

"Seventy five percent of any financial agreement I make is based on a client surviving to the day originally indicated on the CDC database, before the span discrepancy notice was issued. If you – or any – client dies before that time, inexplicably indicated by a span discrepancy notice or otherwise, the great majority of our agreed payment would not be released to me. That is how little confidence I have in those fairy tales, Miss Ying."

Karol knew Ying would have done her research – limited though any information would have been due to the relentless filtering Karol's system undertook second by second across the world. There was a trail of breadcrumbs to follow, all carefully designed to unveil exactly what she wanted others to know of her business, and nothing more. Ying blinked a couple of times, nodded once, then closed the lid on her laptop just as a low chime sounded and Auberon announced the treatment was ready for application.

Karol leaned over the table, slid the hatch cover upwards and retrieved a small phial of clear liquid. Within seconds she had discharged its contents into the two syringes. A couple of flicks of the wrist and the partially filled cylinder was mixed. Both were pressed home into the stainless-steel hypodermic pressure gun.

Selecting the mixture first, Karol bid Ying take off her immaculately tailored jacket and roll up the left sleeve of her cream silk blouse above the elbow. Karol rechecked the applicator was gas charged then gently placed its flat circular nozzle onto Ying's arm.

"This first injection is a combination of my blood marrow extract and white blood cells."

With a sharp hiss and a slight jump of the applicator, the mixture of saline and food dye was forced beneath the subcutaneous layer of Ying's skin into the bloodstream. Selecting the second, clear cylinder on the applicator's carousel, Karol placed the nozzle slightly below the first injection point.

"And this consists of extracts from my pituitary and adrenal glands."

The saline pushed its way into Ying's body with another crack of gas, leaving six tell-tale blood wheels where the harmless fluid had been injected. Karol painted an instant medical sealant over the marks to prevent infection and returned the applicator to the table.

"I need you to stay off your feet for half an hour for the serums to combine in your bloodstream. Please refer to the clock above the entrance door."

Karol nodded to the cool blue ALED numbers projected in front of their digital panel showing the local time to hours, minutes and seconds. For some odd reason, the clock added yet more legitimacy to her elaborate ruse, some clients choosing to sit and watch the time tick by until they dare move. Absurd, but another helpful aspect of their paranoia.

"You are free to undertake any business you wish on your laptop but please stay seated and do not put it away as you will need it later. I will go and prepare the blood extraction equipment and return as soon as it is ready. Please do not replace your jacket as I will be taking the sample from your other arm."

Ying nodded and began rolling down her sleeve. The half hour wait gave Karol time to check her clients' departure details with her front-of-house staff and ensure everything was in order for the financial transaction before they left. By the time she had picked up a sterile blood sampling pack approved for use by the CDC database and re-entered the treatment room, thirty-five minutes had elapsed. Ying continued to sit patiently, the pearlescent lid of her wafer-thin computer resting lightly on her lap. As Karol readied the blood sampling kit, she could see the woman looked even younger than before. Hope, no matter where it came from, was the most remarkable treatment of all.

"If you could please roll up your right sleeve Miss Ying."

Karol took the blood sample quickly, the red-purple fluid bubbling as it flooded into the small vial sticking up from the top of the extraction gun. Applying another instantly drying protective film on her arm, Karol pressed a couple of buttons on the handheld device to begin the analysis, and bid Ying connect to it wirelessly from her laptop. Ninety seconds later, the data was awaiting upload to Ying's CDC account. She looked up from her screen, a hint of nerves creasing around her dark brown eyes.

"Upload your sample, Miss Ying. In approximately twenty minutes, you should receive a span discrepancy notice with much more welcome news than the previous one."

Ying sent the data with a jab of her finger and the translucent keyboard faded to a low glow of Chinese characters.

"Excuse me while I dispose of this equipment. As agreed, your sample will be destroyed. I will be back in a few minutes. Auberon, open secure area. Access code Alpha Zero Four Nine."

Karol allowed the security door to rumble shut behind her before she jettisoned the extraction equipment into a hazardous waste chute built into the corridor wall, passed through the security lock then headed back up the spiral staircase to her office. Within two minutes she had accessed Ying's details, restored her original Cell Death Calculation date and issued a span discrepancy notice, positive this time, with a ten-minute delay. This would allow Karol to be in the room when Ying received it, another subtle way of maintaining the fraudulent veneer the treatment was real. Returning down to the treatment room, she patiently waited with Ying until, finally, the positive notice arrived. Checking her hmail, the old woman smiled. In response to the updated blood sample, her CDC had been recalculated to just under three years of additional longevity. Without it, Ying falsely believed she would be dead in two weeks but now, thanks to Karol's magical elixir, life had been given back to her.

"I shall transfer the first instalment of your payment immediately."

Karol nodded and turned her back as Ying accessed her financial details. Even a quarter of the agreed fee was a considerable amount. One thing Karol had learned with her elaborate scam was patience; she would have to wait for Ying to hopefully die of natural causes in three years' time, when her last will and testament, triply checked by Karol's legal team, would release the remaining seventy five percent of their arranged fee. But as Karol nodded her thanks to Ying and she rolled down her silken sleeve with a look of blissful relief, Karol had a much bigger payday on her mind.

Shybeck, Karol ID KS-P-044F132E-34
DOB 12/21/2034 Kracow, Poland

CDC 03/11/2129
Current date 03/24/2075
Time elapsed since birth: 40y 2m 30 days
Time from birth to CDC: 93y 6m 17 days +/- .5 days
Time remaining to CDC: 54y 3m 15 days +/- .5 days

Press 1 to submit blood sample update
Press 2 to communicate with CDCD support
Press 3 to Exit to previous level

Karol sipped at her coffee and frowned at the screen. Ten days had passed since she had sent out the falsified negative span discrepancy report to Enzo Randall and she'd received no reaction. It wasn't time to panic yet; the longest she'd ever waited was two months, but that particular idiot had been shot the day Karol had communicated with him and spent the next eight weeks in an induced coma. Once he'd got out of it, realising his newly calculated CDC was up in a horrifyingly short three days, he'd worked very fast. That was the only time the two-month margin Karol built into her span discrepancies had nearly lost her business; faced with their impending demise, her clients didn't usually hang around. And then there was the failure rate.

At around 40% of those she selected not 'finding' her, she could easily take the hit. There was plenty of crossover between new clients such as Ying providing their down payment and older ones reaching their restored demise date, mostly bang on the calculated time, releasing the rest of the agreed payment and swelling her coffers to extortionate levels. Randall still had plenty of time in which to act. There was no reason for her to be irritated by his lack of contact. No reason, but she was.

Perhaps it was the audacious amount she'd demand to give back the eighteen months she'd stolen at the press of a button. Perhaps it was because he'd always been at the top of her 'hit list'. Perhaps it was because she was so utterly bored with every other aspect of her life; her self-imposed exile, routine exercise and sex. Perhaps the only thing she had left that offered any real excitement was work. But that wasn't anything new. She'd first realised a way to exploit the extraordinary scientific breakthrough in Cell Death Calculation in the last year of her Doctorate in Advanced AI. Even at the wunderkind age of twenty, work – or her version of it, at least – had been her life.

While the media hadn't at first known what to make of Cell Death Calculation, churches across the world had proclaimed it little more than heresy, taking one of the few remaining great mysteries out of life. Businesses couldn't see how they'd make money out of the information at first but, slowly, when it was possible to determine exactly how much a person might earn and how much they might spend in their lifetime, everything changed; housing, employment, insurance, banking, population centres, everything. When people knew with absolute certainty how long they had on Earth, attitudes shifted. Many still viewed the whole concept of knowing with revulsion, but the majority embraced and planned with it – but not quite in the way Karol had.

Karol exited the CDC database, put her coffee down on a non-active part of the touch-sensitive desk and pushed herself back towards the servers. Looking out the office window, she could see the base of the mountains beginning to show rock through the snow. The weather was improving day on day and she'd not have to fret about the one factor out of her control. It was the best part of the year for her – other than when she checked her various offshore bank accounts. It was still mightily cold, but she might suggest to Giselle they go out for a run now the snow was retreating. That usually took her mind off things. Getting up and leaving the office, she hadn't taken five steps before Auberon chimed in over the speaker system.

"Incoming audio call from blocked number."

Karol's pace slowed, her heart rate increasing at the AI's message.

"Hold."

Someone had found her unlisted number and had enough computing power to hide their identity from Karol's mighty telecom interrogation system. That indicated a very cautious individual who didn't want to wait for responses via encrypted avatars or darkweb messaging. By calling, they were clearly in a hurry for an answer. Turning towards the kitchen, she shouted a delay to Marco for her breakfast and was met with the angry clashing of pans and muffled oaths behind the kitchen door. She returned to her office, activated the privacy screen that sealed off all vision and sound from the interior of the room and stood in front of the window, watching a delivery truck arrive with fresh provisions from the nearby town.

"Auberon. Proceed with audio call."

A couple of clicks, and then seconds of silence.

"I wish to speak with Karol Shybeck."

The voice was rich and deep, the tone insistent. Seven words and Karol already knew who it was.

"Speaking. Who is this?"

Another pause then gentle breathing as the caller considered whether to play games or get on with it. Given the time pressures Karol knew had suddenly been put upon them, the man decided against the former.

"I am Enzokuhle Randall. A mutual acquaintance suggested you may be able to help me with an issue that has arisen."

Randall was word-perfect in the phrase Karol requested any satisfied client might use when passing on her name. It didn't matter a jot who had talked with the man, only that he had called her. For a second she felt light-headed, but took a silent, deep breath then exhaled through her nose, her breath steaming up the glass before her.

"I will be happy to discuss terms with you. If I may – "

"You will see me in three days at six pm your time. The fee will be one trillion. There is no negotiation if you want my business."

Karol turned to face the office. It usually took a couple of weeks to prepare for new clients, to sort out the legal issues, finalise payment channels and for her to ready herself mentally for the full day show she had to put on. Even with such a staggering offer, far more than what even she had thought greedy, three days wouldn't cut it. She had to make it clear she was in charge of this transaction, not him.

"Mister Randall, I'm afraid that timescale isn't – "

"You will be ready in three days. I want my time back as quickly as possible."

Karol felt her heart thumping in her chest. The man's tone had changed to one of menace. From the files she had seen, she knew what he was capable of. Despite the considerable physical protection Karol enjoyed, not least her own proficiency in armed and unarmed combat, she would have to play this extremely carefully.

"Even if I start preparations for treatment immediately, the serums cannot be processed in any less than ninety-six hours. The filtration alone will take – "

"Four days. No further negotiation."

The man was beginning to lose his temper. Fuck him, Karol thought. I'm in charge here.

"Mister Randall, I have certain protocols that need to be observed. I will require your legal and financial – "

"Check your third largest Meridian Account, Miss Shybeck. You will notice it is now by far the biggest."

Karol rushed over to the white leather chair, air hissing in complaint from the deeply upholstered ribbing. After a sweep of the hand to activate the keyboard and a few taps, her mouth fell open at the amount deposited – into an account she had buried so deep, no-one should be able to find it.

"I will transfer the remainder of the funds on completion in four days. Weather permitting, I will arrive at 4pm. There will be no further communication up until that point. Do not disappoint me."

The emphasis on the last few words sounded like a death threat. Karol's heart hammered in her chest. She couldn't remember the last time she had felt frightened.

"Where shall I send my location coordinates?"

The pause was as chilling as the words that followed.

"I know where you are."

A loud click signified the end of the call. Karol stared at her reflection in the sleeping screens before her, oblivious to the low hum of electronics all around. He'd found her account and deposited money without her knowledge. He'd defeated her comms software and called straight to her home. What else did he know about her? Had he discovered her secrets? That would mean all her systems had been compromised and she simply could not, would not believe that. Reaching for her coffee cup, she pulled a face when the cold liquid touched her lips and put it back down on the desktop. For long minutes she sat quite still, willing her heart rate to slow, running the scenario through her head as the sun broke over the mountains and streamed into the room.

No legal, no financial, no transportation control over the client. No arranged payments, no safety nets or protections, no running to her schedule.

One trillion.

Karol got to work.

It was still dark when Karol woke. She didn't bother looking at the gently glowing projected time floating hazily above her pillow; at best she'd had four hours sleep, which was twice as much as she'd grabbed over the last two nights. As she stared at her bedroom ceiling and waited for the dizziness of fatigue to leave her, she thought over the previous crazy three days. They'd been a blur of shouting, demanding, cajoling and pushing everyone around her, whether they deserved it or not, and making demands on herself she'd forgotten she could take.

Giselle had stormed out, vowing never to come back after being treated so rudely, and her remaining two technicians – survivors of her fury over the lab breakdown and surly ever since – finally found the balls to tell her to go fuck herself and her job. Luckily, she'd tipped them over the edge just as they were finishing a full maintenance refit of the lab, so it would still do its useless yet impressive looking business when Randall arrived in – and at that point she relented and glanced at the time – thirteen hours or so.

Thirteen hours. Shit.

Throwing back her heavy silk sheets, Karol padded into the bathroom. Eight minutes later she was dressed and walking down the staircase, head still spinning from a lack of sleep. There were so many checks left to undertake, and she'd not even begun preparing the fake injections. She usually liked to have them on the tray and in the treatment room the day before, but she'd got caught up with a power problem to the Helio pad that had taken up far too much of her time and led to yet another blazing row with someone she'd normally barely acknowledge. They'd probably left, too.

Reaching the second floor, Karol heard Marco arriving and getting the kitchen ready. She couldn't manage a coffee, let alone anything to eat, thanks to the headache and nausea. Some of that was excitement at finally bagging Randall, but most of it was the imbalance created by tablets she'd taken to keep herself going and the recent lack of control over her normally well-ordered life.

Her routine had collapsed; she'd not checked any communications since she'd talked with Randall a few days ago, despite Auberon having notified her on several occasions of incoming messages. Walking, arms folded, towards the panoramic living room windows, she watched daylight struggling to creep over the mountain range. The entire sky was a dark grey, heavy with snow. That was all she needed – unseasonal weather on top of everything else.

Karol shook her head. It was time to enforce some kind of normality, get a grip on those things she could control. She didn't even know if any new clients had been identified over the last few days, which was a stupid way to run a business. Picking up the pace, she entered her office, activated the monitors and asked Auberon if there was any new business. Having responded negatively, she then started up the CDC database hacking process. Wiping her face with a clammy hand, she pulled up her chair and lit up the keyboard. As the hum turned to a whine from the decryption units, she opened her messages. There were dozens, always the same when she didn't check regularly. She was just about to deactivate the screen when one caught her eye, a direct hmail from the DCDC. Occasionally they sent out routine maintenance messages, informing registered users when the database might be temporarily unavailable to their registered users which, naturally, Karol was in addition to being a continual uninvited guest. Knowing such information was useful to avoid hacking the system when part of it might be unavailable, so she opened and read it.

"What the FUCK?"

Karol stared at the screen open mouthed. She couldn't believe what she was seeing.

To: Shybeck, Karol
ID: KS-P-044F132E-34

Negative Span Discrepancy report

Dear Karol Shybeck,

It is with regret the DCDC must inform you of a change to your Cell Death Calculation. Please access your account as a matter of urgency and use the menu system to contact us with any concerns or issues you have over this communication. Please do not respond to this hmail address as it is unmonitored, and you will not receive a response.

Faithfully

DCDC

This couldn't be right. It simply couldn't.

"Auberon. Initiate selected algorithm."

Her voice was little more than a whisper, but the AI

picked it up and undertook its instructions. Swiping the impossible message to a smaller screen on her right, Karol tried to control her horror. The message had come in two days ago and she'd not taken the time to check it. Ignoring her routine had resulted in... whatever this situation was. As she descended through the opening menu screens, Karol had to clench her fists between typing to stop her fingers from hitting the wrong keys. The light intensity in the room notched up a couple of stages, making the glare on the screens more noticeable.

Somewhere at the back of her mind she concluded it must be getting darker outside and, as such, the weather must be deteriorating rapidly – as was her self-control. Furious with herself for breaking her own rigid rules, she focused her attention on getting to her personal information screen to verify the CDC message was authentic. CDC IDs occasionally surfaced on various platforms and were often used to create malicious messages by bored teenage hackers living in their parents' basement. Even though she clung to it, she knew it was a slim hope. Karol knew a genuine communication when she saw one.

Shybeck, Karol ID KS-P-044F132E-34
DOB 12/21/2034 Kracow, Poland

CDC 03/28/2075
Current date 03/28/2075
Time elapsed since birth: 40y 3m 03 days
Time from birth to CDC: 40y 3m 03 days +/- .5 days
Time remaining to CDC: 0y 0m 0.5 days +/- .5 days

Press 1 to submit blood sample update
Press 2 to communicate with CDCD support
Press 3 to Exit to previous level

"No. No no NO."

Fifty-four years of Karol's life had disappeared.

Bile rose in her throat and the text began to sway from side to side. Pushing herself backwards in her chair, she doubled over and retched, but as she hadn't eaten properly for days there was nothing to come up. Her stomach muscles convulsed and then she began to shake violently. Grabbing hold of her flanks, she hugged herself and tried to regain control over her body. The shock was overwhelming, making her panic. Again she retched, her breathing getting more laboured and ragged by the second.

What had happened?

Karol willed herself upright. She had to get a grip, she had to think this through. She pushed herself out of the chair onto shaking legs and over to the office window, resting her forehead on the cool glass.

"Madame… are you alright?"

Marco's voice came from the corridor behind her. It was laden with concern.

"I'm fine Marco. Could you please bring me a glass of water?"

Marco turned and walked back to the kitchen, returning a few seconds later. She didn't want to face him nor prolong the conversation, so she asked him to leave it on the desk and return to his kitchen. As her head cleared a little, Karol returned to her seat, sipped at the cool water, placed it carefully back on the desk then waited for her breathing to return to normal.

The first thing she needed to do was to see if there was any trace of who had issued her Negative Span Discrepancy report. That would indicate if someone else had, finally, managed to access the system illegally. Perhaps it was a warning. Perhaps it had been done to teach her a lesson. After a few hesitant strokes of the keys her muscle memory took over, and she interrogated every corner and crevice of the CDC database. By the time the alarm sounded and counted down for her to exit the system, she had found nothing. Logging out, she sat back in her chair and looked at her reflection in the main monitor. If someone had created the report, they were as good – better, potentially – than she was at hiding their tracks.

But if it wasn't some capricious rival and the report was genuine, that meant she would be dead before the day was out.

No. It had to be someone else. But then, who? Her mind immediately raced to Randall's interception of her bank account. True, it wasn't on the same level of intrusion she was practising on the CDC database, but it was a significant achievement to circumvent not only Meridian's security systems but her own firewalls. Auberon made regular sweeps and checks of potential hacks; attempts were few and far between, and nothing had been flagged between the time she had generated Randall's report and him contacting her. So, whoever he had used to get the information and deposit the money was very, very good. But were they this good, good enough to get into the CDC system?

And then there was the question of why. If Randall had found out he was being conned, he would have sent someone to kill her immediately. Why would he order such an elaborate attack? It didn't make sense. He was a man who acted immediately, often rashly, and always violently. From what she'd accessed of the files she'd stolen, this simply wasn't his style. And in twelve hours – at the far end of the projected window shown by her report – he'd arrive to find her potentially dead.

Karol breathed in deeply. Sweeping a strand of hair from her forehead, she retrieved her water and sipped at it again. Her strength was slowly returning, and while she still had a dreadful headache and her hands were trembling, working the problem made her feel better. Physically, there was nothing wrong with her. She couldn't be in better shape. Her last medical had shown no issues and she regularly used her home body analyser. Even if she had suddenly developed a fatal illness, she'd not uploaded blood work data to the CDC for three years so they wouldn't have known the results if they existed. Looking at her suddenly haggard reflection in the big screen, she suddenly realised this must be precisely the thought processes her victims went through when they received her little gift. If it hadn't been so shit-scarily serious, she'd appreciate the irony. So, if it wasn't a rival presenting their calling card, it wasn't Randall revealing he knew what she was up to and it wasn't updated medical information uploaded by herself, that left only one thing – even more unlikely than those potential explanations.

It had to be accidental death.

But how could it be? How could the system possibly be triggered by an individual's fate? The first non-medical reasons for changes to a person's CDC began to surface a couple of years after the database was initially launched. Headlines had swept the world, claiming some mystical recalculation had occurred for hundreds of people, forecasting their imminent demise instead of dying at a ripe old age of natural causes. Various religious groups had pointed to it as God's way of re-asserting balance over an unnatural human-created imbalance, while others insisted on influences as diverse as aliens and the supernatural. Some believed it, others – Karol included – dismissed it as fringe science at best, a recruitment drive for Mother Church at worse.

Even so, while she dismissed the idea, she'd still incorporated accidental death as a limit to her income. It hadn't happened yet, but statistically speaking, it could. And then there were the few cases Karol had seen which allegedly proved the accuracy of these sudden Negative Span Discrepancy reports. Some had given days for a person to live, the individual duly dying plus or minus twelve hours to the time of their updated calculation. The great majority were clearly frauds, attempts to discredit the CDC or trumpet the existence of higher powers, but that still left a handful that she'd never been able to explain. It had suited her to ignore them up until this point but now, her needs had suddenly, inexplicably changed.

Karol got her mighty machines to work hunting the legitimate and not so legal layers of the web, hunting out the few 'genuine' cases that remained unexplained. The sheer illogicality of it still bothered her deeply but after scanning various reports, a focus of sorts presented itself. She concentrated on instances where people had acted on their imminent demise – and, according to them, had 'cheated' the fates - by ensuring accidents were impossible. Discounting the obviously delusional self-publicists crying for a few minutes of fame, she followed the remaining digital whispers, hoping they might hold some truth.

Within forty minutes, the weather had taken a turn for the worse, Karol had neck ache from craning forwards and scrutinising her screens and her head was pounding. However, after watching half a dozen holo-interviews and a series of borderline contradictory blogs and hologs, she had formed what passed for a plan of action. Before Randall's arrival, she would remove every single possibility of accidental death from her immediate vicinity, shut every non-vital system down and stay put until her client's arrival – if, indeed, he even made it in this weather. For a brief moment she considered cancelling his visit but remembered his final chilling words. It all came together to convince her someone, somewhere, was trying to tell her it was time to retire.

Karol watched from her kitchen window as the last vehicle pulled out of the staff parking bay to the side of her compound. Needing a quick method to get everybody out without any questions, she had triggered the Radon alarm in the basement plant room, the blaring klaxon sounding throughout the entire complex with its urgent instruction to evacuate immediately. Ironically, the only people who might have questioned this event were the two technicians who had walked out on her earlier. Marco had been the last to leave, insisting she get out with the rest of them, but Karol refused, telling him someone had to be there for the specialist company called in to deal with such emergencies. Promising she would not move from her living area until they arrived, Marco had grudgingly agreed, his decision secured by the snow now falling heavily from the slate grey heavens. The road out would quickly deteriorate, and as Karol had messaged the staff not to return for the rest of the day, everyone else had taken the opportunity for a bonus day off with a little more enthusiasm than her chef.

Returning to her living room, Karol waited until Marco's EV had disappeared from view until she began – very carefully – shutting down as many systems as she could. Room by room she turned everything off, wearing double-insulated bioshield gloves for every switch and breaker she had to handle. While the terror of her possible death still raged throughout her body, adopting a methodical, floor by floor approach gave her a goal. Time after time her mind wandered into dark corners; everything she looked at, from the stairs to electrical sockets, was given immediate safety appraisals – could they kill her, could they injure her, what series of events might make the everyday become lethal?

She had to come down hard on herself with these thoughts as they kept bringing her to a shaking halt, throwing doubt on decisions she'd previously not even consider as important. Every flick of a switch and every step was taken with a deep breath in and a sharp exhale out, once the process had proven benign.

By mid-afternoon, everything but the entrance hallway, the fake lab and the treatment room had been isolated. Karol had considered shutting down the power completely to the upper two floors but thought better of it; she needed to keep her office servers running and besides, Randall had to think everything was normal on his arrival. He wasn't to know he would usually have been greeted not by Karol herself but her team, nor would he be able to see the lack of staff Electric Vehicles in the parking bay from the front reception. The lights would be on throughout the complex, providing an impressive display of wealth and style to a man she knew took such things seriously. Randall wouldn't be travelling by Helio – the weather had improved, but not enough for flight, and that meant his 4pm arrival would be delayed. That suited her just fine. Standing in the treatment room, she watched the dummy machines go through their impressive dance behind the airtight window. All she had to do was survive past 6pm and she'd cheat her forecast death. She hoped.

"Auberon. Time."

"The time is five twenty-six pm."

Karol was shaking so hard, the snake-oil mix in her syringe bodies had a froth on them. She'd spent a quarter of an hour trying to work out if picking up the hypodermic pressure gun was an acceptable risk, nearly as long as she'd taken over throwing the big circuit breaker to the lab's power before assuring herself it wouldn't inexplicably electrocute her. Even so, she'd used a broom handle to push it upwards.

The closer she got to the end of the '+/- 12 hours' of her Negative Span Discrepancy report, the worse – not better – she felt. The only thing that acted as a form of safety belt for sanity was the colossal payday Randall promised. It was a suitably enormous sum of money to retire on, although God alone knew what she'd do instead of work.

She was smart. She'd think of something.

"Alert. A convoy of EVs are approaching."

Karol dropped the syringe body onto the gleaming table, only just moving fast enough to stop it rolling onto the clean room floor. Jesus Christ. How had Randall managed to get here so quickly by road? Heart thudding in her chest, Karol lined up the prepped syringes ready for the elixir's arrival at the hatch then straightened up.

Marching out of the treatment room, she activated the big steel door. By the time she had grabbed a thick coat from the hook by the exit, kicked off her Salomons and slipped on a pair of thermal boots, the treatment room was sealed and secure.

The thick glass doors glided apart, welcoming in a rush of freezing air from the fading light. Karol paused, wondering if there was something outside that could be a threat to her and ran through increasingly preposterous scenarios, ending with the approaching EVs somehow losing control and running her over. Stepping out onto the walkway leading to the parking circle, Karol looked to her surroundings like never before. Above, to the left and right behind her stretched the front of her complex, light spilling brilliantly from the myriad windows that didn't have automatic dimming or privacy filters.

Before her, the narrow walkway swept over to the left, joining the wide, empty parking circle with its thick layer of snow. Beyond it stretched white fields to the pine tree line, and past that, the mountains, quickly losing their definition in the sunset. Other than the twinkling of headlights snaking closer through the forest, there was nothing unusual or sinister. Karol felt sick but pushed herself on, reaching the very end of the walkway as the first EV cruised into the parking area, its brilliant white beams picking up flecks of falling snow as it came to a silent halt.

Karol kept as still as she could, hoping her intense shaking could be explained by the cold to the figures exiting the gull-wings of their vehicles. Three men approached, one each from the three sleek EVs, two falling behind the unmistakable figure of Randall. Breath trails sailed into the darkening air, contrasting with the thick, black long coats they all wore. It was all suitably villainous and threatening.

"Mister Randall. Welcome to my facility."

Randall came to a crunching halt in the snow, his dark eyes narrowing and face becoming craggier as he stared through her. Karol took this as impatience to be getting on with proceedings, but given the circumstances, she would not be hurried. She was under enough pressure as it was.

"Cut the shit. Let's get on with it."

Randall began to walk forward, as did his two bodyguards. Trillion or not, Karol put her hand out in a blocking gesture. Randall stopped, stared at her hand, then into her eyes. This time there was burning focus.

"Just you, Mister Randall. No-one else enters the complex until the treatment is over."

Randall continued to stare as he spoke, slowly and deliberately.

"You expect me to walk in there without protection? I don't think so."

One of the men behind Randall rested his hand on what Karol assumed was a very large weapon beneath his bulky quilted coat. The other, doubtless equally well armed, held a small laptop case in his right hand. The move was obviously designed to intimidate, and, for a second, Karol panicked. Could this be it? Was she about to provoke her own murder?

"Mister Randall, you have ignored every protocol I usually employ with my clients. Given the amount of money you are offering, I have chosen to ignore that, although it leaves me extremely uneasy and vulnerable. The actions of your men are doing little to alleviate those concerns."

Karol couldn't control the tremor in her voice. She hoped her genuine fear at the situation would work to her advantage, although with such a killer as this before her, it was the biggest gamble she'd taken to date. What was she thinking, getting rid of her staff and leaving her so hopelessly unsupported? Had she brought her early death upon herself? Was her greed the architect of her own demise?

"Go back to the EVs. If I need you, I'll call you."

Randall barked his orders. The two men looked to each

other, turned around and headed back to the low, curved shapes of their vehicles as the doors swung upwards and outwards to greet them. Karol's anxiety jumped yet further, and she felt herself begin to shake again beneath her heavy coat.

"I require payment once the procedure has been completed, Mister Randall."

"Then he comes in with us. No negotiation."

She wanted to insist Randall bring the laptop in with him to ensure payment, but she could see she was already pushing him too far. All she had to do was survive the next, what, half an hour or so and her Discrepancy report would have expired. By the time they had finished the procedure, she would be well outside the predicted +12 hours for her death. In fact, the longer she played this out, the better. The bodyguard could be invited back in after she'd gone through the procedure. One by one, she was reducing the components outside of her direct control, and this made her relax a little.

"We can sort the transfer out later."

Karol turned back towards the entrance, the brooding form of Randall uncomfortably close behind her. Shedding her boots and coat, she bid Randall do the same and activated the security door to the treatment room, closing her eyes to steady her nerve before the syringe table as Randall marched in behind her. She had shared the room with some very dangerous people, but as the thick steel door closed with an air-tight hiss it was the first time she felt anything other than in total control of events. Given her life-clock was supposedly ticking its last few minutes, it was all she could do to stop herself screaming.

Turning to face Randall, she immediately checked for the outline of any obvious weapons beneath his immaculately tailored dark brown suit. Satisfied, she went into the routine of checking the fake treatments but could see his dark eyes flicking around the gleaming white room, taking in the sealed hatch through which the 'serum' would be deposited, the single chair and table, the devices upon it and the moving machinery behind the glass panel. He stared at all the elements with the intensity of someone who, despite his age, used every heightened sense to absorb as much information as possible. Here was a man who looked for details in everything, something Karol felt she, too, had learned the hard way. Other than that and the ability to make huge amounts of money illegally, the similarities ended.

"Take a seat, Mister Randall, and roll up the sleeve of your left arm please."

Auberon hadn't yet indicated the elixir was ready to be collected from the hatch, but Karol wanted to make it look as if it was business as usual. Staring at the robotic arms doing their mesmerising waltz, Randall slowly took off his jacket, revealing no handgun nor other weapon. Gently placing it on the back of the chair, he quickly removed the glinting gold links on his double-cuffed pink cotton shirt and began rolling up his sleeve. He got about halfway up his thick, muscled forearm when he promptly stopped.

"Should there be smoke coming from that machine, Miss Shybeck?"

Karol followed Randall's gaze through the window to the laboratory behind it. Sure enough, black smoke was drifting lazily around a couple of the thicker piston-like stainless steel arms in the centre of the room. Before she could answer, there was a double chime heralding the AI.

"Alert. Malfunction in Laboratory One. Please attend."

Karol looked to the hatch built into the wall then over to the scowling face of Randall. He wasn't stupid. He could see something was wrong.

"Is this going to affect my treatment?"

Karol stared at the hatch. The fake serum should be released any second, allowing her to get on with the charade of 'treating' Randall, smoking machines or not. Long seconds ticked by, and nothing happened.

"Miss Shybeck. What is going on?"

Her mind was in a whirl. The release mechanism was a simple timer, unconnected to the movements of the machines. And yet it wasn't releasing the pre-prepared phial she had placed behind the hatch yesterday. Looking back to the lab, she saw with horror the smoke was getting denser. Clearly, it had somehow damaged the dispensing mechanism.

"Alert. Heat signature detected in Laboratory One. Activating fire suppression systems."

Even with the double-glazed glass separating the treatment room from the lab, the halon extinguisher system could be heard flooding into the sealed chamber. After a few seconds the smoke began to dissipate and then, with the whine of unseen fans, the halon was evacuated, leaving a picture of frozen machinery partially illuminated by the occasional flash of light from sparking electricals.

And still the hatch did not open.

"You need to go in there and fix it. I want my treatment. Now."

Randall had turned to face her. A thick vein pulsed on his brow, his eyes burning black coals. She tried to ignore the way he was balling his fists.

"Mister Randall... As you can see there has been a malfunction and my staff are not currently available to – "

"Which part of 'no negotiation' don't you understand? I want my time back, I want my life back, I want my treatment."

Karol took a step back and steadied herself on the table behind her.

"I don't know what the problem is, Mister Randall. I can have someone here to – "

She stopped herself mid-sentence. She didn't have anyone to call. She had dismissed both of the technicians who might have been able to fix this and find out why the delivery mechanism had failed. And then, with another wave of nausea sweeping through her, she realised what had happened. They had sabotaged the system before they had left as a grand goodbye 'fuck you'.

"Get in there and fix it yourself. I was told you were supposed to be some kind of genius. Get it repaired and give me my treatment."

Karol looked to the strobe-like flashing in the otherwise darkened laboratory. The bursts of light picked out silhouettes of crazily angled arms and armatures, all still, all totally useless. Then she glanced to the ALED clock above the security door. It was three minutes to six. Could that be the way she died – electrocuted by her own equipment? There was no way she was going inside that room in its present condition. She just had to survive another three minutes and she would be safe.

"I'm not going into that room before I've isolated the electrical supply. Auberon. Open secure area. Access code Alpha Zero Four Nine."

Had Karol not been distracted by the slowly opening door, she might have reacted more quickly to the furious roar from Randall who was now bearing down on her, eyes wide and teeth bared in rage. His left hand grabbed a hold of her throat and she felt herself being lifted from her feet by the momentum of his attack. What air was left in her lungs gasped out as her back slammed into the wall, the fingers tightening around her throat. Her view was filled with Randall's snarling face, the opening door cruelly framing his manic stare.

"You think you can treat me like this? Do you know who I am? You don't do this to me."

Colours and shapes started to form on the periphery of Karol's vision. Grabbing his left wrist with both hands, she pushed her nails into the skin as hard as she could. This only seemed to infuriate Randall further. He leaned his weight into the stranglehold and broke her left wrist with a wrench of his right hand. Karol gurgled back a desperate reply.

"You... kill me and... you... don't get... treatment..."

Randall's eyes narrowed, his face inches from hers. She could feel the heat of his breath, the wet of his spittle on her skin. The colours and shapes surrounding her vision were now turning to darkness.

"You're not the only one who offers this service."

While it was loud and full of hatred, the voice seemed far away to Karol, as if she was listening to it from the bottom of a well. Her world was getting ever smaller, like the iris of a lens reacting to a brilliant light, one which she could now see approaching. Right in the middle of the light, she could just make out the blue figures of the ALED clock above the treatment room door. The numbers suddenly made sense, and she felt strangely peaceful yet sad all at the same time.

Just before the pain stopped, the last thing she saw was 17:59:56.

The War on Trevor

The supply ship was far behind them now, a rhythmically appearing shape on the rising, falling, rising horizon made solid by the slowly ascending sun behind it. Boats had never appealed to nor agreed with Macintyre; even the big one gradually decreasing in size made him nauseated, a feeling amplified by the large rubber landing craft in which he squatted.

If he'd wanted to be a sailor, he'd have joined the Navy and learned how to row a boat, an argument he'd not dare present to the ferocious sergeant sitting directly opposite. He'd been given the task of checking, loading and now ensuring the tightly netted bails of supplies before, behind and underneath him didn't wobble out of the black rubber craft and drop into the sea. Macintyre wasn't worried by the movement of the dinghy working them loose, but his own violently shaking body. Despite the lime green Level A HAZMAT suit he was wearing, he'd never been so cold in his life.

Yesterday had started normally enough. He'd risen with reveille, sorted his kit out, gone for his shit, shave and shower then headed over to the mess hall for breakfast. Not unusually for Aberdeen it'd been raining so he'd be working over in the garage helping to strip down a variety of clapped out light armoured vehicles or scraping the rust off wheels that were pretty much held together by the flaky brown stuff.

This had all changed when the glowering figure of Sergeant Rand, all five feet six high and, many would challenge, wide, came lumbering in, heavily breathing and veins popping in his puce temples, clearly unhappy with the universe at a quarter past seven in the morning. Macintyre didn't think anything of it until, after scanning the half-dozen sorry looking uniformed figures in the dining area, his fiery gaze had fixed on himself and, with a sigh, the sarge had marched up, ordered him to get his overcoat and boots and meet him at the exit to the barracks in twenty minutes.

Macintyre had lived in Scotland all his life but the draughty, noisy drive with the sarge had taken him through places he'd heard of but never visited. When they continued along the A835 past Inverness Macintyre had pretty much given up guessing where they were going but once they picked up signs 'to the coast' it became increasingly clear they were heading west.

After just over seven hours of road rumble and sarge grumble in the knackered Land Rover they'd finally pulled up at Uig on the northern coast of Skye. Given the scarce buildings in the postcard-ready landscape and the few fishing boats moored alongside the pier, it was obvious their final destination was the large supply ship sitting as a grey shadow a few hundred metres out into the mouth of the Little Minch.

Rand maintained radio silence save for the occasional 'every fucking three months' and 'I'm sick of this shit' muttered under his breath, not choosing to volunteer a scrap of explanation in relation to what they were doing. Pointing at the small wooden tender waiting for them at the end of the jetty, Rand grunted 'get in'. Five minutes later Macintyre was clambering up a cargo net - proving basic training had some use after all - and was then directed towards a tiny cabin while a scowling Rand nodded to the officer on watch.

Through the steamed-up porthole facing onto the open deck, Macintyre had watched as words were exchanged and nods given between the sergeant and the officer. As the light faded and the ship nodded in the waves, it was obvious he was going to be spending the night onboard. Unfortunately, any thoughts of a cruise had been entirely destroyed when, on discovering just how useless Macintyre was going to be rowing a dinghy, the sarge had put him to work lugging unmarked and very heavy boxes into the inflatable boat in which he now sat. The transfer had gone on until near midnight, allowing Macintyre three hours of sleep before being awakened by the ship coming to a halt.

Minutes later he had been ordered into his protective suit, wisely keeping questions about breakfast to himself.

Macintyre and the sarge had made the awkward transfer to the heavily laden dinghy in darkness and save for the gentle lapping of the waves against the ship, the only sound was a warning toll from several unseen buoys. Macintyre counted at least six differing volumes, suggesting the buoys were anchored at set intervals for several kilometres in every direction. No explanation was given about them, nor did he ask.

The sounds had slowly disappeared and now, as dawn broke and Rand continued rowing with a look of 'you should be doing this' on his face, Macintyre spotted a tiny scratch of rock a couple of kilometres in the distance. As the sun continued to rise and Rand continued to huff and puff, Macintyre picked out dozens of dark curved shapes bobbing above the water, forcing Rand to zig and zag the closer they got to the island.

Sweat ran down Rand's face but Macintyre didn't dare try to sympathise with the sarge. It was entirely his fault his superior was doing all the work, and he knew he'd be expected to unload the cargo solo when they reached the shore. Looking behind him to the ship, Macintyre could see the shape of an outboard motor under a plastic cover. Freezing and fed up, he turned back to Rand and stared at the long diagonal zip running across the front of his blue protective suit rather than into his eyes. That might not go down too well.

"Sarge… why aren't we using the motor?"

Macintyre chanced a quick look at Rand's face. He was blinking away the sweat dripping from his thick ginger eyebrows.

"None of your business."

The rowing continued. To his left, Macintyre watched as they passed one of the shapes in the water. He couldn't make out details, but it looked as if it had been there for quite some time, given the salt covering its exposed surface.

"What are those things in the water sarge?"

Rand ignored Macintyre, breathing obscenities as he pulled on the thick plastic oars.

"That one's getting a bit close."

Rand followed Macintyre's gaze.

"FUCK me!"

For a stocky man, Rand could move very quickly when he wanted to. In a breath he'd shifted his weight on the bench and was yanking the dinghy to starboard, away from the ominous bump that seemed intent on colliding with them.

"I don't care if you can row or not. Grab that oar and get fucking paddling!"

Macintyre couldn't quite understand what he was being asked to do. Rand's eyes grew wider as he furiously tugged on the left-hand oar.

"It's a mine you arsehole!"

Macintyre grabbed the small paddle attached to the inside of the dinghy and leant over the side, the rubber of his suit squeaking against the outer tubing of the inflatable. As well as shivering from the cold, he was now trembling with fear and glad his stomach was empty. The last thing he needed was to lob up all over his arms.

Getting into the rhythm, he matched Rand's frantic movements to push them away from the device, the movement made all the more uncomfortable by the oxygen canister strapped to his back. After a minute of furious sculling, the two fell back on their benches, exhausted.

"So you're not entirely fucking useless after all."

Rand panted his excuse for thanks, his barrel chest heaving as he ground the words out between uneven, yellowing teeth. Macintyre nodded and looked past the exhausted man. Behind him, the island was beginning to take shape; it was larger than Macintyre first thought. It was also completely surrounded by dozens of the explosive devices.

"Check the seals on your suit lad. Have any of them split?"

Macintyre looked down at his arms and legs, inspected the connection to the tight rubberised gloves at the wrist, and reached down to the gaiters around his boots. They all seemed to be intact.

"No sarge. They're fine."

Rand stared at Macintyre as he regained control of his breathing. Grabbing the oars, he took a brief look behind him then got back into his previous rhythm.

"Open that orange box under your bench."

Macintyre lent forwards, looked beneath his seat and retrieved a large waterproof plastic container marked 'AUTHORISED USERS ONLY'. Flipping the two over-sized steel catches up and to the side, he opened the box lid and stared at the contents.

"Have you used a TASER before lad?"

Macintyre scrabbled at the bright yellow plastic pistol in its foam surround. His thick gloves made it difficult to retrieve, but after a couple of attempts he freed the weapon and weighed it in his hand. It was surprisingly light.

"The trigger guard's been removed, and the safety enlarged for use with HAZMAT gloves. It's pretty easy to work out. Take the belt and holsters and put them on."

Macintyre did as he was bidden and slid the TASER into its sheath with a click. That left one other weapon in the box and a large, empty holster on his left hip.

"That's a CO2 tranquiliser pistol. It's ready to go. It's a sod to reload so you only get one shot. It doesn't matter where you hit. He'll go down like a sack of shite."

This weapon was much heavier, made of green aluminium with the words 'X-2' stamped on the side. Macintyre was on much more familiar ground with this weapon; he'd gone air rifle and pistol shooting with his dad since he could pull back a spring-loaded barrel. Dropping it into the empty moulded plastic encasement on his hip, he tried his best to ignore Rand's casual reference but, with the coast of the island now only a couple of hundred metres away, he couldn't help himself.

"Who'll go down like a sack of shit, sarge?"

Rand stopped rowing and let the dinghy drift forward. Macintyre could see the dark shapes were much denser the closer they got to the rocky beach behind and to the right of the sergeant. He very much hoped Rand was also aware of them.

"Trevor."

Macintyre blinked.

"Trevor?"

"Aye, Trevor. That's the reason we're not using the outboard motor and I'm sweating like a genie in a hot lamp. So he doesn't hear us."

Macintyre didn't know what to say. He thought the weapons were for animals. Rand leaned forwards, his tone even more serious than normal - which was very, very serious.

"Listen, Macintyre. I usually work with someone else, but they weren't available and you were nearest. Anything you see on this island, you keep to yourself or it'll end very badly for you."

Macintyre didn't doubt Rand's words. He nodded once, bravely maintaining eye contact with the sergeant. He wanted it to be clear he understood when he was being threatened.

"Right. Our oxygen's good for around forty-five minutes so we need to chuck this stuff on the beach then get away as quick as we can. He might appear while we're unloading the supplies; he's done that a couple of times but if we're lucky we'll be in and out before he knows it. If he does turn up, ignore him. Don't even acknowledge him. If he approaches you, draw your TASER. Don't speak to him, don't engage him in conversation. If he gets too close, shoot him. If that doesn't work, hit him with the dart gun. And for fuck's sake, keep your facemask and hood on from now until we get back out to sea. Do not take either of them off under ANY circumstances. Understood?"

Macintyre nodded again, pulled on the oxygen mask, and yanked the twin straps on either side of his head. Wriggling the nosepiece into place, he reached behind his head, pulled the oversized hood forward and zipped the suit from bottom right hip to top left shoulder. Turning on his oxygen, a vapour mist slowly cleared inside the Perspex visor until he could see the eyes of the sarge behind his own oval-shaped plastic window and the respirator.

Two minutes later, the underside of the dinghy ground against the beach. Long ragged shadows thrown by low cliffs blanketed the grey rock and shale. The beach was cold, colourless and, from what Macintyre could see through his spray-spattered mask, entirely devoid of life. Not even a gull wheeled overhead. Why the hell anybody would want to live on this barren rock was beyond him.

"Double time Macintyre. We need to get out of here as quickly as possible."

Rand's voice was muffled behind the breathing apparatus and suit hood, but Macintyre got the message loud and clear. Looking at the circular dial strapped to his left wrist, he could see the O2 reading was just under 'full'. Heaving himself over the side of the tubular hull, he helped the sarge tug the dinghy further onto the beach. Once it was clear of the water, Rand gestured for him to get back in and pass out the various boxes and parcels.

Heavy and cumbersome as they were, they proved a lot less awkward to discharge than load thanks to Rand tossing them into a rough heap, giving no thought to the 'fragile' and 'handle with care' signs stamped on the standard military containers. After ten minutes they'd got a good rhythm going, although Macintyre's back was screaming in pain and sweat was running down his face, misting up his visor despite the constant low hiss of oxygen feeding into his suit.

"Hey! Sarge! Is that you?"

Macintyre stopped his rummaging for a box from the dinghy and looked over to the top of the low cliff. He could see the outline of a man waving frantically and with no-one else in sight, he assumed that's where the high-pitched shout had just come from.

"Oh bollocks."

Rand tossed a package onto the untidy heap he'd created a couple of metres up the rocky beach. He reached for his TASER.

"Ready your weapon, Macintyre. Do not talk to him. I'll handle this."

Macintyre did as he was told, unholstering the lightweight plastic weapon and resting his thumb on the safety lever. Looking back up to the skyline, he couldn't see the man anymore. Five seconds later, a figure appeared from between two large boulders. It was still gloomy and he was a hundred metres away, but Macintyre could see he was dressed in rags. His hair and beard were wild and tangled.

He looked like every kid's idea of a castaway; only his thick military issue boots had any semblance of being appropriate to the conditions. With the sharp rocks and shale underfoot and the man's untied laces flapping like mad snakes, Macintyre thought it unwise he had his hands behind his back. At any second he could trip and land on his scruffy face.

"That is you isn't it? Who's this? Is this a new one?"

Rand moved forwards cautiously, weapon drawn and aimed at the pitifully thin figure. Rand shouted through his visor, but Macintyre had to strain to hear what he was saying.

"Just turn around and go back up the cliffs, Trevor. You know the drill by now. We can easily take these back with us."

Trevor continued his relentless stomp, steadying

himself with his shoulders when he was off-balance.

"Has Jenny recovered? You really did give her a nasty smack across the head, didn't you? I thought she was dead."

Rand came to a halt around twenty metres from the dinghy and trained his TASER on the man's chest. The closer he got, the more detail Macintyre could make out. He wasn't just unwashed, he was filthy. With wild eyes, Trevor looked utterly crazy.

"I'm surprised they gave you another one after what happened last time."

Macintyre could see from Rand's posture he was getting nervous. Come to that, given what Trevor was saying, Macintyre was beginning to feel uneasy too. Who was Jenny? What had happened 'last time'?

"Whatever it is you're hiding behind your back Trevor, I suggest you drop it before I drop you."

Trevor scrunched onwards, carefully angling himself so neither Macintyre nor Rand could see behind him. Macintyre wasn't sure of the maximum distance of a TASER, but he was certain the sarge knew.

"Stop there or I swear to God I'll shoot you again."

Trevor took another few steps then stopped around five metres away, swaying slightly.

"No need for that sarge. Hey - I've got a present for you."

Before the sarge could fire, Trevor threw a large rock at his head with all his feeble might. So strong was his effort, he lost balance and fell forwards as the fizzling darts of the TASER sailed over his head and landed on the shale several metres behind him. The rock hit Rand's hood and breathing mask with a loud crack, forcing him to take a couple of steps back, more in surprise than pain. The suits were designed to take a lot of hammer, and Macintyre couldn't understand what Trevor thought he might achieve with such a futile effort.

"Ohhhhh… No no NO."

Even inside his own suit, Macintyre realised Rand's voice was louder than before. For a second he couldn't quite work out why, but Trevor, who had scrambled back upright and was now jumping with joy and clapping his hands, certainly did. He'd managed to crack a hole in the sarge's Perspex with his well-aimed throw.

"Yes yes yes! Come on sarge! Come and get me!"

Rand was staggering about the beach clutching and clawing at his mask through his hood, oblivious to Trevor's goading. Realising he should have moved seconds before, Macintyre threw himself over the side of the dinghy, moved forwards and crouched, his TASER trained on Trevor who seemed delighted for the threat of imminent attack to be doubled.

"That's it! Come on both of you! Have at it!"

Macintyre's breath began to overwhelm the oxygen supply in his suit and his view of the world became soft and hazy through the mist. He could hear his breathing become more ragged as he pushed on over the rocks, the bright yellow weapon bobbing in and out of view at the bottom of the visor. Before he could get what he assumed to be close enough to fire, he saw Rand begin to tear at his hood in a frenzy.

"Sarge! What are you doing?"

Trevor was literally dancing with joy at Rand's mania.

"Take it off sarge! Rip it off!"

Rand grabbed hold of the visor and snapped it in half, throwing his hood back so it dangled behind his head. Next came his breathing mask, which he tore off with such force it detached from the oxygen hose with a pop. Hurling the mask to the ground, he exposed a face purple with apoplexy.

" - going to fucking KILL YOU you FUCKER!"

Rand lunged forwards like a second-rate actor in a second-rate zombie movie. His movements were unnatural, as if he was struggling against his own body. His arms came forward, heavily gloved hands extended, fingers grasping at the air, as Trevor skipped towards him down the rocky beach with undisguised glee.

"That's it sarge! You know you want to! Tear my head off! Smash it to pieces!"

Rand toppled into Trevor, his gauntleted hands clamping around his scrawny neck. The sarge fell forwards over the rough rocks, crushing the air out of Trevor as he landed on him with a thud. Trevor lay there, arms by his side, apparently content for the big man to choke the life out of him.

Macintyre then made the worst decision of his life.

"Sarge! You're killing him! Leave him alone!"

Macintyre was only a couple of metres away from the two now. Rand's face was a picture of purple hatred, teeth bared, drool running down his chin onto his victim's tattered clothes. Trevor's eyes were bugging out like eggs, his face crimson with lack of air. The look he gave Macintyre was far from begging for his help; it appeared more as a warning not to intervene.

"Die fucker! Die die DIE!"

Rand was screaming with rage, his hands closing tighter with every shrieked word. Macintyre couldn't take any more of it. Flicking the safety lever at the top left of the stock, he slipped his index finger through the cut-out slot and rested it on the trigger.

"Sarge I'll shoot you if you don't let him go."

"N...no..." gasped Trevor.

"FUCKER!" shouted Rand.

"Sarge! Last warning!"

"Please... don't..."

"DIE BASTARD!"

Macintyre pulled the trigger.

The two darts thudded into Rand's meaty back, puncturing the suit just above the base of his spine. The electrodes sent fifty thousand volts into the man, who jolted up then doubled over with a yell. Macintyre kept his finger depressed until the big man had shaken and convulsed away from Trevor, who was gasping for air and cursing in croaks. Releasing the trigger, Macintyre slowly approached the sarge, the wires drooping to the stony shore. Crouching, he pushed Rand's unconscious form onto its side and tried his best to get him into the recovery position. Thank God he was still breathing.

"Why… did you do… that?"

Trevor's voice was broken with sobs. Getting to his feet, Macintyre looked down at the pitiful man, his whole body convulsed with grief. Trevor stared into the sky, his tears marking thin white streaks down his blackened face. Macintyre shook his head with incomprehension.

"He was going to kill you."

Trevor gulped in a lungful of air, wiped the tears from his face with a filthy Robinson Crusoe sleeve and met Macintyre's hooded gaze.

"That was the whole point of attacking him! You should have let him finish me… end this miserable sodding life on this miserable sodding island…"

Macintyre's head was spinning. He didn't know if he was hyperventilating from too little or too much oxygen, whether it was because he was exhausted from lack of sleep and food or because this was the most fucked up situation he'd ever known. How the hell was he going to explain to the sarge why he fried his nervous system when - if - he woke up? He could try pinning it on Trevor, claiming the crazy man had taken his own TASER and shot the sarge, but that level of incompetence would probably be worse than his misguided efforts to save the wretch's life from the sarge's mania. What if the sarge was dead? How would he get back to the supply ship without getting blown up or lost at sea? Christ alive.

And then there was Trevor, crying uncontrollably to himself on the least picturesque beach Macintyre had ever had the displeasure to visit. What the hell was he going to do with him? Suddenly feeling guilty, Macintyre threw the spent TASER onto the stony beach with the plastic rattle of a toy gun.

"Look... Trevor... I don't know what you're doing here but - "

Trevor reined in his sobs and pulled himself up to rest on his elbows. He didn't seem to care that he was lying on razor-sharp rocks.

"Oh, so he told you my name, did he? That's nice."

Macintyre was taken aback by Trevor's sudden change in direction.

"What's yours?"

It was ludicrously late to recall Rand's warnings about engaging Trevor in conversation, but he could hear the sarge's voice booming loud and clear inside his hood.

"I'm not even supposed to talk to you. Now piss off back up those cliffs or I'll shoot you with this tranquiliser gun and leave you for the crows."

Trevor looked to the large weapon dangling from Macintyre's belt, rolled his eyes up to the brightening blue sky then back down again. For the first time Macintyre could see his eyes were a deep brown green, not unlike the slime covering his ragged clothes.

"No crows here, me duck. No life at all. Except me."

Macintyre stared at Trevor, who sniffed back his final tears and cleared his throat with a rasping sound.

"Tell you what, slip off your hood and give me a few minutes of your time to talk. I don't get many visitors and I'd like to tell you about why I got here."

Macintyre felt the hairs on the back of his neck begin to rise. He wasn't entirely sure why, but there was no way he was taking off his hood and mask. He really, really didn't want to talk to the man, but the idea suddenly came to him that Trevor might say something that could help him out later, possibly during his reprimand board in front of the Colonel or, God forbid, court martial. Turning warily, he looked to the sarge, sparked out and lying on his side. Shit the bed. What had he done?

Glancing at the indicator strapped on his wrist,

Macintyre saw his oxygen tank was just over half full, past the green and just into the orange. Surely he could give the man ten minutes of his time? If Trevor was as good as his word, Macintyre would be able to haul the sarge back into the boat, set sail and hope Rand recovered as Macintyre tried to learn how to row in a straight line. If Trevor didn't bugger off after his story, he'd pump him full of drugs so he could sleep it off on this miserable excuse of a beach.

"Come on Mister X, just hear me out and I'll leave you in peace to drag fatty here back to the dinghy."

Macintyre continued to stare at Rand's inert form and winced. He was in so much trouble. Taking a breath, he turned to face Trevor, still lying on the rocks as if he was sunning himself on a Mediterranean holiday. Macintyre formed his words carefully, speaking as loud as he could so he wasn't misunderstood.

"The hood and mask stay on. You've got ten minutes. Make a move towards me, I'll shoot you. And if the sarge wakes up, which is likely given how thick his skin is, it's out of my hands. Understood?"

Macintyre watched Trevor carefully as he wiped the tears from his eyes, rubbing a wider white patch across his grubby skin. The raggedy man got to his feet and stood, shaking, for a few seconds. Gesturing to a couple of large boulders nearer to the foot of the dark granite cliffs behind him, Macintyre nodded and took a wary seat across from Trevor, close enough that he could hear him but far enough for Trevor to be unable to do anything fast and stupid. Macintyre pulled the tranquiliser gun from its holster and glanced behind him. Rand hadn't moved and the dinghy was still far enough away from the approaching tide. Turning back to face Trevor, Macintyre motioned with the pistol for him to start.

"What year is it?"

Trevor's simple question shocked Macintyre. It was asked with innocence, in a tone that didn't deserve mockery or sarcasm.

"It's Twenty Twenty-One."

Trevor scratched at his grey-brown beard for a few seconds, tapping his fingers over his lips and on his free hand as he counted inside his head.

"That means I've been here nineteen years. Nineteen years."

Macintyre wasn't surprised. It explained everything he saw hunched before him.

"Let me take you back to Two Thousand and Two. I don't suppose you remember much about the turn of the millennium, do you?"

Macintyre shrugged under his suit.

"I was six."

Trevor smiled, exposing dark brown stumps of teeth that looked as painful as they were ugly.

"Well, back then, things were very different for me. Ever been to Nottingham?"

Macintyre shook his head. The furthest south he'd ever been was Carlisle, and he'd not liked it one bit.

"That's where I lived. In West Bridgford to be precise, just around the corner from the cricket ground. Anyway…"

"So you promise me you're not seeing her?"

Even though Laura looked tired, she was still beautiful. Her light blue eyes were still piercing, her rosebud lips still kissable, and even in a scruffy dressing gown, Trevor could make out the shape that had turned his head the first time she'd squeezed past him in The Bell. Very, very occasionally he had a moment of lucidity when a little voice would say "What the hell is wrong with you? Why isn't she enough for you?" but that voice was quickly shouted down with jeers and various obscene hand-gestures from the shadows of the dominant laddish part of his psyche.

"Laura, honestly, I'm not in the least bit interested in her at all."

Trevor picked up the mug, 'University of Nottingham' emblazoned on its side, and took a slurp as he rested his weight onto the kitchen worktop.

"Christ, did you put sugar in this?"

Laura's eyes widened and her jaw jutted forwards as she stepped up a notch of anger. Trevor had only seen her this cross once before, and even he'd had to admit he'd gone a bit far back then. For the life of him he couldn't see the similarity. Laura, clearly, could.

"Honestly? Honestly? You don't know the meaning of the word Trevor. You keep secrets, you cheat, you lie to me… you even steal."

"Steal?"

Trevor stared at the large red teapot sitting on the drainer.

"Is there any more tea in that pot?"

The kitchen wasn't that big, given the narrow nature of the terraced house. Laura had done a lot with it, creating what was fashionably known as a galley-style workspace, posh magazine talk for 'small and narrow'. She'd tiled it herself in dazzling yellow and black after waiting for Trevor to do it for three months, one of the many promises he'd made on moving in. None of them had been kept, even though he'd genuinely meant it on a couple of occasions. There had always been something better to do with his time than go to work or DIY. Drink, for instance. And shag as many girls as he could.

"Trevor! Just drink what I've given you, from my tea made with my electricity and paid for with my money. And yes, steal. What about that time I found you taking my underwear as a present for Michaela? Or that business with my shoes."

Trevor looked forlornly into his mug. Probably best he didn't throw his drink away, seeing as Laura was now a poking finger in the chest away from him and working up a proper storm.

"You haven't got an honest bone in your body."

Laura swept her curly blonde hair back behind her ears with an angry Miss Piggy flick and folded her arms. Trevor wasn't sure how he was supposed to respond, so he decided to go on the offensive.

"Don't you talk to me about honesty. You won't even tell me what you do at work!"

Laura's eyes flashed with anger. Pulling her worn grey dressing gown about her, she retied the belt with angry fingers.

"Every time we have an argument you bring this up. You know very well where I work and what I do."

Trevor knew she knew that was a lie. At first he'd found Laura quite mysterious, but after a few weeks the vague answers and inconsistencies grew annoying. She'd suddenly get called in at four in the morning and often not come back until early the next day. Other than not being there to regularly cook for him, this was irritating because he couldn't rely on her being out when he wanted to bring girls back to the house.

Even now, she had only just got up after being away for nearly thirty-six hours. If he could depend on her not being at home, it'd be great, but he had no way to track her movements or know when she was coming home. All in all, it was getting really, really inconvenient.

"You work at the University, in a part that's got barbed wire around it and great big fences. I'm not even allowed past the gate to see you!"

Laura wasn't having any of it.

"In five months, have you ever tried to meet me from work? You haven't even attempted to come and see me! When you worked at the warehouse, you know, before you became the freeloader you are now, could I have just walked into it unannounced? Of course not."

Trevor winced at the memory of work. It really wasn't for him.

"I work at a pharmaceuticals company. There are a lot of them in Nottingham, dickhead. Hear of a little company called Boots the Chemist? Where do you think most of their research is done? In the back of their shops? The reason you can't visit is because most of the building is sterile. It's clean of nasty, dirty, filthy germs and parasitical organisms - like you!"

The attack was turning towards his failure to contribute since he'd moved in. Having absolutely no defence, Trevor glanced at the oversized clock above the stripped oak door and decided on a hasty, tactical retreat. Luckily it was giro day. By the time he'd picked that up, it'd be at least half-past beer time.

"I've had enough of this. I'm going out."

Trevor took one final slug of the rapidly cooling tea, pulled a face, and slammed it onto the worktop. In a deft move, he was out of the back door and halfway down the narrow passage before Laura had time to begin her tirade.

"I'll put a stop to you, you freeloading, cheating bastard. Do you hear me, Trevor? I'll put a stop to you!"

Macintyre could feel the cold from the rock creeping through his HAZMAT suit and fatigues into the bones of his backside. Despite the sun's rapid rise, he and Trevor were still in shadow thanks to the cliffs and the angle of the beach. Trevor was staring into space, having abruptly stopped his story at the mention of beer. Trevor licked his cracked and blistered lips, catching on the wiry hairs of his beard and moustache. Macintyre risked a brief look behind. The dinghy was still mostly on the rocky shore, but the water was creeping up behind it on the incoming tide. Rand hadn't moved a muscle. God, he hoped he was still alive. Or not. He couldn't make his mind up which might be preferable.

"You see, the thing is… the thing was… I liked to play the field a bit. Laura was great - well, she had her own place, and it was somewhere to keep my stuff, and the first month or so was really good but then, well… you know how it is, right?"

Macintyre shook his head. He didn't know how it was at all.

"Oh. Okay. Well anyway, I cashed in my giro and - "

"What's a giro?"

Trevor blinked a few times, not understanding why Macintyre couldn't understand.

"UB… Unemployment Benefit cheque. You take it to the post office and cash it. Then you have money. Yeah?"

Macintyre shrugged again. He'd come from a household where everyone always worked. He'd joined the army not because it was expected of him, but because he wanted to. He saw it as a potential career, having done badly at school despite trying his hardest. The idea of taking money for doing nothing wasn't in his makeup. Trevor's obvious delight at sponging off the state didn't do a great deal for Macintyre's sympathy. Nor did his attitude to women.

"So anyway, I found myself heading into town. Yates's Wine Lodge was always a good bet for girls leaving work and having a drink. It was opposite The Bell so if it was quiet in there, I'd always be able to find someone I knew to drink with across the road…"

Even though it was one of the biggest pubs in the city centre, Yates's was always heaving on a Friday from mid-afternoon onwards. Despite the bunches and groups of shouting, gesticulating people making it difficult to swerve through, Trevor quickly got served with a pint of cider and black. He spotted Jackie on the crowded ground floor, three exes back from Laura, already onto her third Malibu and pineapple and unsteady on her feet.

At first she'd waved him off, telling him not to bother her when she was having a good time, but after offering her the drink he'd been promising her for the last two years, she finally left her gaggle of disapproving girlfriends and headed up the stairs with Trevor to find a booth. A group of students was just vacating a table in the corner and, while they left it awash with Newcastle Brown Ale stains and empty bottles, it was a good spot for bird watching. Trevor cleared a space for their drinks, threw his Harrington jacket onto the stained and torn velvet seat beside him and began a charm offensive on a tipsy yet still-wary Jackie.

"I still want to strangle you."

Jackie pointed the tip of the broken yellow cocktail umbrella at Trevor's nose. Trevor laughed and sat back, drinking in the view before him. Jackie was a lot older than him, but she was in good shape and, apart from wearing too much make-up, she was a handsome woman. She'd probably had as many blokes as he'd had women over the last few years, and theirs was a relationship of two very large eccentric orbits that occasionally met for a glorious, if short lived, liaison.

Sometimes the meetings were accidental, sometimes not so - like today. He'd sought her out in the crowd and could have easily remained unseen, but given the argument with Laura, he had to look to where he might crash over the next few days until things calmed down. That just left the problem of how he'd left things with Jackie. Even he had to admit he'd been a bit of a bastard to her.

"Come on Jack, we had a few laughs, and you weren't exactly faithful to me, were you?"

Jackie feigned hurt, scrunching up her nose and flicking her short dark hair out of her eyes with a toss of the head.

"Only 'cos you went out with my lodger!"

Trevor took a sip of his dark concoction and placed the pint glass back in the gap he'd made between the students' detritus. This time of day, it was unlikely the table would get cleared until closing.

"And I paid for that didn't I? She nicked my wallet and my car."

Jackie brayed with laughter. Despite having never smoked in her life, she had a coarse, rasping voice that only got rougher and louder when she found something funny. Which, to Jackie's credit, was often.

"That was my idea."

Trevor pulled his own hurt face but then smiled, using his Nottinghamshire-famous winning grin and twinkling eyes to the very best effect. If only he'd had time to put on a splash of his favourite cologne before bailing out of Laura's, he would probably have been in bed by now.

"I knew it! She really was a nasty piece of work, not warm and loving and kind-hearted and beautiful like you."

Jackie's eyes narrowed. Sipping the remains of her coconut delight through her chewed plastic straw, she put her glass down and leaned forward, giving Trevor a deliberate flash of her deep and inviting cleavage. How Trevor loved a woman in a tight silk blouse.

"I smell bullshit. Let me guess. You need somewhere to sleep."

Trevor looked over to the iron columns that formed the spine of the roof of the first floor. The place was full of men and women shouting, laughing, pushing and generally having a drunken good time. For a few seconds his vision doubled, and he felt the ground spin beneath him. It was his body telling him he'd had enough to drink, which was odd because he'd only consumed around half his normal volume of snakebite.

The view came back to normal although his head still felt floaty. Briefly wondering if it was because he was getting old, he proved to himself he was still the virile man-about time by fixating on a young girl in a bright yellow dress on the opposite side of the bannister. By the time he'd looked her up and down, his focus returned and he felt back in the room. Rain began to spatter on the grimy windows forming the apex of the roof high above where he and Jackie sat. With his head clearing, he concluded he could do much worse than press on with Plan A – a brief hiatus from Laura and pray she didn't change the locks – and dialled his charm to 'full'.

"Well it's funny you should say that Jack. Oh wait."

The biggest reason he didn't spend more time with Jackie suddenly came back to him.

"What about that shitty-arsed rat dog of yours?"

Trevor wasn't a great fan of dogs at the best of times, but he absolutely hated Yorkshire Terriers. Jackie's was by far the worst he'd ever encountered. In addition to constantly yapping at him and generally getting in the way, it'd also left a stinking gift in his shoe on more than one occasion. He despised the creature, and he had no doubt it felt the same way about him. Jackie's face lit up with the mere mention of the thing. Forget about the wrinkle and the laugh. By far her biggest character weakness was her love for that mutt.

"Poppy? Oh she'd love to see her Uncle Trevor again!"

Macintyre took another glance at his oxygen meter. It was heading towards the end of the orange banding and into the red, meaning he only had about fifteen minutes left of breathable air. It was clear Trevor was relishing having someone to talk to - well, talk at - but he wasn't entirely sure what this had to do with anything other than prove what a dick he'd been all those years ago. Add the fact Rand would be waking up soon, Macintyre's patience was getting thin.

"Look Trevor, I'm running out of time here. Can you get to the point?"

Trevor frowned and shifted on the slick granite rock. If Macintyre's arse was numb through his various layers, God only knew how freezing this unfortunate's backside must be.

"Yes, yes I'm getting to it. It'll all become clear real soon. Okay?"

Macintyre waved the muzzle of the dart gun again.

Trevor stared at the cracked and peeling ceiling of Jackie's bedroom. But for the muffled tweeting of the dawn chorus through the velvet curtains, the only sound was her rhythmic snoring. Thanks to a sliver of light forcing its way through the window covering, Trevor could see the duvet rising and falling in time with the grunting. Flicking his eyes around the room, more of Jackie's faults came back. Clothes were everywhere, over the battered antique dresser on the wall facing him, on the floor to his left and draped across the chair behind Jackie to his right. There was also a really strange smell, one he'd never quite managed to work out despite having slept in this room several times before. Reaching out with a lazy hand, Trevor grabbed his Nokia 3210 and squinted at its scratched LCD display. The keypad glowed a sickly green, making it difficult to read the scuffed screen. After angling it a few times he saw he'd got typically poor reception for that part of town, so Trevor contemplated his next move with a sigh.

He could stay there and wait for a greeting from Jackie's ferocious morning breath and endure a truly appalling cup of instant coffee and a slice of burned toast, then either spend the rest of the day back in bed or go out Saturday drinking. Given the amount of money he'd spent last night and his uncertain residential status, he decided against both of those ideas. Instead, he resolved to sneak out of Jackie's house, take an early morning stroll to the Crematorium, nip over the wall - Fridays were always good for funerals - and steal the best flowers he could find to fashion a 'sorry I'm such a shit' bouquet for Laura.

Edging out from the duvet, Trevor dressed quietly and deftly, only slowing to latch his belt in case the chink of metal awakened the gurgling Jackie. All that could be seen of her was a tuft of black hair sticking out from under the bedclothes, which continued to rise and fall with her muffled noises. The cheap cord carpet didn't mask his movements but years of sneaking out of bedrooms had given him a certain weight balance and transferral technique that, in his opinion, could only be matched by the most practiced and artful Ninja. He'd also set his phone to silent before slipping it into his back pocket. He'd been caught out with a comedy timed ringtone on more than one occasion.

Allowing himself a self-satisfied smirk, Trevor gently closed the fake woodgrain door with a soft click of the latch and turned onto the gloomy landing. Strictly speaking he needed a shower - for some reason he was sweating more than usual - but that would certainly wake Jackie up, even if the shower was downstairs past the kitchen. There were probably clean clothes, some perhaps even belonging to him, in the spare room's broken drawers but the longer he stayed, the greater the chance of death by Nescafe, so he made his way towards the stairs, taking some of the weight off his socked feet by leaning on the upstairs banister as he stepped. Just as he turned to go downstairs, the growling began.

Poppy stood on the landing step, looking up at Trevor with wide, staring eyes. She was shaking with fury, baring her little needle teeth and curling back her top lip in a display of absolute hatred. He'd never harm an animal intentionally, but for Poppy there was always the very real possibility of an exception. Right at that moment, it wasn't the laughable display of hostility that bothered him. It was the noise.

"Shut up you mutt."

Trevor hissed at the mess of brown and black fur. Jackie was attuned to the gentlest whining of the creature from any part of the house. Under normal circumstances the dog would have been encouraged to jump into bed with her and whoever might be keeping her company at the time. At least Jackie had the decency to remember Trevor wouldn't have any of that if he was staying the night. She feigned concern for the creature's delicate sensibilities

The growling got louder and the shaking more violent. He had to act fast before the wretched animal woke Jackie up.

"I swear Poppy, I'll drop-kick you off this landing if you don't - "

Trevor had seen the rat-dog move fast before, particularly when he'd caught it finishing off its business in his new trainer, but it was nothing compared to the blur of motion it suddenly became. Pin-like teeth started to chomp at the bottom of his jeans. Carefully clipped nails scratched and clawed at his leg. On any other occasion Trevor would have laughed it off but there was something quite sinister about Poppy's actions. Her eyes had a glassy, vacant look to them that Trevor found disturbing. She was absolutely committed to this attack, and was putting her entire, negligible weight behind it.

"Will you - OW - shut UP you OWW."

Despite trying to keep his voice an urgent hiss, Trevor knew the attack was only going to get louder. With her teeth caught on Trevor's turn-ups, he dragged Poppy by her head towards the airing cupboard across from the stairs, her claws catching the carpet as she gamely attempted to pull him back towards her. Opening the door as quietly as he could, he brought his leg around so the gap was behind the crazed dog. With a flick of his foot, Poppy hit the hot water tank jacket with a wheeze and landed on all fours. Shaking her head, she rallied herself for another attack but was thwarted by the door slamming in her face.

"What's going on?"

Framed in the bedroom doorway, Jackie pulled her ancient brown dressing gown around her body. Her hair was sticking out like a greying tiara and the remnants of her makeup were unevenly distributed across her face.

"I was just going get a glass of water. Do you want one?"

Despite his years of practised treachery, he winced as he said it. Was that really the best he could come up with? Jackie yawned and scratched her head.

"I heard Poppy. Is she up here?"

"I don't —"

The timing couldn't have been worse. Muffled yaps and mad scratting from behind the door signalled the game being well and truly up. Jackie looked to the airing cupboard then back to Trevor, her crusty mascara widening in horror.

"What have you done to my poor darling? You'd better not have hurt her."

Trevor took a step towards the stairs as Jackie advanced on him. They'd had a few skirmishes in the past and he knew she knew how to hurt him. She'd go straight for the fleshy bits.

"She was being a pain in the arse Jack. She tried to bite me!"

As Jackie advanced, her face changed. The look of incredulity changed to one of fury, her eyes now wide and staring, through and past Trevor to something unseen.

"I'm sorry Jack. Look, I'll let her out and – "

"You…"

Jackie's face was twisted with rage. Raising her hands, she flexed her fingers like an eagle ready to pounce on a fieldmouse.

"I am going to kill you."

"Now hold on Jack – "

"KILL YOUUUUUU!"

Jackie threw herself at Trevor, clutching and slashing with her nails. He was so surprised at her sudden rage she landed a perfect gouge across his cheek, the pain jolting Trevor back into reality. Realising she could easily knock him down the stairs, Trevor moved forwards, grabbing hold of Jackie's flailing wrists and pushing her arms apart to stop her from taking more flesh from his face.

This was a bad move, as it left his groin exposed to a frontal attack, which duly came as Jackie's knee darted out, a direct hit only just avoided by him twisting to avoid the killer blow. Jackie was raging now, unbalancing herself in an attempt to kick and claw Trevor, spittle flying from her smudged lips, her eyes fury saucers. Hearing her mummy in obvious distress, Poppy's yelping and clawing became more frantic from behind the cupboard door, feeding Jackie's frenzy and attempts to dismember Trevor with her bare hands.

"For God's sake Jack, what the HELL is wrong with you?"

"KILL! KILL YOU!"

Trevor took a good hold of Jackie's wrists and pushed her towards the bedroom. As he turned and ducked and heaved, her dressing gown worked its way open, exposing Jackie's naked body. Normally he'd be happy to watch her gyrate and wiggle, but her movements seemed unnatural, as if she was being remote controlled by someone who didn't know how to use the buttons. Jackie was dripping with sweat with the ferocity of her attack. Again she tried again to claw at him, but the attempt was clumsy and Trevor saw his chance.

Pushing at her with as much strength as he could muster, he threw her backwards onto the bed, grabbing hold of the dressing gown cord and pulling it free as she toppled over onto her back. Before she had time to recover, Trevor jumped on top of her (something they'd enjoyed many times in the past), flipped her over and tied her hands behind her back (again, something they'd enjoyed many times in the past).

"BASTARD!"

Jackie kicked and screamed and tried to turn herself onto her back, but Trevor pushed down with all his weight. Within a minute she was trussed up like a turkey. Sweat trickled down into his bleeding face and he wiped it away with the back of his hand, cursing as he saw how much blood she'd drawn in her attack.

"I don't know what's got into you Jack but I'm not having this. I'm off. Call me when you calm down – or better still, don't."

"DIE! DIE!"

Jackie twitched and writhed on the bed, but the more

she pulled on the cord the tighter it became. Heaving himself up, Trevor marched out of the bedroom, past the door behind which Poppy still snarled and yapped, down the stairs and out into the cool early morning air.

"I couldn't get out of there fast enough. It was the weirdest thing I'd ever experienced, like someone had thrown a switch and the whole house had gone mental."

The HAZMAT suit had a full-faced visor and only his eyes were visible through the breathing apparatus, so Macintyre wasn't sure if the ragged man could see just how unimpressed he was with the story. Up to this point in the sorry tale, all Trevor had proven was his casual cruelty to animals and his ability to subdue then tie up a rightly furious woman. If his purpose was to generate any level of sympathy, it was failing badly.

"Sounds to me like you had that coming Trevor... from the dog AND the woman."

Trevor looked genuinely hurt.

"That's not very fair. I was only defending myself. I didn't want to harm anybody, and I don't think I actually did."

Macintyre sighed and glanced at his wrist. The indicator was just into the red.

"I think the best thing for me to do is sink a dart into you, get the sarge loaded up and get off this bloody island."

Trevor heaved himself off his rocky seat, eyes pleading, hands outstretched. Macintyre had the muzzle of the pistol aimed between his eyes in a flash.

"Please don't, not until I've told you the rest."

Macintyre sighed. Reluctantly, he had to admit he was intrigued. Trevor hadn't yet given any insight into his current situation, and for the life of him Macintyre couldn't work out how a spat with a woman and a dog ended up nineteen years later on this dreadful rock. Behind him, Rand hadn't made a sound so, concluded

Macintyre, what harm would it do to spare Trevor a few more minutes? Sensing Macintyre's permission to continue, Trevor eased himself back onto his damp stone seat, stroked his disgusting beard and cleared his throat.

"I knew I'd have to get myself cleaned up before I went back to Laura's. I was covered in scratches and could feel bruises coming up on my thighs and shin. I was starving, too. It was too early for a bus to the gym, where I could get a shower and had some clothes stashed for just this kind of occasion, but I couldn't call a cab because I'd dropped my Nokia at Jackie's during the scuffle. I knew there was a payphone a few streets away and as I headed for it, I saw a milk float – "

"A what?"

Macintyre had no idea what Trevor was talking about. Trevor opened his mouth to speak, closed it, then continued.

"An open electric truck that delivers milk. Even back then they were a rare sight. I'm guessing they don't really have them any longer?"

"I've never seen one."

Trevor sighed, picked at a scab on his forehead and raised his eyebrows.

"Anyway, I saw this milk float…"

The small van came to a rattling stop near the junction with the main road, the bottles shifting in their crates as the milkman jumped out of his cab. He deftly swapped two empty bottles for two full ones on a nearby doorstep as Trevor approached the rotund, blue and white-aproned man.

"Morning chief. You wouldn't have a pint and some yoghurts I could buy off you, would you?"

The portly man rose and examined Trevor's bleeding cheek and dishevelled appearance.

"Walk of shame is it?"

Trevor looked the man straight in the eye. It occurred

to him how much of a state he must look.

"Something like that, yeah."

After a few seconds of laboured breathing the milkman smiled, lighting up his ruddy face.

"I can check me list me duck. Might be able to spare you a liquid breakfast."

Trevor smiled back and nodded. Stepping out of the way, the milkman leaned into his open cab, pulled out a clipboard and flicked through the pages with stubby fingers. Trevor leaned against the cart, his mind drifting to how he was going to eat a yoghurt without a spoon. It was the silence that drew his attention back to the milkman, whose chest was heaving as he stared at his delivery notes.

"Are you alright mate?"

The milkman's smile had gone, his face had turned to a dark purple and sweat was dripping from under his white peaked cap. Trevor thought he might be having a stroke or a heart attack. He wasn't in the greatest shape for someone who spent their working lives on the move.

"You…"

The milkman dropped his clipboard and turned to face Trevor. His face was dark with rage, flecks of froth bubbling at the sides of his mouth. Trevor moved away from the cart as the big man advanced on him.

"BASTARD!"

A huge and meaty hand, massively powerful through years of lugging crates and carrying bottles, clamped around Trevor's neck. In a surprisingly fast move for someone so big, the milkman pushed Trevor into the rack of crates on the open rear of the float, his hand squeezing tightly. Trevor had been in a few brawls before; he knew when people were seriously trying to harm him, and this was definitely one of those occasions. When the milkman's left hand joined the right and he felt two thumbs pushing into his windpipe, Trevor panicked. He had to do something right now. So intent was the milkman on killing Trevor, he didn't notice him grab a bottle of gold-foiled milk from a crate. When the bottle came crashing down on the milkman's head there was a brief look of surprise in the man's face before he fell to the floor, blood pouring from the wound on his scalp. The milkman muttered something that sounded like 'Pasteurise... Sterilise...' but Trevor didn't wait around to see if he'd seriously injured the man. His morning was going from weird to downright dangerous and it was time to get far away from this part of town.

Trevor broke into a jog he doubted the milkman would be able to match even in the best of circumstances and headed off down the quiet road. When he reached the phone booth at the end of the street, he pulled out a handful of change and shoved a ten pence piece into the slot for a local call. The first taxi company was engaged and, despite his protestations, the second wouldn't pick up from a phone box. As they were the only two numbers he knew off heart, Trevor grabbed the tattered remains of a phone book and hoped 'T' hadn't been yanked out completely.

He had just completed his call to DG Cars when Trevor became aware of a high-pitched humming and violent rattling build behind him. Turning inside the cramped and stinking phone booth, he blinked a couple of times as he peered through the scratched windows. The milk float was driving directly towards him at full speed, the puce face of the milkman in stark contrast to his yoghurt pot-circumference staring eyes. The float mounted the kerb, crates flew off and crashed to the pavement, milk and orange juice exploded across the flagstones. Trevor only just flung himself from the booth before the float smashed into it with a tremendous explosion of glass and thick sliced loaves.

Trevor staggered into a nearby hedge, slick with dairy produce. All around the terraced street curtains twitched. It was only a matter of minutes until the police or ambulance turned up. He quickly surmised he'd look like the kind of person who would cause an accident such as this, so he decided a quick sprint towards the route most likely for the taxi to arrive on would be the best bet. Unfortunately, the milkman had different ideas.

Untangling himself from his crushed cab, the bloodied man lumbered out of the wreckage, a thousand-yard stare fixed on Trevor with lethal determination. Blood poured from his head and his arm. His apron had been torn and his blue tunic was covered in butter, but it didn't stop his progress. He reached down blindly to the ground for a weapon and rose like an avenging angel, his chubby hand wrapped around a large block of cheese.

Holding it like a rock, the milkman staggered forwards, clearly intent on Red Leicester homicide. Trevor would have laughed if it hadn't been so utterly bizarre and horrifying. Instead, as the milkman slipped in a pool of pouring cream and fell onto his face, Trevor turned and ran. Two minutes and three street lengths later, he saw a cab driving towards him and, flagging it down energetically, he hoped like hell it was the one he'd just called.

"Taxi for Trebor?"

Trevor nodded at the wrinkled face, jogged around to the passenger side, and jumped into the green Vauxhall Cavalier.

"Beer to, bate?"

The thin man began coughing violently, slapping the smooth-worn steering wheel as he tried to get over his sudden consumptive attack. From seemingly nowhere he took a long drag on a cigarette, coughed a couple of times then stubbed it out in his overflowing ash tray.

"Are you alright?"

The taxi driver wafted the last few wisps of smoke from his face and wiped tears from his bloodshot eyes.

"Gob mab flu or somethib. I'b okay."

In the distance, the wail of a siren drifted on the morning air. Trevor concluded he was one beggar who wasn't in a position to be a chooser.

"Castle Boulevard, the gym. Is there a corner shop anywhere nearby? I'm starving."

"Therb a pebrol stashin halb a bile abay. Gob Pork Farms pies."

"Good enough for me. Let's go."

The car revved into life, U-turned to face the opposite direction and headed towards the centre of Nottingham. As they approached the promised petrol station, an ambulance screamed past, closely followed by a fire engine and a police car.

"They're ib a hurry."

The taxi driver exploded into a coughing fit as he pulled over in front of a petrol pump. Trevor waited for him to recover, thankful for the anonymity given the emergency response they had just witnessed. How they'd write up the scene awaiting them was beyond him.

"Goib to fill ub whibe you go to the shob."

Exiting the car at the same time as the driver, Trevor walked across the empty forecourt and went to open the door of the petrol station shop. It was locked. A tap on the window from the cashier a few yards away and a sullen pointing to the Perspex screen and small hatch in front of her told him the shop wasn't yet open.

As he approached, the young woman eyed Trevor with suspicion, reaching into her handbag on the counter as he loomed closer to the transparent screen separating the warm and cosy inside from the petrol fume-smelling outside. When he shouted all he wanted was to buy some food, she relaxed a little, withdrew her hand from her bag and conducted their savoury transaction through half an inch of plastic. A few seconds later he had the wrapper off the pork pie and the meaty delight stuffed into his salivating mouth. By the time he got back to the taxi driver, it had been consumed in its crust and jelly entirety.

"You nearly done? I need to get to the gym."

The taxi driver snorted. Trevor looked down at the

crumbs on his shirt. Pork pie for breakfast and then the gym? Training regime of champions, clearly.

"Okay. I'b nearly dub."

As Trevor stood next to the cabbie and wiped the crumbs from his shirt, the man stood upright and sniffed the air with a snotty rattle. Slowly, he turned to face Trevor, his wrinkled face changing as quickly as the weather at the seaside. His eyes glazed over and he began to sway, dislodging the diesel dispenser from the neck of the Vauxhall's petrol tank and liberally splashing fuel all over the side of his car and the floor.

"Watch what you're doing!"

The taxi driver's face distorted into a scowl.

"Youuuuub…"

Trevor couldn't believe it. Exactly the same look as Jackie and the milkman, except this time it wasn't a ratty dog or lump of cheddar being used as a weapon. It was a black hose full of inflammable death. Trevor jumped backwards away from the old man who began waving the metal gun around like a club.

"Oi! What the hell are you doing with my pump?"

The young woman appeared in the shop's doorway, five foot one of red-haired fury and clearly in no mood to be messed around with at the end of her nightshift. As she marched forwards, Trevor backed away from the advancing taxi driver whose entire focus was on Trevor.

"Put that pump back you fucking idiot! You're getting diesel all over the place!"

Trevor had read once that, despite their tiny size, wrens could make a noise so loud they could startle a cat. Both he and the taxi driver jumped at her shrill tone, but it only seemed to enrage the old man more. Now he was pointing the dispensing nozzle like a pistol, the hose nearly at full stretch from the pump and straining the joint with the dispenser. If that came loose, the whole garage forecourt would be flooded with fuel. Not happy at being ignored, the feisty attendant barged Trevor out of the way and slopped through the spreading puddle of stinking fuel towards the taxi driver. It was then Trevor noticed she had her mobile phone in her left hand, knuckles white with the grip she had around it.

"Turn it off! Or I'll turn it off for you!"

The woman stood between Trevor and the driver, shaking with anger.

"Kill! Kill him! DIE!"

The taxi driver lunged forwards, slipping on the diesel and catching the woman as he fell. Both crashed to the ground, and in the man's attempt to get back to his feet, the woman clearly thought he was trying to attack her and swung the hand holding the phone towards him. Except, in a moment of supreme television-quality close-up clarity, Trevor realised it wasn't a mobile phone at all. It was an electric stun-gun, the small handheld type that could be bought for a few quid on holiday and sneaked home on the plane in hold luggage.

The more the cabbie kept screaming and thrashing in his bid to reach Trevor, the more the woman kept on shouting her threats until, with no thought of her fuel saturation, she thrust the prongs of the device into the man's shoulder. Trevor backed away, but not fast enough. He heard the fast click of the electrodes as they zapped the hapless cabby and saw him twitch as he screamed in pain. Then, he saw the fuel ignite.

Two seconds later, just as he'd begun to run as fast as he could away from the thrashing figures, the world went orange and white, and he felt the giant hand of God lift him up and throw him into the air. It felt like a dream of flying, like when he was a kid, but the flight was brief and the landing on the far side of the road very, very hard. He didn't even see the cyclist who braked violently to avoid him.

Trevor lay face-down for a few seconds, trying to decide if it was worth the risk of moving lest something had snapped or been torn off. There was a dreadful smell of singed hair, the source of which was revealed when he gingerly felt the back of his head. It felt crispy, like the seaweed he liked in a Chinese restaurant. He winced at the pain from his torn hands but still managed to prop himself up. Directly before him, the garage was consumed in flames, with no sign of the cashier or the cabbie. To his right, curious people were emerging from their houses to see why their windows had been blown out of their homes. To his left, a man dressed in hi-vis work gear lay on his back, his twisted bike on the pavement behind him. A couple of people were running towards the carnage to see how they could help. Looking back at the raging inferno and bits of Vauxhall strewn about the place, Trevor couldn't even begin to suggest where they'd start.

Macintyre was getting edgy. He'd heard the sarge's breathing change a few seconds beforehand, and his air supply was getting dangerously low. He fully realised he should shoot Trevor, grab his boss, get in the dinghy and row as fast as he could, but he had to know what happened next. Sod's law Trevor took an opportunity to go quiet and look reflective.

"Well?"

Trevor jumped at Macintyre's impatient prompt. He looked exhausted, sad, deflated, beaten by life. Looking down at the rocks, he nudged a couple of stones around with his battered boots.

"Hindsight's a wonderful thing. You might be sitting there thinking 'couldn't he see a pattern emerging here, that everyone he's met was trying to kill him', but I didn't. I was so... confused doesn't even cover it... so overwhelmed I just sat there in the road as all these people came towards me to help."

Trevor snorted to himself.

"Except, of course, after a few seconds they didn't want to help at all. At first there were concerned mutters of 'are you alright duck' and 'you were lucky to survive' but then... have you ever seen An American Werewolf in London?"

Macintyre raised his eyebrows. Finally, a reference to something he understood. He'd always been a big fan of horror films, particularly those made in the eighties. He knew the film well. The reference, however, threw him a bit.

"Yeah, why? Did you turn into a werewolf?"

Trevor hacked out a strange, cracking noise that almost passed for a laugh.

"That's funny! No... there's a bit in it right at the start when the two hitch-hiking Americans walk into a pub on the Yorkshire Moors, and everyone stops what they're doing. It was just like that. There was even a bald bloke staring at me who looked like Brian Glover."

Macintyre couldn't help it. Air indicator and potentially homicidal sergeant be damned. He had to keep listening.

"So?"

"They attacked me. Every one of them. I got hit with fists, newspapers, handbags; anything and everything they either came out of their houses with or were carrying with them to work. I couldn't move. I was pinned down. Luckily the scrum was so large they mostly ended up hitting each other, such was their fury and rage and lack of coordination. But I knew I wasn't long for this world, so I just curled up in a ball and waited for the end."

Macintyre waved the muzzle of his tranquiliser gun impatiently.

"And then?"

Trevor's head dropped to his chest. Slowly, he raised his face, his eyes brimming with tears.

"I got rescued."

The blows rained down so fast on Trevor, he couldn't distinguish one from another. Had they not been so crowded together, the mob might have been able to get a proper swing at him but such was the crush, the punches and kicks lacked the impact they might have delivered. Had they been more accurate, he'd have been dead by now. The road was filled with the thunder and crackle of the petrol station blaze and cries of 'KILL!', only interrupted by violent coughing brought on by the air, thick with black smoke and the smell of burning fuel. Trevor knew he couldn't take this for much longer – someone would get him in the' temple or crack his skull sooner or later – so he decided to try and crawl his way out. That didn't go down well. As soon as he moved, a roar went up around and above him. The uncoordinated assault increased in speed, if not ferocity, and in that instant he realised he was well and truly done for.

And then, the ground beneath him began to shake. Deafened by the screaming and the ringing in his ears, Trevor couldn't make out what was happening. But then he became aware of a new sound, a deep growling rumble that quickly built in volume, making the road vibrate more violently. A rhythmic squeal pierced its way through the calls of the murderous crowd surrounding him and, somewhere in the back of his memory, Trevor put it all together – it was a tank, and it was heading straight towards him. Strangely, his homicidal mob didn't seem to care about it at all.

The squealing stopped and an amplified voice began shouting. Between the pulsing of the ground from the machine's idling engines and his attacker's sustained rage, Trevor tried to make out what was being said. Whatever it was, his assailants weren't listening. Another brief few words followed, again ignored, and then a change in tone, orders of some kind, were called out. Seconds later, a staccato series of loud hisses and pops exploded all around, closely followed by yelps, screams and thuds. Despite having his eyes closed and arms over his ears and head, Trevor gradually became aware of sunlight above him and the thumps and kicks decreasing until they stopped. Uncovering his head, all Trevor could hear was the growl of a very big engine, the crackle of the petrol station fire and… snoring.

"Stay where you are. Do NOT move."

Trevor's head was throbbing. Every part of his body hurt but he managed to pull himself to a sitting position. Only then did he dare to open his eyes and look at the four-deep ring of unconscious bodies surrounding him. Behind them were a circle of camouflaged and gas masked armed men, two very large Armoured Personnel Carriers with their back doors open and, yes, a tank, sitting on top of which was an olive-drab figure holding a megaphone to his respirator.

"Cordon off the area. Get the recovery team in here and put the QMC on alert. Keep your masks on until we've sanitised the area. Move it."

All but two of the suited men split off in different directions, some taping off the width of the road, others grabbing the arms and legs of the sedated mob and dragging them towards one of the APCs. The remaining two walked straight towards Trevor through the path freshly made between the bodies. Both had tranquiliser and real guns slung around their shoulders. All he could do was look up at them and stare with his mouth open.

The first of the men to reach him pulled out a piece of cloth and threw it onto Trevor's lap. He looked down at it dumbly, then back up, trying to see some features behind the two owl-like circular windows in the hood.

"There's two ways to do this Trevor. You can either put this bag on your head – "

It had been a rough morning. Trevor had been attacked by a rat dog, chased by a milk float, blown up by an exploding petrol station and nearly beaten to death by a gang of early morning shift-workers and local residents. It took the shock of hearing his name from this spookily anonymous figure to make Trevor jump. Shaking the concussion away for a few seconds, he frowned at the man until he realised just how painful it was to move his face.

"How… do you know my name?"

The quiet hooded figure turned to face the muffled speaker. After a moment of silent communication, they both turned back to face Trevor.

"The second way then."

Clearly deciding any further dialogue was a waste of time, the second figure drew his tranquiliser gun and pulled the trigger.

Trevor was more confused than ever when he woke. Given the stainless-steel walls, the skeletal surgical bed on which he was lying and the dazzling strip lights in the ceiling, he clearly wasn't sitting on a road in Nottingham anymore. After a few seconds looking around, he attempted to sit upright. He wished he hadn't the second he began to move. Every muscle, every sinew, every part of his body hurt. He could see bruises on the tops of his hands and bare feet and guessed his entire body would look the same had he not been wearing a wrinkly paper boiler suit. Ignoring the stabbing pains, he pulled himself upright and took a good look around.

Other than the James Bond villain vibe, the most disturbing features were the apparent lack of a door and a sinister darkened window running across the wall to his right. Trevor went to run his fingers through his hair, only to discover the reason his head felt so cold was because he was now bald. A squint at his reflection in the glass confirmed someone had shaved his head which, surprisingly, upset him the most about his current predicament.

"Good afternoon Trevor."

The voice was very calm and soft. Just like a Bond villain's.

"Good aft… What the HELL? Who is this?"

After a brief pause, the hidden intercom reactivated.

"My name is Colonel Wilberforce. I was the chap on the tank."

Trevor blinked a few times and shook his head, which made his neck hurt. If this was some half-arsed way to say 'we've met', he didn't appreciate it.

"Okay, doesn't help me at all. Where am I? How do you know me?"

"First part of the question I can't answer I'm afraid, other than to assure you you're quite safe now."

Trevor frowned.

"Safe? From what?"

"We're going to need your full cooperation Trevor, or we won't be able to sort you out."

Despite the utterly alien situation, Trevor began to get angry.

"Sort me out? What does that mean? And you haven't answered my question. How do you know who I am?"

Another pause, longer this time.

"Hello Trevor."

Trevor's mouth fell open.

"Laura?"

"Yes. Laura."

Trevor's mind reeled.

"What's going on? Why are you here? What I have done?"

The intercom clicked off and then back on again.

"You've not done anything wrong Trevor. We just – "

"Not done anything wrong? Not done anything wrong?"

Laura's voice was breaking with fury. Wilberforce's reply was sharp and brutal.

"I'd keep your mouth shut if I were you. You're in enough trouble as it is."

"I couldn't care less what trouble I'm in. I've had it up to here with being quiet and taking it. He had this coming."

Trevor realised somebody still had their finger on the intercom button. A very angry somebody.

"I told you I'd put a stop to you, didn't I?"

Laura was shouting now, her voice distorting the speaker.

"Look at you now! How does it feel to be on the receiving end for a change?"

"Laura, I'm warning you – "

"What are you going to do? You couldn't make my life any more miserable than he did!"

The intercom snapped on and off a few times. Then it came back on to the sound of grunting and shoving.

"No more... ooof... the big 'I am', no more... agh... sleeping around, no more anything because... give me that microphone... you can't go anywhere – "

"Guard! Get her out of here!"

There was a loud shuffling, a yell and a rustling.

" – you can't be near anyone or touch any living thing ever again!"

"Get her OUT OF HERE!"

Trevor looked to the huge window but could see nothing other than his own terrified reflection.

"Wha... what do you mean? Laura? What are you talking about?"

Laura's voice trailed off as she was dragged away from the mic.

"I got you Trevor. I've put a stop to you for good!"

With that, the intercom clicked into silence. Despite the pain coursing through his body, Trevor pushed himself off the gurney, staggered over to the one-way window and hammered on the glass with his raw hands. It didn't take long for him to use up what little energy he had so he skulked back to the metal bed, voice hoarse from shouting every obscenity he could think of.

For several minutes Trevor listened to the hum of the lights and his ragged breathing, trying to calm down and make sense of his situation. Failing, he took to staring at the wall until, without warning, a door slowly opened with a release of air, framing three green HAZMAT suited figures. The one in front walked forward, turning to stop the other two who stepped back and allowed the seamless door to close in front of them. Unmoving, the figure regarded Trevor for long seconds.

"Sorry about that."

The voice was muffled behind the green hood and respirator but was recognisable as Wilberforce's.

"Laura doesn't work for Boots, does she?"

Even though Trevor could only see the eyes framed by the breathing mask behind the suit's visor, Wilberforce managed to look embarrassed.

"No. She works for us."

"Us being…?"

"I can't tell you that."

"I thought not."

Wilberforce put his black-gloved hands behind his back, as if he was briefing a group of cadets on their new drill.

"What you have to understand is we're doing everything we can to fix this. I'm terribly sorry for what she's done."

Trevor shivered. He didn't want to ask, but he had to.

"Which is…?"

Wilberforce shuffled from one foot to another.

"I don't… it's hard to know how to put this. It's all rather… complicated."

Trevor folded his arms. It made his elbows throb.

"I'm not stupid."

Wilberforce sighed, then took a rasping breath.

"Right. Well. Our job is to… Our mission is… a few months back, my team discovered a tiny section of noncoding DNA, an ancient dormant gene that everyone has. Completely overlooked until now by all the researchers across the world. Remarkable really."

Trevor tried to look enthusiastic, but his face muscles were too busy presenting a mask of trepidation.

"Anyway… in the great majority of the population it's inactive. Occasionally it kicks in around adolescence for some unfortunate teenagers, leading to… difficulties. In adulthood it's rare."

Trevor didn't like the sound of this at all.

"Go on."

Wilberforce looked down. His suit crinkled. He looked back up again.

"Have you ever met someone you just wanted to hit? Didn't like their look the second you clapped eyes on them?"

Trevor thought about it. There had been a bloke, couldn't remember his name, who he'd very briefly worked with – briefly as in he'd briefly been to work. He'd hated him for absolutely no reason he could think of then or now.

"Yes… why?"

Wilberforce's body language suddenly changed as if he was now talking to someone who would understand exactly what he was saying, that some basis of shared knowledge had been reached which, of course, it hadn't. The Colonel clearly also didn't appreciate how terrified Trevor was.

"Ah well, you've probably encountered what we call an Omega, someone whose gene is active. Such people broadcast a pheromone that makes others react to them in a hostile way."

Trevor raised his eyebrows.

"They smell that bad?"

Wilberforce chuckled somewhere behind his hood.

"Not exactly, no. It's odourless, but very, very powerful – even after thousands of years of mutation and dilution."

Trevor sat back on the gurney and considered what he was being told.

"Well I can't have it… I mean I can't be active. I'm no Omega. In fact… I'm pretty popular with the ladies and I've never had… well… a reaction like that. Until the other day."

Wilberforce nodded.

"Yes. I need to debrief you about that at some point. It'll help our research considerably."

Trevor stared at the Colonel, waiting for him to continue – which he didn't.

"What research?"

Wilberforce shuffled uneasily again. Trevor didn't have to be a scientist to tell this wasn't a conversation he was enjoying.

"After we identified and isolate it, we carried out a few experiments and concluded this gene once played a crucial role in the development of humanity. Around five thousand years ago it was effectively responsible for weeding out the human race to what we have now."

Trevor was quite taken aback by the gardening reference.

"Weeding out?"

"We examined the remains of ancient graves where the individuals had met a violent death for no obvious reason – not in battle, or a natural catastrophe, that kind of thing. What we found in the majority of cases was astonishing. Their DNA had this gene pumping out reactive pheromones like a violent aphrodisiac, likely resulting in someone coming along and killing them without any justification whatsoever. It was some kind of global gene pool cleansing. No idea what instigated it or why it happened. It just did."

Again, Wilberforce fell silent. Trevor could hear him breathing inside his suit, reluctant to get to the point. Trevor couldn't stand it any longer. With a dry gulp, he closed his eyes.

"What's this got to do with me?"

Wilberforce cleared his throat.

"We not only found a way to activate this dormant gene in an inactive individual, to effectively turn them into an Omega, but a method to dramatically increase the virulence of the chemical signal they broadcast. An Omega Plus, if you will."

The Colonel sounded pleased with his analogy. Trevor shook his head in disbelief.

"You found a way?"

Wilberforce stepped forwards in his excitement, but quickly stopped himself and backed away against the steel wall.

"Yes. What's more, we worked out how to weaponize it, to make it into a transferable agent."

"Transferable agent?"

"A way to give it to someone, a target individual – Hussein, Gaddafi, Bin Laden if we ever find him, whoever... Slip them a drop of it, walk away and then bang! They transform into an Omega, their own people turn on them and kill them within minutes of target ingestion."

It sounded ingenious. Trevor was impressed. There was just one utterly hideous point he had to clarify to enjoy the science lesson to its best advantage.

"Okay, but I still don't know what this has got to do with – "

In a flash, Trevor saw Poppy's snarling hairy face.

"Does it make dogs react the same way, too?"

Wilberforce was taken off-guard. He considered for a second.

"In theory it could provoke a reaction from any mammal."

Images filled Trevor's head - Jackie's frenzied eyes, the milkman's murderous dairy intentions, the cabbie's relentless diesel attack and the screams of 'DIE BASTARD!' from the petrol station mob.

The conclusion was clear. He'd been given this wonder drug.

Trevor looked down at his raw, road-rash blistered hands.

"It works on dogs. It doesn't seem to do much for around six hours from first contact with the Omega, then takes seconds to kick in."

"Really."

Wilberforce's voice was hushed with wonder. Trevor almost felt a part of his absurd team. He wasn't trying to be helpful but Wilberforce nodded slowly, as if he'd just been given vital pieces of information. Which, in fact, he had.

To hell with him, Trevor thought. This isn't about him.

"Surely… someone could taste if they're being given it…"

"Apart from a slightly sweet aftertaste, it's undetectable as a substance. Looks and acts just like water. You could easily mask it with some sugar."

Trevor felt sick.

"My tea. My bloody tea."

So this was Laura's revenge, her way of 'dealing with him'. Jesus Christ. Talk about an over-reaction.

"But hold on a minute… how did Laura get a hold of it? And how did she get it out of a top-secret establishment?"

Wilberforce sighed.

"She got a hold of it because she works – worked – in the lab where it was developed. And she got it out of here because, well, it's undetectable."

Wilberforce sounded embarrassed. So he should, thought Trevor. The two regarded each other in the shiny metal room, the sound of Wilberforce's respirator breathing and the buzzing of strip lights echoing off the polished walls.

"It's getting late Trevor. You've had a very hard day. Try to relax."

The rectangular doorway magically appeared as the airtight door began to swing outwards. Wilberforce turned to leave.

"Wait a minute… You've got a cure, right? An antidote?"

Trevor felt stupid for not thinking of it earlier. Wilberforce paused as the two identically suited guards –

both armed with real weapons, not tranquilisers this time – kept a wary eye on him.

"We'll talk again in the morning. Run a few tests. Do a few blood samples. That kind of thing."

Trevor felt anger rising in his chest. He didn't like this. Not one bit. Struggling to his feet, the two guards stepped closer, rifles immediately brought to bear. Trevor swallowed as Wilberforce breezed past them and the door swung closed.

"You have got a treatment haven't you?"

Macintyre watched the tears running down Trevor's crusty cheeks.

"So you're telling me you're here because you pissed off your girlfriend?"

Trevor wiped his eyes with the back of his hand and nodded.

"I've been here for nineteen years without the company of a single living creature. Anything that comes near me wants to kill me, so they put me on this anthrax-soaked boulder thinking it was a kindness. It isn't."

Macintyre couldn't help it. He felt sorry for the man.

"Surely though… they must be working on some kind of cure…"

Trevor's eyes bored into Macintyre's. They were as bleak as the island on which they sat.

"Where did the supplies in that boat come from? Special delivery from some shady lab, or just taken as stock from the nearest supply dump?"

Macintyre looked back at the parcels. They were all standard issue, nothing special.

"They're not working on a cure. They don't want a cure. If they get a chance to pop whichever despot or terrorist or government they want rid of, they don't want any chance of it failing."

There was no denying the sense in it, ghoulish though it was. Why create a way to screw up a potentially perfect weapon? Macintyre hoped no-one else had their own version. COVID had been bad enough.

"This is it for me. Forever."

From behind, Macintyre heard a low moan. Rand was waking up.

"Okay but why haven't you tried to... y'know..."

Macintyre pulled a finger across his throat. Trevor laughed, showing his stump teeth and making Macintyre wince.

"Top myself? Chuck a seven? You're going to love this. One side-effect of the boosted Omega Plus virulence they discovered after my... tests... was increased self-preservation. Even picking up that rock earlier to clobber the Sarge nearly made me collapse. I can't kill myself. Believe me, I've tried."

Trevor leaned forward, his gaze still burning into Macintyre's eyes.

"Someone has to do it for me."

Trevor's words hung in the air.

"Well now hold on a minute Trevor..."

Trevor jumped up, wild with movement. He looked like a neanderthal trying to surprise a buffalo in a cave painting.

"Look, I am doomed to walk around this barren rock until something falls on me, I have an accident or get terminally ill. I'll die eventually, but only after a lingering, unpleasant and agonising wait. Much like the last nineteen years in fact."

In addition to the soft swearing amongst Rand's moans from behind, Macintyre could see his visor steaming up. His tank was pretty much out of air.

"You can finish what everyone started that morning."

"Trevor... you little... shit..."

Rand would be fully conscious and angrily mobile in seconds. Macintyre stood and faced Trevor, who had clasped his filthy fingers together and was pleading for release, lip quivering, tears rolling down his face.

"Just pull off the hood and take a deep breath. Come on Macintyre… my pheromones will do the rest."

"I don't…"

"Tell the sarge I ripped your hood off or something."

Trevor stared wide-eyed over Macintyre's shoulder to Rand's twitching body.

"Please."

Macintyre couldn't take it anymore. Holstering the tranquiliser gun, he reached over to his left shoulder, fumbled for the zip beneath the HAZMAT head cowling then pulled it down to his right hip in a single tug. Flipping the visor and hood over the back of his head, it rested on the top of the empty oxygen tank as he undid the straps of his redundant breathing apparatus. Pulling the mask up and over with a squeak of rubber, Macintyre enjoyed the cool morning air on his sweating face.

Taking one final look at the clapping, dancing Trevor, Macintyre closed his eyes and took a deep, long breath.

Computational Error

"Hell and damnation."

Faldo stared at the smouldering carcass of the android, most of its boxy metal torso embedded in the windscreen of his recently beautiful Porsche-E4. One V-shaped foot twitched erratically, fanning the smoke curling up through the shattered glass canopy now crazed and opaque from the violent impact. Until a couple of minutes ago it had seemed a lovely morning.

But then, just as he'd stepped out of the gleaming new vehicle and admired the sleek gull-wing on the yellow sportster, the wall of his battery recycling factory had erupted in a shower of sparks and shards, ejecting a two-ton industrial robot at considerable speed through the freshly generated exit. Had he been in the vehicle, he would probably have been killed which, at this point, gave him little consolation. He had argued down the insurance coverage of his facility so accidental damage to anything, including hugely expensive latest-gen electric sportsters, wasn't covered.

On top of all that, he had a hangover.

"Looks like another battery explosion to me, sir."

The voice had just the wrong hint of 'I told you so'. Faldo didn't turn to look at Jefferson. He spent most of his working day - or, more accurately, morning - avoiding the supercilious engineer. That's why he always met with him first thing, to get it out of the way and let the factory get on with whatever the hell it did to make him money. Given the extent of the damage to the battery disassembly section's wall, that wasn't going to happen today.

A faint sizzling started from inside the car, probably the sumptuous red leather seats beginning to fry. Faldo couldn't watch any longer. He walked over to the robot-width hole punched out by the ballistic droid and sighed. He had a history of writing off cars, reckless driving, reckless behaviour, reckless *everything* and were they to witness this sorry scene, his so-called 'friends' wouldn't even register surprise. They'd shrug it off in their rich-beyond-comprehension way and point out that, were his boasts about the profit he made from his hapless machines and corners he cut at every turn true, he'd be able to afford another car in a month. They didn't know the half of it. In reality, were he to push his hapless machines yet further, he might even achieve it in a fortnight.

"Best take a look at the damage, I suppose."

Ignoring the very few safety protocols he had to maintain to continue operating, Faldo stepped through the twisted panelling into the interior cavern of the factory. Flashing orange lights indicated something unfortunate had taken place, their insistent rhythm outlining the triple set of roller belts stretching from one towering metallic wall to the other. The two furthest production lines were working as normal, with dozens of machines, all as decrepit as the one that had just trashed Faldo's Porsche, juddering and shuddering as they dismembered an endless conga of discarded car, truck and super-heavy batteries.

They had one task - to dismantle these exhausted power supplies, strip them down to their components and send them to the next section so their precious metals could be extracted and recycled. It was a job even the most sophisticated, well-maintained and programmed machine would struggle to do at the speeds he set them, let alone the motley heap of junk Faldo employed. But why should he spend money on good machines when bad ones did half as good a job at a quarter of the price?

Faldo spotted the lurking shadow of Jefferson in his peripheral vision. For a few seconds they both studied the blackened crater in the centre of the closest production line, the remains of one robot trying gamely to get back on feet that no longer existed. The damage to the building and its automated workers was significant, but not unfamiliar.

"Sir, we're going to have to shut down the other lines to effect repairs. We need to call the Inspectorate and - "

"I need those units replacing and line three up and running as soon as possible. Increase speed on the other

163

two to compensate. Get M-5 on to it."

The pulsing beacons brought the younger man's pinched, sallow features into sharp relief. Recently graduated engineers were cheap and mostly eager to learn. Jefferson was all these things, with the added bonus of being a brilliant mechanic and software designer. Unfortunately, he also had a conscience, something Faldo saw only as an impediment to making as much money as possible in the absolute minimum of time.

"Mister Faldo, M-5's still under repair from the last time we sent her in like this. We really need to stop processing and update every droid's AI. They're simply not careful enough in battery disassembly. And the production line speed *must* be reduced. This is the third time we've had an explosion like this in the last four months. It's unsustainable."

Faldo stared at Jefferson, and Jefferson stared back at Faldo. How could the young man actually *care* about these lumps of metal?

"How much time will it take?"

Jefferson's beady eyes widened with enthusiasm.

"I've got an ingram recording system I designed for my PhD. I've been wanting to use it for years. I can hook it up to my cortex, filter out the relevant brainwave patterns then transfer them. Shouldn't take longer than a couple of days start to finish."

Faldo scowled as he flashed a few thousand numbers through his head. More careful machines meant slower machines. He had to reduce the impact on reprocessing times as much as possible That would cut the time he had to wait for a new car. Hundreds of batteries came to him every day from around the world, many requiring a 'no questions asked' policy. Anyone who shared his impatience to make a buck, even in 2186, was welcome. There were still plenty of ways to avoid the gaze of Big Brother, including a factory on land no-one else wanted to buy or, for that matter, visit. Perhaps he'd tell Jefferson the real reason he only stayed on-site for a few hours at a time. One day.

"Two *days*? You've got to be kidding me. Isn't there a faster way?"

Jefferson looked as if someone had just told him his puppy had died.

"Well yes, I could use off-the-shelf public domain safety patterns to modify their behaviour rather than my machine, but I'd have to repair M-5 first, then programme her so she could speed dump the new code into the droids. If you helped it'd take even less - "

"I'm not helping. I don't know how this all works, and I don't really care. Do the ready-made thing as long as it's quicker."

"But my ingram download machine is free, it's really easy to use – "

"And the belts on lines one and two get reduced by no more than five percent. Any more loss in production comes out of your salary. Understood?"

Despite being a novice when it came to social interaction, Jefferson knew a financial threat when he heard one and chose to stop arguing.

"That shouldn't be a problem sir."

Faldo nodded once and turned to leave. The pained expression on Jefferson's face made him pause. Clearly, there was something else to be discussed. He knew he'd regret it, but he asked him what was on his mind.

"We could really do with installing new battery packs into the droids rather than the best of the shitty used ones that I have to sift through in the yard every day. They can't operate off-grid for more than twenty minutes."

"Hell and damnation, Jefferson. Don't push it. The power won't go off, so they won't stop working. We don't need them operating autonomously of the grid. They're never going to leave the factory, are they?"

"No, but if the power did fail – "

Faldo didn't hear the rest of Jefferson's sentence.

Leaving the ruined building the way he'd come in, he looked at his watch and then at his smouldering car. He had a headache, and he needed a drink.

Faldo sat with his arms folded in his usual position at the lavish table and fumed. Hooking up with his so-called peers had lately become more of a chore than a pleasure. Regardless of it being 'one of those things he had to be seen at', he'd not conducted any major business within the group for months. Gone were the various handshakes and winks that could quickly secure a favourable contract or avoid a huge slice of taxable revenue.

Finishing off an appalling day with these appalling people was trying his limited patience. He'd hurriedly munched his way through his starter and main course, finishing as he always did well before the rest of them with the hope of getting to the bar and completing his evening in the preferable company of hard liquor. These people irritated the hell out of him at the best of times but, with a swig of his wine, he had to admit to himself that wasn't the real reason he was so pissed off.

Unusually, uncomfortably, the factory had been playing on his mind since he'd abandoned his ruined car that morning. God only knew what liberal, stay-safe and stay-well bullshit Jefferson was readying to install into his machines in his quest to make a happier world for his mechanical wards. Draining his drink, Faldo gritted his teeth and placed the empty glass on the table. The first clanking rust bucket that wished him 'good morning' would find a spanner wrapped around its oblong head.

Faldo looked at his timepiece. It was nearly nine. Usually this would be the start of his evening, but not tonight. Since getting home from the factory, pouring himself a drink, changing, pouring himself another drink, changing again, pouring himself a drink then finally getting to this swankiest of restaurants, he'd been running the numbers. Perhaps, just perhaps, if he did slow the droids and the lines a touch, the productivity wouldn't be too badly affected, and he'd delay the recovery of his losses but increase his profit margin. He hated to admit Jefferson might be right, but the rate of attrition on the worker robots had become too high, even with Jefferson treating them like a group of robo-infants under his kindergarten care.

Despite Faldo getting most of the machines for next to nothing, the bottom line was he couldn't keep them going for free. Losing nine in the last few weeks was a big financial hit, and while he'd replaced them fairly easily, for once in his life, caution might make sense – and that was what bugged him the most. Hell and damnation, perhaps it was time for *him* to slow down a little.

"Hey Faldo, where's that new car of yours? I thought you'd turn up in it, being the massive show-off you are."

Faldo looked down the long, highly polished table, past the forest of near empty wine bottles, half-filled glasses and the dozen sharply dressed businesspeople facing each other in two uneven rows. The noise level had, as it always did when they met, risen to the point where Daisy had to shout, even though she was only three people away. Some turned and looked towards Faldo with a smile, others continued with their meal or their own conversations. Faldo raised his glass and effortlessly rolled out a lie.

"I didn't like the contrast stitching on the seats so I'm having them picked out and replaced with a better colour. It'll be in the shop for a few weeks."

Daisy pulled a face and looked to the bearded man opposite her. They laughed uproariously. Faldo balled his fists under the table and tried to keep calm. There was no way they could know about the accident… was there? Daisy wiped the side of her mouth with her napkin. She was such a sloppy eater.

"If you come to next month's meet-up, I'll have my new Tesla 99. Got it in orange just by talking to old man Musk myself. It'll eat your Porsche alive."

Daisy loved cars almost as much as Faldo did. Shame she was so ugly.

"If I've got it back by then, we'll see."

The bearded man, Corrin, looked at Daisy and laughed again. Faldo didn't like that one bit.

"What's so funny?"

Corrin put his cutlery down, took a drink as a robot waiter removed his plate, and placed his glass unsteadily back on the table.

"From what I hear Faldo, there's a bigger chance of you wrapping your latest toy around a tree than turning up in it. Why you insist on deactivating the auto-motive system when you clearly can't drive is beyond me. But hey, if that's the way you furnish your scrap battery empire, by smashing up your own cars with a heavy foot on the accelerator, good luck on that for a short-term business model."

Daisy put her hand across her enhanced mouth and teeth, her false-coloured eyes wide with mock shock. Faldo had been the butt of many a joke about how he made his money and had lost count of the times he'd been teased about only having one speed – too fast. Several witty and a couple of profane retorts flashed through his head. Instead, he pushed himself up to his feet and weaved his way to the bar, ignoring the jeers from his 'friends' and raised eyebrows from other select diners dotted around the cosy boutique interior.

By the time the triple neat vodka had been dispensed by the gleaming silver bartender, Faldo had completely changed his mind about slowing his factory or his life down. A normal person would have understood they had nothing to prove to such shallow, materialistic people, but Faldo was the most avaricious of them all. As the fiery liquid slid down his throat and he walked on unsteady legs towards the exit, he decided he was going to shift up a gear, not down.

Faldo squinted as the old man stroked his snow-white

goatee with one hand and shone his baton-length torch into his face with the other. Faldo couldn't remember the last time he'd visited the complex in the dark. The only reason the ancient guard stood before him was a decrepit safety clause that insurers still required for fully automated facilities. He'd tried to find a broker who would allow the machines to get on with it twenty-four hours a day without any kind of human overview, but not one would take him on, so – naturally – he'd gone for the cheapest option, which was this old boy now peering at an image of Faldo on his cell phone. Exactly what he would or could do in an emergency – such as another explosion – was open to debate.

Right now, Faldo was losing patience. He needed to get into the programming suite while he was still good and drunk so, unless he pushed the doddering fool aside, he'd have to wait for the identity check. With a whistle suggesting poorly fitted dentures, the guard finally recognised him and let him pass with a string of tuneful apologies.

Faldo entered the complex and navigated his way upstairs to Jefferson's lab. Pausing to steady his spinning head, he looked down to the gloomy disassembly section below. Sparks and flashes picked out the machines working on the operational lines, but one third of the enormous hall was in darkness, the unseen machines awaiting their reprogramming next morning.

Anger surged through Faldo as he pictured Jefferson stroking and cooing over their angular frames, whispering sweet digital nothings into their audio receptors or whatever the hell passed for ears. Shaking his head in disgust, Faldo marched towards the heavily secured programming suite, waved his wrist at the RFID locking mechanism and pushed his way through the slowly hissing door.

More lights, brighter than the rest of the building, crackled into life and Faldo had to shield his eyes from glare amplified by the mirrored wall of windows that had been sealed and coated to block prying eyes. Exactly who would want to watch Jefferson fawning over a load of knackered robots, Faldo still didn't know, but Jefferson had insisted on this security protocol along with the door and because it hadn't cost very much, Faldo had agreed. Now, as it happened, it meant he could do what he wanted in total secrecy so, with a smile, he walked past the steel benches covered in robotic limbs and torsos, wires and monitors, and went to the recovery area for the best, most advanced and hardest working robot of all.

Roughly seven feet in height and weighing in at half a ton, even Faldo had to admit M-5 was a beauty, faded to be sure, but widely regarded as one of the greatest marques ever to come off the Daystrom Corporation's production line. Powerful, lithe and agile, the machine could run for ninety-six hours on a single charge. She was capable of being fully serviced within six hours and could take a tremendous amount of beating thanks to her honeycomb alloy construction, most of which was exposed and corroded due to the outer skin having been sloughed, blown or sliced off over the last twenty years.

Most of these models had been retired long since, having served their duty proudly and diligently to whichever careful owner had cherished them, but M-5 had been bashed and abused long before Faldo had bought her. On Jefferson's first day he'd actually cried when he'd first set eyes on the towering, slender robot, tracing his fingers over her leaking joints and cracked, tarnished head, tenderly wiping years of grime from her two oversized circular visual receptors. He'd been slowly renovating her ever since, bringing bits of outer casing he'd salvaged or bought with his own money to restore her to her former glory. The idiot.

Faldo traced a long, thick yellow cable from the base of her skull to a recharge/recalibration module. Unhooking it with an impatient yank, he listened to a pulsing electronic hum die to nothing. Cable still in hand, he set out to find Jefferson's magic box, the one which would allow him to *properly* reprogramme not only M-5 but his entire factory. After some bad-tempered rummaging he found it, connected the cable, turned the machine on and watched as the robot began to twitch as it cycled through its interfacing checks.

With the 'Please wait' message gone, the monitor built into the device's aluminium case began giving instructions on how to position a series of pads around the brainwave donor's head. These would record those parts of the subject's psyche deemed appropriate for translation into a robot workforce – caution, diligence, bravery – that kind of nonsense. Jefferson hadn't lied; it *was* easy to use and, despite Faldo's deliberate ignorance of all that transpired in his own factory, he grabbed a hold of the network of wires and pads, singing to himself as he stuck them onto his face and neck.

Faldo opened his eyes and glanced at the clock. It was just before seven. Galvanised into action, he threw off his clothes, showered, changed and jumped into a waiting cab, eager to reach his factory before Jefferson. As his ride pulled up the wide drive of the factory, huge automated trucks were already lined up, ready to discharge their toxic and valuable cargo.

Right at the front, he saw Jefferson's vehicle waiting for the main gate to open. The shuffling figure of the night guard was clearly in no great rush to clock off and get home. Paying the cab, Faldo jumped out, jogged down the path in the long shade of the lumbering trucks and got to the gate just as it was grinding its way open. The guard waved Jefferson through, gave Faldo a curious look as he strolled past, then, without a word, turned to his own beaten-up vehicle and drove off.

Jefferson eased his way out of his car, stared at the hastily repaired panel next to the Porsche-shaped scorch marks on the floor, then cocked his head. If Faldo was hoping to surprise Jefferson, he failed. His greeting was cut short with a raised hand and worried look from the engineer.

"What – "

"Shh."

Jefferson moved towards the patch and put his ear to the overlapped plates. His frown deepened.

"Something's not right."

Faldo tried his very best to keep a straight face.

"What do you mean?"

"The rhythm isn't right. It's too fast. Far too fast."

Faldo assumed Jefferson was talking about the output speed of the lines, betrayed by a pulsating, low frequency throb that thrummed through the floor. On more than one occasion Jefferson had 'felt' a problem before seeing it while working upstairs in his lab or making one of his routine inspections, but Faldo knew the reason the machines were working faster – and they must have been doing so for hours. Porsche showroom, here I come.

Just as he put on his best poker face, a loud bang came from inside the battery disassembly area followed by a series of clangs and crashes. Jefferson sprinted towards the factory entrance with the urgency of a father realising his children were in danger. Faldo was right behind him.

Faldo reeled from the rattling and shrieking of metal on the factory floor. Every operational status beacon had gone from orange to red, the scarlet light bouncing off the steel rollers and the girders that kept the dilapidated building together. The intensity of the lights silhouetted Jefferson's mortified face, but that wasn't what most struck Faldo.

All three lines were running at least four times faster than he'd ever seen before. Closest to him, suitcase-sized truck battery packs were rocking violently on their feed belts. Several fell to the concrete floor, gouging out chunks of the surface. Those units that made it to the frenzied robots fared little better. Their cases were smashed open by heavy steel fists, their innards ripped out in a violent flurry of electrical flashes and discharges. An explosion to the right threw two robots in opposite directions, anode and cathode plate fragments whistling through the air as lethal shrapnel. A massive cobweb of conduit and cable wrapped itself around the rollers and manic limbs of the mechanical workforce as it desperately tried to match the frantic pace.

Faldo spotted M-5, lurching between the second- and third-line robots, pushing and shoving them to work faster, urging them like some crazed sports coach. This just made them clumsier. One robot of the same model that had destroyed Faldo's car became entangled in the battery it was taking apart and was dragged onto the speeding conveyor belt, its legs kicking uselessly like a competition swimmer. It disappeared through the hatch to the next section of the factory, sure to make an even bigger mess.

"We have to shut it down! Shut it all down!"

Jefferson screamed over the cacophony, his eyes bulging at the horror of it all. Faldo nodded in agreement, his head buzzing with the scale of just how much he'd screwed things up with his guerrilla programming. Jefferson ran towards the emergency shutdown station set into the outer wall, a rusting metal cube with a master kill-switch set at waist height. Before he could reach it M-5 spotted his plan and unsteadily vaulted over the lines to intercept him, her glowing round eyes suddenly sinister and full of malice.

Faldo shouted a warning, but it came too late; M-5 smashed into Jefferson, crushing him against the station's casing then leaving him to crumple in the dent he'd just created. Satisfied with her work, M-5 limped back to harry the wretched droids closest to her. Faldo had to make a decision; try the same approach as Jefferson, who lay unmoving on the floor, or isolate the entire power supply to the factory. Slowly backing into the corridor, he turned and ran down a passageway into the open courtyard where the massive trucks were busy disgorging their lethal loads.

Everywhere he looked, piles of batteries sat in untidy heaps. Spider robots scurried between them, more victims of M-5's reprogramming which, in turn, had come straight from Faldo's alcohol-soaked 'go faster' brain. They were picking up six battery packs at a time instead of their usual two, using their rear legs to heave themselves along the rusting metal floor grids. All three reception bays were overflowing. The spiders couldn't know that they were delivering units faster than they could be processed by the cranked-up disassembly lines further down the factory. That kind of sophisticated communication cost money.

"Hell and damnation."

Faldo soberly realised if he didn't do something radical, he'd lose everything.

The complex's power supply came up through the floor of the seething courtyard into a small hut tucked into the corner of the unloading area. Running over and tearing open the door, he stared at the tall banks of transformers humming loudly to his left from behind thick rusty caging. Ignoring the 'danger of death' signs, Faldo smashed down every lever he could find until the noise from the electrical equipment began to wind down.

Running back outside into the early morning air, he watched as the huge steel gate to the awaiting line of trucks rumbled closed on its emergency shutdown protocol. The spider robots continued to scuttle and ram battery packs into the over-stuffed bays but at the rate they were working, without the energy grid, they'd soon run out of internal charge. Score one point for being cheap on their batteries.

With the power disconnected, Faldo dashed back to the disassembly area. Worryingly, Jefferson hadn't moved. Despite the reprocessing lines having stopped, those robots that weren't hopelessly entangled in their own mess were still operating on their quickly discharging power supplies, even without new units delivered to them. M-5 was nowhere to be seen, and Faldo hoped she had gone off to continue reprogramming the soon to be lifeless workforce. Crouching down, Faldo pulled Jefferson to a sitting position with his back to the shutdown station and gave him a shake. The last thing Faldo needed was a lawsuit on top of everything else Relief swept over him when Jefferson groaned and opened his eyes.

"Are you okay?"

Jefferson winced and put his hand to his side.

"I think I've broken my ribs."

Faldo lost interest the second he knew Jefferson wasn't badly hurt. He now had to try and cover his tracks so that no-one discovered this whole mess was his fault.

"The grid's off. These droids will run down in a few minutes, but M-5 needs shutting down and wiping. God knows what's got into her."

Jefferson pulled a face as he breathed, his face lit with intermittent sodium lights running off the emergency batteries around the gloomy interior.

"You'll have to send a deactivation signal. If she's within five kilometres, it'll shut her down. Then we can retrieve her and get her hooked up to diagnostics and find out what's happened. I just don't understand it."

Faldo looked away in case his face gave anything away. He knew exactly why she was tear-arsing around the place and pushing everything past its limits. *That* was the part of his mind he'd given her.

"You wait here. I'll go up to the office and call an ambulance then shut her down. If you need to – "

The lines started up again with a judder.

"Oh Christ. She's put the power back on!"

Jefferson was frightened. Faldo was heading the same way.

"I'll be right back. I'd suggest you don't touch that lever. She might not like that."

Jefferson nodded and swallowed. Faldo hadn't taken

three steps before M-5 appeared from the access corridor and blocked his way.

"Get to work."

The voice was rasping, a rudimentary vocoder designed for single syllable responses. Her detached calm was terrifying. Faldo stared into the glowing orbs, anger building at his own stupidity and the increasing danger he was getting himself into.

"I don't take orders from you. You do as *I* say. Now let me pass."

M-5 looked past Faldo to Jefferson then back to Faldo.

"Work fast. Work hard. Earn money. Buy car."

Faldo's mouth fell open.

"How in the hell – "

M-5's slender arm shot out, her long, steel talons crushing Faldo's upper arm as she pulled him towards the nearest production line and threw him between two thrashing robots. A metal limb connected with his shoulder and spun him around onto the conveyor belt. Seeing his chance, he threw himself backwards towards the second disassembly line, ducking under more flailing machines as he nursed his useless left arm. Showers of sparks surrounded him as he tried to get away, but he moved too slowly; M-5 was upon him again, shoving him back towards the line and a teetering stack of hefty industrial battery packs.

"Work fast. Work hard."

Faldo turned on M-5, teeth gritted in defiance.

"I can't do it, you idiot. I don't know how."

M-5 looked to Faldo, then to one of the battery units.

"Watch. Learn."

M-5 rammed her arm into the rusting carcass of a huge super-heavy battery, making it rock on the line despite its weight. When the casing didn't give way, she continued to pummel it with both piston-powered arms. As the casing distorted and peeled away from its toxic innards, Faldo's eyes bugged. The interior was glowing.

"Stop! Stop it! The battery's on fire!"

Faldo tried to run but M-5 grabbed hold of his bad arm, making him shout in pain. Pulling him closer, M-5 continued to smash the now smoking battery pack with her free hand. Faldo pulled and struggled against the robot in a frantic attempt to escape.

"Work fast. Work hard. Earn money. Buy car."

There was a loud 'popping' sound then a rage of flashes. M-5 stopped what she was doing and stared at the ruptured battery with unblinking eyes. Her robot voice didn't even get to finish the sentence.

"Hell and dam – "

There was a brilliant flash, then Faldo felt himself rising into the air. At first his view was obscured, but as the fractured body of M-5 sailed in different directions high above the factory's blown out roof, he realised where he was. He didn't feel any pain. For that matter, he didn't feel anything and, just before he began to fall and everything went dark, Faldo was convinced he could see the Porsche showroom in the distance.

Computational Error

The World Above

Azral stared into the sky, watching the clouds gathering in the darkened heavens above the sacred ground on which she stood. It seemed fitting the congregation surrounding her were cloaked in darkness. It matched her mood, and that of her fellow warriors. Closing her eyes, she breathed the incense from the lamps dotted around the ancient clearing, listened to the crackle of the fires around the perimeter.

Despite being relatively young, she had witnessed many of these ceremonies; death in battle was the highest honour to her people, something to be celebrated with those departing this world and those surviving them. As the sweet smell wafted on the breeze, she squeezed her eyelids tighter to stop a tear rolling down her cheek plates, not from any sadness for the celebrant, but the number of farewells she had attended since the lowering of the sun.

One after another, those mortally injured and left for dead on the battlefield that day had been silently readied for their final journey, such was the shock of their defeat. Every survivor of the massacre had been pressed into service, young or old, fighters or clerics or farmers, to prepare the dead. Her entire tribe – what was left of it, at least – had rallied together in an unspoken bond to send those fatally wounded to The World Above, and Azral knew the same would have happened in their neighbouring tribes.

Notwithstanding their heavy losses, Azral knew things could have been far worse. The rising of the sun that day had brought with it a sudden and unexpected breach of their border, but they had been quick to respond, sending as many warriors as they could. It had not been all of them, thank the Mighty Keeper because, up until that day, the Govor had been a relatively easy enemy to vanquish.

Had been.

She knew on that battlefield, along with the other survivors of the attack, she had witnessed an extraordinary shift in power, one that created questions without any answers. Her people had been defeated in battle before; they were not invincible and, on occasion according to the Elders, they had even lost to the Govor before. But that had been centuries ago and in that time her people had adapted to their most hated enemy, learned their weaknesses, and held the advantage in battle. Azral herself had slain many of them since her ascension to adulthood, and had she not been there to witness the catastrophe that befell them that day, she would have dismissed it as a fantastical tale, akin to those she dreamed up as a child.

Azral opened her eyes, lowered her head and looked at her fellow warriors. Despite their best efforts to maintain their fiercest demeanour, the shock of what had happened was literally painted across their faces. In the flickering firelight, she could see the ridges of their neck gills shift from blue to orange then back again as they attempted to contain their emotions, with one of the youngest fighters holding his long, slender fingers over the top of his skull plates to hide the discoloration and shame displayed across his brow.

Standing at his shoulder, Trova, Azral's oldest friend and comrade in arms, gently reached up and pulled the youth's arms downwards. Such movement would normally be construed as a sign of disrespect but, given the circumstances in which the remains of the tribe found themselves, even the dying Timku, around which they stood in a perfect circle, forgave the indiscretion with a weakened wave of her hand.

"I commit my soul to The World Above. Receive me, Mighty Keeper."

Timku's voice was barely a whisper, but Azral heard her, nodded, then knelt beside her shattered skull. Both of Timku's lateral cheek plates had been snapped off, exposing a network of tissues and nerves that lay like tiny snakes over her bleeding gills. The twin top plates that swept upwards and backwards over the softer tissue of her skull were badly fractured, the right one hinged on the remains of cartilage that had refused to tear. Further down her face, at the bottom of the deep U-shape that formed the top of her central nasal ridge, one eye stared blindly. The other, glossy and black as the night sky above her, looked upwards without blinking, while her tiny mouth moved soundlessly. Azral looked down the length of Timku's long, slender body. Most of it showed similar signs of damage, but it was the trauma to her chest exoskeleton, torn open to expose her failing organs, that had brought her down.

Azral looked back to Timku's face. The mightiest of not just their tribe but one of the greatest of their entire people had been slain. Death, of course, came to all, and welcome it was too, but the way in which she and so many others that day had been left to die was beyond comprehension. There had been so few of the Tok Govor – the name her people gave to the Govor when they encountered them in battle – they had barely seemed a threat. Scouts had picked up their violation of the border and signalled the need to repel them as soon as they had stepped foot onto their territory, with a defensive force mustered from her tribe, The Tribe Nubar, and the tribes closest north and south as they were nearest to the violation.

They had rendezvoused and met the small force before the sun had reached its zenith, with all who marched upon them confident the engagement would be over quickly. If only they had paused to question the strangeness of it all, to take breath before charging into the fray. The sun had barely moved before a quarter of their warriors had been slain and half lie dying, the Tok Govor inexplicably retreating as suddenly as they had arrived. Had they pressed their advantage, one of savagery and skill never seen before in the hated enemy, all would likely have perished – including Azral.

Why had they withdrawn back to their own lands when so many of them had been defeated so effortlessly? Why hadn't they slain them all on the battlefield, and instead allowed her tribe and their neighbours to take their mortally wounded back to their sacred grounds and ease their way to The World Above? And how was Azral going to cope with the changes that would now be thrust upon her? Looking down at the dying Timku, she knew her fate was sealed.

With every faltering breath of her beloved guardian, Azral came closer to becoming the leader of The Tribe Nubar, charged with protecting her people and the tactically vital Vale of Grey. Only yesterday, her tribe would have thought themselves protected, invulnerable even, in its network of natural stone corridors and caves. Now, after the onslaught they had faced, Azral wasn't even sure she knew what 'safe' meant. She had always known her ascendance would come one day; she had been trained and mentored for it over most of her life. She just never expected it would be so soon – nor in such catastrophic circumstances. For so many reasons, she was not ready.

"Azral."

Trova's voice was firm and low, intended to bring her friend back to the dreadful truth before her. It worked. Azral spoke the words she did not want to say.

"We commit our sister Timku al Hedra to the Mighty Keeper of Eternity with joy, and in the safe knowledge we shall fight together in The World Above."

Azral's voice was soft, but loud enough for the thirty warriors surrounding her to begin humming in unison. Standing to take her place back in the circle, she took a breath and diverted the dry, smoky air of the clearing through her top two gills, making them vibrate to produce a single rising note that grew louder as the tribe sang their farewell to their leader of so many decades. The colours on their thickly ribbed necks changed, this time in accordance with custom, as did the tips of their skull plates, turning lighter then darker in faster succession until their inky black eyes and small, rosebud lips were framed in a deep red glow. With the tone reaching a crescendo, Timku's desecrated head also began to change colour, shifting through the spectrum from green down to blue then a final rich violet. With a wrenching crack, what was left of her thick brow plates parted above her eyes, exposing the frontal lobe of her brain to the Mighty Keeper. A sphere of pulsing blue light drifted upwards and hovered over her lifeless face, seemingly reluctant to continue its journey.

"Go!" shouted the warriors surrounding her. The orb hovered, illuminating Timku's lifeless eyes.

"Go!"

Timku's soul ascended into the clouds, and on to The World Above.

"What happened?"

It was a simple question, one that had consumed the thoughts of not just the tribal leaders that sat with Azral, but their entire people. Azral shuffled on the cold sandstone seat, unable to lean back fully because of the twin scimitars lying diagonally across her back. Even if she had taken them off, as many of the other tribal leaders had done with their own weapons, she was still unaccustomed to sitting for more than a few minutes between hunting, eating and fighting.

She had travelled overnight to be here, as swiftly as she could on foot, and the rising of the sun outside the chamber had left her with another problem – one of trying to take in the scale of the largest interior space she had ever seen. In addition to her new position, one accelerated in appointment with the death of Timku, it was one of many things she would have to become accustomed to – if she survived that long.

"The High Council recognises Suvri al Noghi of The Tribe Cotal."

The Speaker's voice boomed around the vast interior of the Council's chamber, its red stone walls amplifying the top frequencies of his words, making them sibilant and bright. Light streamed in through the naturally formed holes in the ceiling high above, projecting dozens of shafts of light onto the dusty floor. Azral had heard Timku talk of the wondrous cavern at length over the years. Words did not do it justice. It was magnificent.

As the Speaker's voice died back and the colour of his gills returned to their neutral grey from a deep green, he threw back his heavy ceremonial robes and took his seat on the third tier of the amphitheatre, a gift made by rivers and lakes from The Mighty Keeper to all her people on The World Beneath. Little had changed in the thousands of years representatives had met in this place, save for the addition of the top tier four centuries past to accommodate several new tribes. Despite their increase in numbers, wars and pestilence had on occasion taken a heavy toll, so over half the upper layer's one hundred seats remained empty. With the beating they had taken two moons past, the hope they would eventually be filled by leaders of new tribes now seemed a forlorn one.

Because Azral's tribe was one of the oldest, she sat on the lowest tier, but because of the chamber's oval shape and the angle with which the seats had been hewn into the soft rock around its perimeter, there wasn't a bad sight line in the enormous hollow. All could see and hear all, as was intended.

Azral turned to her left as Suvri strode down the steep steps to the open floor below, banging the end of his battle spear on the hard rock in time with his descent. Timku knew – *had known* – Suvri well. As leader of the closest tribe to the Vale of Grey, he had visited their settlements frequently, and Azral had witnessed first-hand his legendary impatience on several occasions.

It had frustrated and amused Timku in equal measure that someone could speak their mind so freely. Given the lack of surprise expressed at his shouted question mere seconds after the Speaker had pronounced the beginning of the emergency assembly, it appeared those gathered in the chamber also knew it to be his nature. Truth be told, no one was in any mood to procrastinate; their crushing defeat had to be scrutinised, no matter how painful to anyone's pride.

Suvri took to the centre of the floor, swishing his heavy robes behind his battered armour and opened his arms outwards in an expression of greeting and respect, the tip of his spear pointed downwards in a sign of kinship. One slow rotation later, he looked upwards to the Speaker and the Elders, three of which were supposed to sit either side of the Speaker. These seven seats were positioned at the narrowest part of the oval, providing a commanding view of the entire chamber. The chairs were larger and elaborately carved, reminding all that, following their people's early violent history of in-fighting, their word, regardless of popularity, was final. Suvri nodded to the Speaker, who bowed his head in response.

Two seats to his left and one to his right were empty, another painful reminder of the events two moons past.

"We have lost to the enemy in combat before, but never on this scale."

The edges of Suvri's skull plates turned a deep blue, flushing a few seconds after his neck gill display. Such a colour shift was rarely seen outside the battlefield, the speed of the transition revealing his fury.

"Many in this chamber remember the first time we faced them as the Tok Govor. Up until that point they were weak, no threat to our lands or our way of life, but their avarice for what we possess led them to dark alchemy. For a time, they had the upper hand thanks to their unnatural work. We sustained losses, but gradually adapted to the aberrations encasing them because, despite their repugnant invention, they still could not fight as we. Resilient, yes, and harder to kill, but still no match. Until two moons ago."

Azral was only into her thirty fifth alternation, so she had only heard stories of the great shift in power between the Govor and her people. The Tok Govor were perversions of nature, living protective armour capable of withstanding tremendous punishment from her people's arrows and spears. However, as Suvri pointed out, the Govor creatures that cowered within their protective sleeves still could not fight – their skills with blade and bow, with finger, foot and fist, could not match her people's speed and agility.

There were, occasionally, individual Govor soldiers, results of mutations and heretical experimentation no doubt, but they had been few and far between, singled out by the tribes and targeted for extinction. But what they had experienced such a short time ago was something more fundamental, more basic and worrying. The Govor's ferocity had taken them completely by surprise.

"So I ask again, what has happened? What has changed?"

Suvri turned again, arms outstretched, long, powerful fingers twitching around his battle spear as he looked to the scores of solemn faces before him. Colours shifted from neck gills to face plates and back again in a wave. To the Speaker's left, Quwru al Ghada rose, hand shaking on her ever-present staff. As one of the oldest members of the Council, indeed oldest of her people, the Speaker did not insult her with announcement, and Suvri immediately bowed and returned to his seat.

Back bent with her advanced years and skin loose over her skull plates, Quwru was nevertheless still formidable thanks to her unnatural height, and her eyes still sparkled like onyx pools as she slowly regarded the assembly before her. Silence fell over the chamber like a blanket.

"Your questions have no answers, Suvri al Noghi. Currently, only whispers and supposition exist. Nothing *anyone* says at this juncture is based on fact, other than what we witnessed in the Vale of Grey. The Govor tore us apart, much as we have done to them over the millennia. Had they not retreated when they did, our losses would have been greater still. That action in itself is of great concern."

A murmur rippled through the tiers of assembled leaders. Nothing seemed to make sense, from the Govor's new-found battlefield prowess to their baffling tactics. Given how ferociously each individual had fought, why had they sent so few in the first place? For every Tok Govor brought low that day, ten of their people had been slain. Some had noted the way in which the enemy had moved was different, and others commented on how new the vile armour looked. All agreed it was something unseen that had been transformed. Quwru raised her staff and the chamber fell silent.

"Our scouts report no activity on our borders, but I fear this will not be the case for long. If they return in greater numbers, whether they kill our warriors outright or leave them to die of their wounds on the battlefield, they have the numbers to initiate a pogrom upon us. We will be exterminated."

Not one of Azral's people feared death, only to die without honour or purpose. They knew their soul would, under most circumstances, be released in ceremony or on the field of battle, with only the unlucky few denied their final journey to The World Above. All had witnessed it in their brethren, lovers or friends, and all believed it, even though not one of the departed had ever confirmed their ascension to the side of The Mighty Keeper of Eternity.

There were far more things unknown than known, something that had frustrated the younger Azral and caused many arguments with her Elders. They accused her of wasting her efforts on dreams, she accused them of lacking imagination. As she had grown older, her questioning nature had been forced into remission. Too many times Timku had warned her to think of the impossible made her too close to the Govor, whose quest for territory and resources was matched only by their attempt to distort and master the natural world. This had wounded Azral; being compared to those honourless reptiles wasn't something she would tolerate, and gradually she had seen the sense in suppressing her natural curiosity. Even so, Azral couldn't help thinking an unconventional approach might help the examination of their defeat. The Govor had an extraordinary and sudden advantage. The Council had to consider all possibilities to ensure their survival.

Quwru looked to the two remaining Elders and the Speaker, then back to the chamber.

"Our priority is to redistribute our forces, for those who have lost many to be supported by those who have lost few. We shall not attack until we understand what we are facing."

Quwru stared down at Suvri, who glowered with anger.

"I call upon all leaders to provide numbers to the Speaker while we Elders consider how best to discover the truth of the matter. We shall reconvene at daybreak tomorrow."

Quwru slowly lowered herself back into her seat. Glances were exchanged, flushed colours of confusion showed on gills and skull plates, but all in silence. Suvri, clearly furious with the lack of immediate action, made to stand but was held back by fellow tribal leaders seated on either side. Before their exchange could escalate into something more physical, the Speaker rose and ordered all the tribal leaders to gather in The Counting Room at the far end of the chamber from his position to compile the census of available fighters.

Subdued by the abruptness of the meeting's end, the representatives rose, filed down the steep steps to the dusty floor then out towards a large natural exit set beneath the bottom tier. While Azral's tribe was senior, she herself was amongst several hastily promoted leaders so, as protocol demanded, she awaited her turn to join the line filing into The Counting Room. She was only a few steps into the short walk when she felt fingers gently wrap around her upper arm from behind.

"Azral. A moment."

Azral turned to see the Speaker standing before her. Startled, she forgot to bow having been directly addressed, her neck gills turning yellow as she attempted to control her embarrassment. He waited patiently until she remembered to show her respect, looking down at his robes until her colouring returned to normal.

"I need you to come with me."

Azral blinked a couple of times, aware the rest of her fellow tribal leaders had exited the main chamber. Azral had been in battle many times, but never had she felt so vulnerable, not even in the fight two moons ago with the Govor.

"Of course, Speaker."

Azral followed the towering figure in the opposite direction to The Counting Room towards a small wooden door. Descending into the shadows beneath the Council's tiered seating, the Speaker rapped loudly on the timbers then pushed it open with a creak. Turning, he beckoned Azral to follow him. Entering the darkened room, Azral's eyes had barely adjusted to the candlelight before Quwru spoke from her seat at the end of a long, rectangular table.

"Azral al Harta of The Tribe Nubar. Sit."

The Speaker nodded to one of the dozen large wooden chairs arranged around the table, a respectful distance from Quwru's position but close enough so she did not have to raise her voice to be heard. As Azral sat, the Speaker closed the heavy door with a creak of dry hinges then seated himself directly opposite, forming a triangle between the three. Azral did not know where to look, so stared at the table, watching the gaps between the rough planks widen then tighten with the dancing of the candle flames. Through her peripheral vision, she saw Quwru scrutinising her through subtle movements of the Elder's head.

"My condolences on the loss of Timku. Our sister

fights besides our ancestors."

Azral nodded slowly to the table.

"Timku spoke very highly of you, daughter."

Azral was glad of the darkened room to mask her colour shift. The use of such a personal term was entirely unexpected from one so elevated, particularly on a first meeting. She worded her reply carefully to honour the time Timku had spent readying Azral for her new role.

"And she spoke of nothing but admiration for your wisdom and strength, Quwru al Ghada."

"Indeed?"

If she hadn't known better, she would have sworn on the name of her tribe the Speaker snorted a laugh at Quwru's wry answer.

"We have a task for you, Azral. A very dangerous, very unpleasant task."

The Speaker's voice was as cold as the room in which they sat.

"I live to serve my tribe, my Council and my people."

It was the stock phrase expected of anyone being given a directive, whether they liked it or not. Azral delivered it with as much sincerity as she could muster. Regardless of what was being asked of her, the answer could only be in the affirmative. One rarely had the option of saying no.

"I must caution you. This task has not been sanctioned by the Council, nor has it been discussed with the other Elders. It is between we three in this room. Do you understand?"

Azral nodded once. She knew little of the Council's etiquette, but immediately suspected this was not the usual way of conducting the affairs of her people. Dangerous times often called for unusual approaches, and she felt vindicated in her earlier thoughts about looking at things from a different perspective. Of course, Timku had instilled respect for the laws that held the tribes together, cryptically referring to 'flexibility' and 'interpretation' when it came to circumstances that called for it. Even so, Azral felt uncomfortable. It seemed fitting they were talking in shadow.

"Does the name Brima al Duhul mean anything to you?"

Quwru pronounced the name with a strange emphasis Azral did not understand. The Speaker shuffled in his seat, clearly uncomfortable to hear it spoken.

"It does not, Quwru al Ghada."

"Look at me, daughter."

Azral lifted her eyes and turned her head. Candlelight framed Quwru's head, throwing her ancient features into wrinkled relief. The voice belonged to someone a tenth of her age.

"Brima al Duhul was banished from your tribe two hundred alternations ago. He and Timku al Hedra were well known to each other. At one point he had been her rival for the leadership of the Vale of Grey. When the Govor first appeared in their living armour and engaged us in battle, we were taken completely by surprise. As our losses mounted, before we changed our ways to combat their dark magic, Brima suggested a controversial path – one of research and knowledge, to discover how they had created these abominations. Timku flatly refused to entertain his notions, accusing him of thinking too closely like the enemy."

Azral grew uneasy. She thought she knew all there was to know about Timku, about her life, her victories, her struggles, but she clearly did not. In all her years of mentoring and training, of discussions long into the night as she was groomed and readied for taking over the tribe, she had never revealed the extent of her relationship with the leader of the Council nor mentioned Brima's name once. Neither had anyone else for that matter. Azral felt uncertain, disconnected from what she once knew to be the truth. So much in her life was changing, and she was struggling to keep pace with it.

"Timku was convinced our superior combat skills,

either individually or as a collective, would restore the balance of power. She was, up until recently, correct. However, that did not stop Brima from approaching the Council and proposing he try to learn the ways of the enemy, to understand how they created the Tok Govor."

Azral had seen Timku challenged on several occasions as leader of The Tribe Nubar. She had never claimed to be the perfect leader, and had undeniably made mistakes that had led to disagreement with and disgruntlement of some of her fellow warriors. However, all accepted Timku acted with the best interests of the tribe in her hearts, and they had eventually found common ground and forgiven her. But this Brima... he approached the Council against her wishes. A subordinate taking it upon themselves to do such a thing was unheard of.

"They were uncertain times, much like we face today, so the Council overlooked the gross insult presented by Brima and heard him out. Of we six Elders, five dismissed him the same way Timku did. I, however, felt there was a disturbing wisdom in his thinking. I approached him via the Speaker to discuss his thoughts in more detail, unknown to the other Elders or any member of the Council. Particularly Timku."

Quwru nodded once to the silent figure opposite Azral. The Speaker did not react.

"He never returned to The Tribe Nubar. I agreed to secretly provide him with every help and facility he required to discover the truth behind the Tok Govor, while agreeing with the other Elders he should be banished for his insult to Timku. They agreed, Timku's honour was satisfied and Brima got what he wanted. As did we, eventually."

Azral's head spun with the intrigue. Timku had once described the Council working like the layers of rock they so often saw in the valleys and caves of the Vale of Grey, that sometimes fractures and fissures formed only to be squashed and repaired in time, but the scale of subterfuge being suggested by the Elder of Elders was… Azral didn't even have the word. The Speaker cleared his throat, the edges of his gills rippling downwards in a rhythmic pattern. Azral took it as an invitation to speak.

"Quwru al Ghada, what you have told me is difficult to reconcile, but as you have spoken it, then I recognise it as truth. I have so many questions, but only one of consequence. What do you want me to do?"

Quwru looked to the Speaker, who rose from his chair and disappeared into the gloom behind the candles mounted in clusters on the wall. Azral heard the rolling of parchments and papers, suggesting some form of library stored in the depths of the room. A final tidying rustle, then the sound of a container being opened. Apparently satisfied with the unseen actions of the Speaker, Quwru nodded to herself and took a breath.

"You shall journey to Brima and task him with solving this riddle of our defeat. We must know what has changed in our enemy, and how we may best combat it. Once discovered, you shall return with this knowledge to save our people."

Azral had been ambushed on a couple of occasions in her life. She thought she knew what surprise was, until this point in her life.

"I do not… understand…"

The Speaker cleared his throat once more.

"It is quite a straightforward task, Azral. What is there to be confused by?"

Azral knew she was way out of her depth, but despite her deep respect for the two, she did not enjoy being made to look a fool.

"Speaker… Quwru al Ghada… What I meant to say was, I do not understand why you have selected me. Surely a more experienced warrior and leader such as Suvri would be a better choice?"

The Speaker leaned forwards and placed his hands on the table. He was clearly in no mood to be questioned.

"Should we require your counsel on who we select to represent our interests, we will ask for it."

Azral looked down at the table, ashamed of the sharp rebuke. Quwru sighed deeply, suddenly sounding old.

"Daughter, your skills are known to us as a hunter and a tracker. We also know you to have a curious mind, one that is more open to the… unusual than most others."

Azral looked up sharply, as if she had been caught doing something forbidden. Memories of her being chided for her flights of fancy as a young warrior swept through her, and she could hear Timku's voice uncharacteristically harsh in her warnings of the dangers inherent in unconventional thinking. Clearly, she had seen some of Brima in Azral's nature and had done her best to repress it.

So many things suddenly made more sense, and Azral abandoned controlling her flushing colours. Yes, maturity had brought with it an erosion of her imagination, but it was still very much there. Timku had taught her to channel it into her fighting skills, something that had surprised her opponents and given her an advantage on many occasions.

Clearly, it had been recognised that, while buried deep, her nature hadn't entirely been defeated – and it had clearly been a point of discussion between Timku and Quwru. Azral wasn't sure how many more surprises she could take. There were so many things she wanted to say. Instead, she stiffened her back and regained control of her emotions. There was no point in trying to be anything other than she was; to try would be to lie.

"My apologies. I did not mean to speak out of turn."

The Speaker got to his feet and headed back towards the shadows behind Quwru's seat, muttering darkly. Quwru folded her bony fingers into an apex and spoke with urgency.

"You need to travel light and fast. There will be little time for preparation."

Outside, past the door to the main chamber, Azral heard a shower of rocks falling onto the floor of the amphitheatre. Neither Quwru nor the Speaker reacted to the noise, so she dismissed it as a natural occurrence. They were, after all, deep underground in a cave with holes in its roof. The Speaker took over the conversation from the Elder as he rummaged in the shadows.

"You shall not speak of this meeting nor the information you are being provided to anybody. Your second, Trova al Yuval, will be informed you are working with the Council on a strategic plan to combat the Govor. It has more than an element of truth to it."

"I understand."

The sound of papers being prepared stopped. The Speaker emerged from the gloom and placed a short, hide-wrapped cylinder carefully onto the table before Azral. Quwru leaned forward in her seat, her skull plates silhouetted in the soft light behind her.

"We have not communicated with Brima for some time. You may find him… difficult at first. Despite his faults, he is one of our most brilliant minds and, if the Mighty Keeper of Eternity wills it, still loyal to his people. His location is isolated, so it is unlikely he will know of our unfortunate circumstances – or be expecting a visit."

The Speaker tapped a couple of fingers on the cylinder resting before Azral.

"This contains maps and a warrant for travel lest you be questioned by other tribal leaders or their representatives. There is also a letter for Brima. Ensure he reads it."

Outside, the rocks fell again. The impacts were louder, suggesting the debris was larger. This time, Quwru looked to the Speaker, whose pursed mouth turned down in a puzzled expression.

"It is unusual to have falls this late in the season."

Quwru had barely risen from her seat when a loud series of thumps repeated in quick succession. Shouts of rage and the drawing of weapons could be heard from the far side of the chamber outside, then something else – a frantic scraping noise, like rock on rock. Except everyone in the small room knew it to be the sound of scale on stone.

The sound of Tok Govor.

Azral was first out of the room, ducking a whirling throwing axe that sailed past her head and embedded into the wooden frame a fraction away from the Speaker's astonished face. Before her, half a dozen black scaly forms were rushing across the open floor towards the entry to The Counting Room which, having been alerted to the attack, had a slew of tribal leaders thundering out of its doorway.

As Azral unsheathed her twin scimitars and broke into a sprint, it became clear how they had been taken by surprise – more dark forms fell through the holes high in the chamber's ceiling, curled into a ball like a pangolin. On impact, the living exterior absorbed the force, preserving the cowardly, amphibious forms of their wearers but after a few stunned seconds, the armoured shell recovered from the shock and, controlled by the will of their masters, the first of them to fall rose to their full height, their diamond-shaped scales clacking and clicking over each other to form a near-impenetrable barrier.

Azral had heard the tales of how so many of her people died trying to find the weaknesses in them two centuries before. Since that time, every warrior old enough to carry a weapon knew where to attack – the backs of the knees, under the arms, the eyes, breathing glands on the underside of the chin and the top of the shoulders behind the neck. All were impossibly small targets but were you to concentrate on any other part of the body, all you did was blunt your blade or waste your arrows.

But this, of course, was before they had somehow learned to fight, to move with a confidence and balance never seen before. Given that change, Azral knew she had to attack the forms on the amphitheatre's floor just as they recovered and unfurled. Those rushing to engage the charging tribal leaders were already too far away for her to make any real difference.

Azral roared as she threw herself into the air, arcing downwards on the last of the fast-recovering Tok Govor before it had time to get into the fray. Pivoting the blades of her sword downwards, she used the momentum of her fall to drive both into the shoulders of the creature. One just missed the entry to the vital soft tissue beneath the plates and angled sideways, but the other penetrated beautifully, gliding its way downward to the hilt of her sword. Flipping herself around so her back met with its back, she heaved the heavy creature over her head with the embedded blade, screaming with the effort and withdrawing the blade with a spurt of green blood as it flipped over and smashed to the ground.

Catching her breath, Azral rotated both swords to the upright, waiting to see if she had delivered a killing blow. If the occupant died, so did the living armour, but not immediately. As such, Azral watched the creature carefully, lest its death throes caught her unawares. She had seen many a warrior injured - or worse - as they celebrated what they believed to be a victory.

Azral spotted the Speaker racing towards the melee, having recovered his spear from inside the meeting room. Ten scaly creatures were hacking and gouging their way through the tribal leaders with breath-taking ferocity, still shocking despite having witnessed it not three moons before. The speed at which these Tok Govor fought – and the ways they feinted, twisted, tricked and attacked - amazed her.

Had the Govor created a super-army, or had they brought in mercenaries from across the Great Water to fight on their behalf? How could anyone be convinced to wear a living creature, to join with it and control it like a puppet? Who could bear to be so entombed in living flesh and bone? Imaginative or not, such thoughts were as appalling to Azral as they were her fellow warriors.

Satisfied she had slain the Tok Govor lying at her feet, Azral calculated the best way to join the fray in the middle of the chamber's floor. Steeling herself for the attack, she heard two loud thumps behind her. Turning instinctively and crouching low, she beheld a couple of Tok Govor uncurling on the ground. However, instead of moving towards Azral and the main battle, they headed for the meeting room from where she had just come.

For a second Azral could not understand why they might do this, but then she remembered Quwru would likely still be in there – and the scrolls, including the one sitting on the table waiting for her take, may also be a valuable prize. Azral threw a glance over to the Speaker but he was too busy grappling with the enemy and out of earshot. Tackling two Tok Govor out in the open would be a bad decision, so Azral allowed them to gain entry to the cramped confines of the room, hoping Quwru would have the strength to keep them at bay for the mere seconds she needed to surprise them from behind.

Azral threw herself into the room, scimitars drawn and ready for blood. The two creatures had been forced to split either side of the meeting table, their scales scraping along the sides of the walls as they advanced on Quwru, whose trusty staff had transformed into a lethal defensive pike. Crouched behind her chair, she waved the point of her weapon at their dome-shaped heads, still more than capable of driving it with lethal force despite her advanced years.

Whoever cowered inside their shells were clearly experienced warriors; they moved as a pair, as hunters, looking for an opportunity for one to strike while the other drew their prey's attention. Something in their posture alerted Azral she was out of time to plot any kind of clever attack, so she jumped onto the table and ran in a crouch to avoid the low ceiling, kicking the hide cylinder containing her instructions into the darkness behind her and, swept both of her blades outwards in a desperate attempt to hit the breathing glands under both creatures' chins at the same time. Neither connected properly, but it did give them something new to think about.

The creature on the left spun and looked upwards in surprise, allowing just enough of the underside of its scaly chin for Azral to kick into it with the toe of her boot. It fell backwards more in surprise than pain, taken off-balance as it instinctively covered the two slits through which it breathed. Azral threw herself onto the Tok Govor, sending it into the wall, trusting Quwru would be able to keep the other at bay.

Regaining her balance, she whirled her blades before her and ducked under a swiping claw, feeling its forearm graze across her right skull plate and take off some skin. Quwru grunted behind her, and Azral heard wood scraping along the stone floor. Either the Elder had pushed the chair out of the way to launch an attack, or it had been tossed aside by the foe. There was no time to look.

With her own aggressor pushing itself up from the wall, she thrust forward with her left hand, the blade of her scimitar easily batted away by an armoured fist. There had been a time when such a move would have resulted in her enemy being dispatched, such were the feeble skills of the Govor hosts. Not anymore.

Azral dropped low as the Tok Govor lunged forwards, avoiding both of its lethal talons. Spinning on the balls of her feet, she thrust upwards with her blades, directly under the chin of the creature. This time they hit the glands, and while the penetration was not deep, the blow was enough for it to clutch at its head in pain and spin off to one side, staggering out of the doorway and back into the amphitheatre. It would only be a temporary retreat; the Tok Govor had the ability to regenerate at a tremendous rate, that was why it was always preferable to try and kill the host rather than the outer shell. For now, she'd got it out of the way, allowing her to go to Quwru's aid. Vaulting towards the Elder, for a second she thought she might succeed. But then the creature's claws lashed out and tore across the lower, fleshier part of the ancient one's face, dealing her a fatal blow.

Quwru staggered backwards, blood pumping from her ruined mouth. She tried to steady herself but fell over the upturned chair she had used as a barrier and onto the floor. Azral screamed at the creature to distract it, but its mission was clear – to kill the oldest of their people, to deal a blow to their leadership. It was an entirely logical move, one the Govor had tried many times before but this time, with their new-found ferocity and fighting skills, it was very likely they could succeed. Azral had one choice.

As the abomination descended to complete the kill, she waited until its razor-sharp claws were busy tearing into the flesh between Quwru's now shattered breast plates. Calling to it again, the creature turned its head – and gave Azral the chance to thrust her right scimitar into its eye. Pushing forwards, she drove her blade as deep as she could into the socket, past the soft tissue of the Tok Govor, through the membrane that formed the inside of the armour, and into the leathery skin of its host's skull. A muffled scream could be heard, then the Tok Govor dropped like a sack of grain, crushing Quwru beneath it.

Azral stared at the unmoving form of the enemy, panting for breath. Behind her, the sound of battle was just as furious as when she had entered the room and, realising there was nothing more to be done, she turned to help in the defence of the Chamber. A hand clutched at her ankle and tugged at her foot. Crouching, she could barely make out Quwru's shattered form. Barely able to breathe with the weight of the slain Tok Govor upon her, the Elder had to force out her final words.

"Flee daughter… We have… so little… time… "

Azral was torn. She wanted to throw the hideous body off the Elder's broken form, witness her soul's ascension to The World Above and join her fellow tribal leaders in the battle outside. But Quwru was right. One extra person here would make little difference. They had to know how to redress the balance, to restore their dominance on the battlefield to preserve their existence. Scrabbling in the shadows beneath the table, Azral found the cylinder given to her by the Speaker, threw its strap over her shoulder then, with a final bow of respect to the dying Elder, ran into the chamber.

It was littered with dozens of bodies, but the Tok Govor raiding party hadn't been big enough for them to claim a victory. She could see the Speaker, bloodied and exhausted, directing the mopping up of the remaining enemy pinned against the wall of the chamber. Azral knew they would claim the day – but at a dreadful price. Whether she liked it or not, she had to leave, read her map, and move as fast as she could while she still had a people to save.

By the time Azral had reached the Eastern Border, the moon had risen to its highest point in the cloudless sky. Given the distance she had travelled and the steady speed she had maintained, it was good progress. However, with no idea what the Govor might already be doing across all the tribes that made up The World Beneath, she might already be too late. This fear had been a constant companion inside her head, over river and stream, incline and descent, and she had wasted too much energy trying to fight off thoughts of impending doom. Her body ached, but her mind hurt even more.

Luckily for Azral, the moon's cycle was at his fullest, casting a light not dissimilar to twilight or early morning. It was more than enough to navigate by and, if the situation called, to fight in. She had only seen her people twice and had to show the Council warrant once to pass without frustrating, time-consuming questions through the tribal lands bordering the Vale of Grey. This was the furthest she had ever travelled, well south of the boundary her land shared with the Govor and nearly to the coast. With the attack at the Council still vivid in her memory, it was obvious no part of their lands was safe from the emboldened enemy although, given enough warriors, they were still capable of victory – for now at least. This had been the main counter to the fear trying to eat its way into her and, as she hauled herself up yet another steep and smooth rockface, it gave her the energy to reach the plateau at its top.

Now on flat ground, Azral paused to get her bearings. Looking to the heavens, she quickly located the stars she needed to calculate her position, and she again thanked The Mighty Keeper of Eternity for a clear night. According to the constellations before her, she was very close to her goal. In fact, it should only be –

"I expected you earlier."

The voice came from the shadows to Azral's right, at the base of the unscalable peak of the mountain on which she now stood. Without thought, both scimitars were drawn and readied, their curved blades catching the brilliant moonlight as she adopted a classic defensive stance. She could feel her gills turning dark blue, the flush of colour rushing across her face to the crest of her skull plates. That was the only warning she would be giving to her unseen visitor.

"Show yourself."

Azral's voice was low and full of menace.

"Did Quwru send you? The Speaker? Or has the whole Council finally come to its senses?"

A chuckle, but devoid of humour.

"Be that the case, their realisation comes too late."

Azral gripped the handles of her weapons tightly, even though she knew it had to be him. Staring into the darkness, she could just make out the outline of his body.

"Brima al Duhul. I have been sent by the Speaker and Quwru. It was her last wish."

A pause.

"Quwru is slain?"

Azral heard regret in Brima's voice.

"The Tok Govor attacked the Council itself. She is, along with countless others."

Brima stood motionless for some seconds. Azral shifted her weight, unsure of his intentions. She had not expected to feel so tense. Something about his sudden appearance, about this place, troubled her deeply. Quwru had been right to warn her about Brima. Under any other circumstances, she would have attacked first and asked questions later.

"That is of little surprise."

Brima stepped into the moonlight, his shadow falling back into the gloom as if it were maintaining his connection to the darkness. It was difficult for Azral to read his colours; the moon gave a false light, with most shades appearing the same. Instead, she read his posture, an awkward gait suggesting a life of crouching and creeping, of stealth and avoidance rather than confrontation and combat. Brima walked like a scout, indeed wore the minimal hide armour of one. Standing before her, he straightened and had the audacity to look her up and down with clear disdain.

"And you are…"

"Azral al Harta. Of The Tribe –"

"Nubar."

The word was spat rather than spoken. Azral flushed with anger and hoped Brima could see her warning colours. How dare he talk to her like this? She was about to challenge him when he turned and spoke with a strange inflection, not exactly dismissive, not exactly complimentary.

"Follow me, *warrior*."

If his way of speaking was meant to be an insult, she wanted to know why. However, getting into an argument wouldn't be the best way to start this extraordinary task, and to show he could upset her with mere words would be unwise. Rather than throw more questions or retorts, she opted to fall in behind Brima as he squeezed his way into a narrow fissure in the rock face. Sheathing her scimitars on her back, Azral swung the hide container by its strap behind her and followed, feeling her way along until, a few steps in, her path was outlined by a faint orange light in the distance. Only Brima's silhouette before her obscured the detail of the passageway's slick walls and floor.

Despite trying to master her emotions, the further they continued into the depths of the mountain, the greater her anxiety grew. It wasn't the confines of the passage nor the fact Brima had still not confirmed his identity or intentions – she was more than confident he could be bested in a straight fight. It was the nature of the light getting brighter with every step. It did not flicker like fire or candle but remained constant, like the sun. Despite her curiosity, she found it unnerving.

"Steel yourself for the unfamiliar."

Azral's stomach dropped at Brima's instruction. Was he capable of reading thoughts? That had not been mentioned by Quwru. It would be yet another secret withheld from her. So many things had changed in such a short period of time, she felt disconnected from the people she once knew. Come to that, she felt disconnected from herself.

Ahead, a roughly hewn rectangle of orange light framed Brima's form. Above her, Azral noticed the ceiling begin to angle upwards. At least she would be able to unsheathe both blades without impediment if she had to. Brima had not given any indication he was still loyal to his people. If Azral suspected otherwise, she would dispatch him and leave this dreadful place. There had been nothing in her instructions to stop her from killing a traitor. As the thought finished in her head, Brima stopped without warning and turned to her.

"You may see and hear things new to you, warrior. Do not approach or touch anything without my permission.

Do you understand?"

Azral flexed her fingers behind her back, readying herself to draw her scimitars.

"I understand."

Brima turned his back on Azral and walked through the entrance. Azral took a breath and followed. As she stepped into the light, any confidence she could cope with anything she saw vanished.

It wasn't the size of the chamber or the smaller rooms visible through hollowed rock portals along one side of the cavern that staggered her, nor the roughly built benches along the opposing wall to the entranceway on which sat myriad unrecognisable devices and objects. What really unbalanced Azral were the lanterns, hanging at regular intervals from the gently domed striated ceiling. Within their transparent containers were orbs that glowed with an unwavering, orange-yellow light.

She had only seen a room so well-lit twice before, and both had been great ceremonies where every available candle and torch had been brought in from surrounding homes and other encampments as a temporary measure. Any one of the lanterns she now gazed at would replace twenty of their pitch-soaked torches. This was utterly alien to her, and as she struggled between astonishment, admiration and fear, Brima walked over to a small cage in the middle of the bench, bent down to observe its contents. Tapping it a couple of times, he straightened to look at her, his colours now much more visible on his skull plates and gills. Following her gaze towards the lanterns, he seemed pleased at her wonder.

"Ah. They are called *uphanii*. It is a mineral, altered by the Govor with various potions and substances to make them absorb sunlight in the day and release light at night."

Azral closed her mouth when she realised she had been gaping like a child at their first view of combat. She felt foolish and knew it would be showing in her colours.

Wonderment got the better of formality, and she regretted blurting out her question as soon as she had said it.

"Why do we not have such things? They are…"

"Beautiful? Practical? Clever?"

There it was again. Amusement without humour.

"They are all of those things, yes."

Brima tapped the cage again once more, eliciting a small mewling sound from its unseen contents, then walked towards Azral, staring up at the string of lights as he did so. She could see he carried no weapons which, along with the strange contraptions within his unfamiliar home, made her feel distanced from him despite their kinship.

"The Council would call them heathen, unnatural, a violation of nature. In fact, this was one of the first things I attempted to show them when I first undertook my… adventure here."

Azral shifted her gaze to Brima, who was still scrutinising the lamps as if it were the first time he had seen them.

"Point of fact, they said all of those things and flatly denied their adoption for our people. I even learned how to renew the mineral once they are exhausted. A pity."

Azral frowned, her upper skull plates sliding closer to each other. She felt she had to say something that showed she represented the views of her people, even if, very deep down, she didn't necessarily agree with them.

"They are unnatural. No light should glow like this at night."

Brima slowly shifted his gaze to Azral, a look of disappointment in his colours and face.

"But that's where you're wrong, warrior. There is nothing unnatural about the process at all. It is how natural elements are combined that creates the effect. Just because we have not discovered it does not erode its potential usefulness."

Azral could tell Brima was probing and watching her

reactions. Spending so much time on his own – if, indeed, he had been on his own – had done little for his subtlety. She was beginning to recognise him as a mass of contradictions, and while her unease had not receded in relation to his true intentions, she understood why Quwru had not sent someone like Suvri on this mission. He would likely have run Brima through the second he stepped out of the shadows. Whether she was more open to the unusual than her fellow warriors, Azral nevertheless needed convincing of his principles.

"You sound as if you admire the enemy, Brima al Duhul. I wonder if this time in isolation has distorted your loyalties?"

A flash of blue and purple exposed Brima's anger. This pleased Azral. Perhaps she had misjudged him. Up until that point, he had been extremely difficult to read. She needed to get his guard down to reveal the truth of his motives and this approach seemed to work.

"The Govor are creative. They have had to be in the face of our might and superiority over the ages."

Azral might have been young, but she knew her history and would not stand for an attack on her people.

"We have only ever reacted in defence of our lands, Brima. We have never encroached upon theirs."

Brima snorted air through his gills, a look of pity on his face.

"You really shouldn't believe everything your Elders tell you, warrior. Timku and I conducted several raids into Govor territory when we were younger than you. Granted, those actions have reduced considerably over the last couple of centuries, but we're not quite the benign people you have been led to believe."

Azral tried to mask her colours, but to no avail. Mention of her beloved mentor by someone with so little respect infuriated her. She was angered even more by the ease with which he had garnered her reaction.

"You will doubtless be happy to hear Timku was

amongst those who perished at the enemy's hands."

Brima blinked a couple of times and looked to the sandy floor. Surprisingly given what Azral had been told of their history, his colours changed to sadness. More contradiction.

"That is... regrettable. But it does not change the truth of what I am saying."

Azral did not want to trust nor believe this man's damning words, but something about the way in which he said them had the feel of Quwru's tone. What he said may well be true, but that gave her another problem; she wasn't sure how much more distortion of her beliefs she could take. Brima raised his head and fixed his gaze on Azral, the soft glow of the lamps' pinprick orange spots reflecting in his large, round eyes.

"Do not misunderstand me, warrior. The Govor are overtly antagonistic and aggressive, but we are not blameless, and conflict has a way of accelerating technological progress. The Govor create the Tok, then our Smiths harden the steel in our weapons to counteract. It was inevitable they would attempt to gain the upper hand once more. Now, some of their conceptions are sophisticated and benign, like these lights. Others, however, are as horrific as they are brilliant."

Azral had never thought about the struggle against the Govor in such terms. But that sounded like admiration in Brima's voice, and she did not like it one bit.

"Your knowledge of the enemy disturbs me Brima. You have spent more time in their company than of your own people. Perhaps you do not realise just how suspicious your words sound."

Brima began to speak but then promptly snapped his mouth closed. Looking down, he clasped his hands behind his back, exposing the top of his skull plates and the softer tissue beneath. His words sounded as if he was trying to convince himself.

"It is one thing to admire the ingenuity of the enemy

Azral, but quite another to subscribe to their heresy."

Azral sensed a shift in their short relationship and pressed the offensive.

"How did you know I was coming? Are you aware of events across The World Beneath?"

Brima took in a slow breath, his gills dilating widely then folding back into place as he looked up once again.

"I can surmise. Several moons ago, I witnessed a group of fresh-born Tok Govor leave their main citadel on the coast. This was lucky happenstance, as I was there trying to investigate something they have been developing in secret. They headed north, only a relatively small group, but the way they moved was... unusual."

Azral felt a cold sensation creep across her chest.

"That would be the force we encountered when they invaded our borders. They do, indeed, move differently."

Her words were laced with bitter understatement. Brima folded his arms across his narrow chest and listened intently.

"They decimated our forces, Brima. Tore us apart then left as quickly as they arrived. Why they did not press home their advantage and finish us all is a mystery, but one we are grateful for."

Brima's black eyes narrowed as he considered what he was being told without emotion. Frustrated at his lack of surprise at her revelation, it was Azral's turn to snort through her gills. Was he, after all, so detached from the suffering of his own people? Had his banishment – which clearly hadn't been quite as straightforward a severance from the Council and his people as she had been led to believe – turned him cold to their fate? Something occurred to Azral and she stepped towards him, pointing an accusatory finger as she moved.

"What do you know of this?"

Azral did not mean to raise her voice, but it echoed around the warm stone chamber. Brima did not retreat. Instead, he shifted uncomfortably from foot to foot.

"I have... suspicions at this point, nothing more. Pieces of a puzzle I have been trying to assemble for a considerable time. Suffice to say, the strange actions of the Tok Govor convinced me something dreadful was about to befall us."

Azral was incredulous.

"And it did not occur to you to send us warning?"

Brima stared into her eyes and shook his head.

"I am banished, remember? No one is supposed to talk to me. How could I warn those that would not listen?"

It was Azral's turn to shake her head, this time in disgust. He should have tried harder.

"Besides, I anticipated the Council – or Quwru at the very least - might be calling upon me again, so I remained here. Hence my lack of surprise when you arrived at my door."

Brima's eyes flickered to the strap resting over Azral's animal hide armour. Azral stared straight through him in an attempt to come to some conclusion as to what she should do. Should she trust him or kill him? Closing her eyes, she took a deep breath and waited for her head to clear. She'd not travelled all this way to end up no wiser than when she had left. There was so much at stake, the weight of it threatened to crush her. Brima said nothing, did nothing, as she attempted to find some kind of clarity of thought.

Fatigue overwhelmed her and, with a sigh, Azral detached the parchment cylinder and handed it over to Brima. Prizing off the lid, he retrieved the letter from Quwru and tossed the container onto the nearby bench, spilling out her map and warrant as he walked away to the rear of the room and read it. He returned moments later, the parchment limp between his fingers and his face a mask of concern.

"The Govor are hunting for something across The World Beneath. Quwru mentions several tribes spotting Tok Govor scouts in places they have never previously ventured, fleeing into the night when discovered and mysteriously disappearing. But this was all before the attack on your – our – lands. It must be connected, but I do not see how."

Brima paced around the chamber, looking to the smooth stone floor as he did so. Azral suddenly felt very tired and very hungry. She hoped he had food he might share and a place she might sleep, if only for a short while. At the far end of room, before entering the gloom where the lanterns did not illuminate its darkened wall, Brima turned.

"You say the Council was attacked? They entered the great chamber?"

Azral nodded. Brima walked back to her position and looked to the warrant and map unfurled on his work bench.

"And Quwru died where?"

"In a smaller doored chamber, on the opposing side of The Counting Room. Two of the Tok Govor mounted an assault on it after the first raiding party engaged with the Council. They made no attempt to join them."

"Ah. The Repository."

Azral nodded. She had not heard it described as that before, but with all the parchments The Speaker had been sorting through in the shadows, it made sense.

"I found it strange they headed straight for that room, away from the battle with the other tribal leaders. Could it have been the main target?"

Brima looked surprised, then pleased, at Azral's deduction.

"Yes… yes indeed. Although it contains so many documents, it is hard to know what they might have been looking for."

From one of the rooms set off from the main chamber, a strange grinding noise began then stopped. Brima looked back sharply, then turned his attention to Azral once again.

"We need to discover the truth of the situation and

save our people from disaster. It will be fraught with danger, but I have an idea where we may find the answers we seek. But first, you need to eat and rest. You will need all of your fortitude for what is to come."

Azral blinked in surprise. Perhaps he *could* read minds after all.

The food had been hot, strange, but welcome, as had the opportunity to rest her body. Azral was a hunter and a tracker, accustomed to fatigue and pushing her body to its limits. As such, it took her little time to gather her strength. While she had eaten, Brima had busied himself between the smaller rooms off the main chamber, muttering to himself and transferring items between one part of the long bench to another, picking things up, considering them, then putting them down again. He also returned several times to a large scroll, set on a clear part of the bench closest to where she sat and ate, scribbling words down then crossing out others as he referred to documents strewn across the rest of the rough wooden tables.

As Azral placed the bowl down on the floor, Brima disappeared into the darkened far end of the main chamber, leaving her alone in the room for the first time. Seconds later he returned, completely naked.

Azral was used to seeing her fellow warriors and tribespeople unclothed. They often bathed communally, and some rituals were conducted with the minimum of attire, but for some reason his appearance shocked her. His long, willowy limbs showed the signs of his age, confirming he had been a contemporary of Timku, but his dark skin, stretched taught over his slender rib cage, bore scarring the likes of which Azral had never seen. She had plenty of reminders across her body of battles hard won and occasionally lost, but nothing like Brima's. It looked as if he had been cut a thousand times, fresh scar tissue forming over older pucks and mounds. He had suffered greatly, regardless of whether he carried himself as a warrior or not.

"We must journey to the Govor citadel by the coast, warrior. It is not far, and I have a route that will mask most of our progress."

Azral assumed they would be going out on such a mission, but one glaring issue had to be addressed.

"And what happens when we arrive at the citadel, Brima? How do we move about those... creatures... without detection?"

Azral could tell Brima knew the question was coming.

"Disrobe, then follow me."

Azral paused, then stood and unpicked her battle armour with nimble fingers. Gathering it up and placing it on her chair, she reached for her scimitars leant against the wooden frame of the bench before her.

"You will not need those."

Azral snorted with disbelief.

"You want me to go on a mission to a Govor citadel *unarmed*?"

Brima smiled.

"You will not be defenceless. Come."

Azral's opportunity for further protest was cut short as Brima disappeared into the darkened rear of the room, picking up a lantern resting next to the large document he had scrutinised so carefully and placing a heavy cloth over it to diffuse its light. Azral followed him into the gloom, past the smaller rooms with their unknown contents, until she was in near darkness. Brima stopped before a large open doorway, through which she could see nothing despite her eyes having quickly adjusted to the lack of light. However, she could hear, and smell, something strangely familiar.

"Prepare yourself warrior. Do not fear that which you do not understand."

Brima stepped into the room and pulled off the lamp's covering to reveal two large stone sarcophagi resting upright against the far wall of a small cave. Their doors had been removed, revealing a single Tok Govor within each. Azral recoiled in horror, instinctively reaching for weapons that were not there. Turning to flee and retrieve them from Brima's workshop, she felt his hand wrap tightly around her arm. She lashed out with her free hand, aiming her fist between his eyes, but he deflected the blow easily, caught her by the wrist and twisted it backwards.

"Traitor! Heretic! I should have killed you when you started spewing your vile lies about the Council!"

The more Azral struggled, the more her fury grew at her own stupidity. She could not believe she had been so easily led to the enemy. She deserved to die, uselessly and unwitnessed, in this dismal hovel below the ground.

"Azral. Calm yourself."

Brima's sharp words had no impact. She lashed out with her feet, tried everything she could to break his grip on her. Instead he twisted her wrist back further, making her yelp in pain as he spun her to face the Tok Govor and pushed her roughly to the floor with surprising force, maintaining his grip and keeping her at arm's length.

"Look at them."

Azral hurled every curse she had ever heard at Brima, but she could not ignore the pain in her wrist which, with one more push, would surely snap.

"*Look at them.*"

Reluctantly, she raised her head, panting with the exertion of her struggle. She felt utterly defenceless and resigned herself to their attack. The release would be welcome, a fitting end to her failure.

But it did not come.

The Tok Govor stood, unmoving, the orange light picking out the details of their black, diamond-shaped scales within their open cocoons.

"They are inert, warrior. They are without their Govor hosts, and no threat to us whatsoever."

Azral felt Brima's iron grip on her wrist ease. He was

right. They had not moved a fraction since they had entered the room. Breathing heavily, Azral tugged her hand away from Brima's grasp, releasing her from his control.

"I have fed and nourished these for many alternations. I have studied their secrets since they were first born. Thanks to them, you know how to disable and kill the Tok Govor."

Azral flexed her sore wrist a few times and scrambled to her feet. The cold ate into her naked body but that was not the reason she shivered. The sight before her was appalling, and yet strangely fascinating. She had never been this close to the living armour without having to defend herself. And then, Brima's statement registered, and she turned towards him in surprise.

"What do you mean by that?"

Brima stepped forwards as he spoke, bringing the light source closer to the towering, powerful forms.

"I identified the weaknesses in the Tok Govor and shared them with the Council. I thought it would be enough to end my expulsion, but Timku had other plans when Quwru told her the source of the information. Timku believed – entirely correctly – I would return as some conquering hero, ascend the Council quickly then be able to make her life extremely miserable."

Brima's small mouth set into a sneer.

"So instead, she argued against my return, claiming it would destabilise the Vale of Grey and I would inevitably reveal the subterfuge I had been a part of with Quwru against the rest of the Council. Quwru claims she agreed to maintain my exile reluctantly. I am not so sure."

Azral scrutinised the overlapping scales on the living armour, the dome-shaped head, the razor-sharp talons at the ends of the powerful arms. She saw a thick animal gut tube connected to their hips running through a pitch-sealed hole in the side of their sarcophagi and followed the tubes across the floor into a large open barrel of gently bubbling liquid. Bile rose in her throat. This was obscene. Azral could not believe they had played any part in her people's history, let alone victory. Swallowing down her revulsion, she shook her head in denial.

"The tactics were hard-learned in many battles. That is a fact of history Brima."

The bucket belched and gurgled a couple of times and one of the Tok Govor twitched within its container. Azral swallowed hard with the realisation they were feeding.

"My information was tested over several battles, to see if it was true. Some of them were ruses, to make it look as if it were trial and error to the enemy. Many warriors were sacrificed to maintain the lie."

Azral stared into Brima's eyes. It was the closest she had been to Brima since she had arrived. There was no deceit in his face or colours.

"Besides, had we suddenly become victorious, the Govor would have known something was amiss and likely become alerted to my presence. Getting in and out of their citadel is difficult under the best circumstances so, in a way, I suppose Timku's untruth did us both a favour. Although I yearn to prove myself to my people, even after all this time."

Brima's voice was rueful, as if it was something he'd repeatedly tried to convince himself was a good thing. It was the first time he had showed any real desire to serve The World Beneath, and Azral had to wonder if he had he misjudged him. If half of what he said was true, his treatment at the hands of the Council and Timku had not been fair.

Then there was the fact he had not killed her on sight, which he could easily have done from the shadows on the plateau. Could these actions mean he wanted to atone, to make amends? Azral turned back to the Tok Govor. Several disconnected thoughts suddenly clicked together, and she felt her stomach lurch at a sudden realisation. It was a question she did not want to hear the answer to, but asked it nonetheless.

"How… are we going to enter the citadel undetected?"

Brima took in a deep breath through his gills then exhaled slowly, making a low, humming sound.

"In those."

Azral fell again. The sensation was unnerving, as if she were moving in a dream. Reaching out, she half-felt the rocks below her and pushed herself upright, but misjudged the power coursing through the Tok Govor's muscles and flipped onto her back. She felt the slightest pressure along her spine, like falling on a pile of freshly woven blankets, and then it was gone. Taking a shallow breath, she tried to concentrate as she had been told on controlling her movements, but instead another wave of claustrophobia swept over her and she began screaming inside the creature. The living creature.

Even though Azral understood the logic of her situation, that wearing the Tok Govor was the only way they could move freely amongst the enemy, the reality of it was overwhelming. Back in the cave, other than her total revulsion at the idea, several other questions had poured from her – how could they fit inside the creatures if they had been bred for the smaller, reptilian forms of the enemy? How would she breathe? How would they communicate? Why did they both have to go on this ghastly undertaking?

Brima had been forthright as he disconnected the feeding tubes from the entities and laid them gently on the ground, the remnants within the opaque gut umbilical leaking putrid fluids onto the floor with a revolting gurgle. They would fit because, over several alternations, he had adapted their interiors to mate with their own. There were limitations on what they could do compared to the normal Govor hosts, and they would have to move carefully so as not to attract attention while wearing them, but he had walked amongst the enemy on countless occasions without suspicion.

Azral would be able to breathe thanks to tendrils, carefully cultured and adapted by Brima, that would creep their way into her gills to supply her with air, by far the most problematic part of the adaptation because the Govor's breathing slits were in a different position on their body compared to theirs. If she over-exerted herself breathing would become difficult, but they worked well enough to sustain the wearer for quite long periods.

They would communicate through the silent signing all their people learned as children when hunting or stalking prey; the hands on the living armour were highly articulate and would translate their ancient nonverbal language perfectly.

And as for why they both had to go... in case one of them was killed, so the other could present any discoveries to the Council. But Azral knew that anyway.

Brima had concluded his preparations just as Azral had exhausted her protests. Other than not wanting to go through with it, there had been nothing more to say. With a satisfied nod, Brima had whispered something into the tiny holes on the side of the Tok Govor's conical head chosen for her to don, and she had watched in horror as it had stepped out of its sarcophagus and stood motionless for a moment before the scales on its featureless face had slid apart to reveal rudimentary, deep-set eyes.

Blinking into life, the creature slowly turned to face the now vacant container and opened. Azral had heard tissue and bone splitting before, but nothing compared to the wet wrenching sound as its back split open and folded back to reveal glistening red innards. She had tried to keep down her meal, but as Brima coaxed her forwards, she had bent over and threw up the contents of her stomach onto the dusty stone floor. Brima had waited patiently for her to recover and then talked her through the insertion process. Arms outstretched, she closed her eyes, held her breath and willed herself forwards. When her skin first touched the inside of its arms, she panicked and tried to pull away but Brima pushed her into the living sleeve and within seconds it had enveloped her in its warm, slick embrace.

That had been the first time she had screamed.

It was as if a thousand insects were crawling over her body. She became aware of a muffled voice, Brima's, urging her to open her eyes and to focus. Doing so, it was like looking through a window, but one that showed everything in exaggerated colours. Brima had warned her senses would not be the same, because the Tok Govor's hearing, sight and touch would merge with her own thanks to a bundle of nerves resting on the top of her head, and that one of the limitations would be a lack of smell or taste.

As she fought to control her panic, she found this a small mercy. Azral flinched as the breathing tendrils entered her gills but once in, the sensation was not as unpleasant as she imagined, and she quickly justified it as breathing through a reed when submerged. Outside of those crude analogies, she had no other way to explain how she felt. Testing her movements, she turned to see Brima disappearing into his own armour. Fully encompassed, he had signed her to follow him.

This proved to be far more difficult than it sounded; he had warned her walking would be difficult to start with, but she would soon adapt. If she kept her own movements relatively subtle, the suit would do the rest. Getting out of Brima's home had been a very steep learning curve, but they had finally made it onto open ground and, as they had broken into a run down the empty slopes at the base of the mountain range and headed towards the citadel, it was then she began to understand the power of the Tok Govor. Understand, but not like it.

Particularly when she kept falling over.

Azral tried looking to the sky to get her bearings from the stars but Brima's adaptations revealed yet more restrictions to her normal movement. It felt as if she was wearing a heavy ceremonial mask, the kind used during betrothals and naming ceremonies. Vision was clear enough but permanently framed in a tight oval, and the lack of peripheral vision would hinder her in a fight. Hopefully, it wouldn't come to that. Stealth and darkness had been their friend over the wide-open desert plains, but the closer they came to the coast, the greater the chance they would encounter the Govor. Sure enough, Brima abruptly stopped and signalled for her to drop to her knees. She tried to do so and landed on her face.

Furiously righting herself, Brima spelled out their proximity to the Govor capitol. They would be encountering tracks leading to the city very soon, and the first of many observation posts, many of which had sprung up over the last couple of alternations and fuelled Brima's conviction the enemy were developing something worth protecting. Azral signed she understood, and Brima paused. Asking if there was a problem, Brima's body language was impossible to read inside the dark, scaly suit.

His final sign before he set off puzzled Azral – 'do not be surprised or afraid of my actions – trust me.' With that he launched himself towards the twinkling lights of the citadel in the distance, with Azral following close behind.

A tower began to take shape on the horizon, its skeletal upper section picked out by the same strange orange-yellow light of the *uphanii* in Brima's home. Figures moved within its flat-roofed canopy, and Azral suddenly felt vulnerable on the exposed ground sloping gently down to the unseen ocean. Crouching instinctively, she expected Brima to do the same. Instead, he increased his pace, making no attempt to hide his movements.

Azral felt her stomach tighten; he was heading straight for the tower, whose light had suddenly focused into a cone that projected outwards onto the ground below it. Speeding up, she tried to attract Brima's attention but realised another limitation over the usual Govor host – she could not call out to warn him of the situation. But then, surely, he could see where he was going and that it was only a matter of time until he was spotted. And then the light was upon him, and through the basic ears of the Tok Govor Azral heard the hisses and shrieks of the hated enemy calling into the darkness.

Despite Brima's proximity to the tower, the guards clearly didn't distinguish his Tok Govor as one of their own. One figure began unleashing arrows at Brima's charging form as another unveiled a second, much brighter light and shone it into the distance towards the Govor citadel. Azral pushed forwards, unseen by the guards who were distracted by Brima's rapidly approaching form.

In the distance, a light answered the tower's signal, followed by a line of orange dots that strung their way towards the citadel barely visible on the horizon. Azral assumed them to be warning beacons, which meant every Govor in the area was now alerted to their approach – thanks to Brima.

But why would go through such an elaborate ruse just to reveal himself a traitor now, when he could have killed her on their first meeting? Was it to make a daughter of the Vale of Grey suffer the indignity and heresy of donning this vile creation? Were that the case, she would kill Brima with her own hands – not the puppet claws she currently inhabited – as soon as this absurd situation allowed.

Azral closed on Brima with fury in her heart, coming dangerously close to suffocating herself as the basic breathing system struggled to match her exertions. By now Brima had reached the base of the tower and was looking up to the Govor through a trapdoor in the upper platform. Clad in its traditional light chainmail, one of the lookouts was descending the rough wooden ladder to join their spy, having clearly not recognised the Tok Govor armour despite their powerful light. Readying herself for an attack from the two, she opened the claws on her suit, unsure how successful these rudimentary weapons would be against one of their own. She would kill the Govor first and then take her chances with Brima, the traitor. But then, Brima thrust his talons through the wide, green neck of the lizard creature, threw its dying body to the floor then turned his attention to the ladder, which he smashed into splinters with one mighty blow.

Turning, he threw himself at the closest upright support pole, rocking the flimsy tower with the force of his attack. Spotting Azral, he invited her to join him in destabilising the structure and despite her utter confusion she did just that, ramming the wooden post until it cracked under their blows. They barely got out of the tower's shadow before the whole thing smashed to the hard ground, Brima quickly dispatching the remaining Govor with a mighty blow as it staggered to its webbed feet in the debris.

As Brima regarded the tower's remains with apparent satisfaction, Azral lashed out against his scaly arm and angrily demanded to know what in the name of the Mighty Keeper of Eternity was going on. Why had he thrown away their element of surprise? Surely, they could have avoided the tower and crept into the Govor citadel, their true forms masked by their armour?

Brima pointed to the twinkling line of warning beacons in the distance. Yes, she was right the enemy were preparing themselves for attack, but that was all part of his plan. If they had passed the tower without incident and walked into the citadel wearing their disguises, they would have immediately raised suspicion because the Tok Govor were only worn for campaigns – or in times of attack. Brima had to alert the enemy and give them enough time to don their armour so, when they did arrive at the gates, there would be so many Tok Govor they would blend into their numbers and be able to move more freely.

Azral saw the simple brilliance of it and signed her understanding. She just wished he had told her that was his intention. Brima nodded once, and the two set off towards the citadel, Azral's suspicions of Brima's intentions again assuaged – for now, at least.

Azral could not believe the sight before her. She had visited many hamlets and townships of other tribes across The World Beneath, many of which had been forced to construct large communal and municipal buildings where their local cave systems had not been capable of adaptation. Some of these structures had been imposing, impressive even, but compared to what she saw in the Govor citadel, they were matchstick houses.

The scale of the countless structures soaring into the sky before her was overwhelming. Concentrated around the major tributaries running out to the sea, rows of wooden towers stood shoulder to shoulder, some shorter than others, some wider, but all showing distinct signs of life. Shadowy figures flitted behind myriad open-shuttered windows, the distinctive soft glow of *uphanii* everywhere.

The narrow streets were filled with Govor, some darting, some striding, some armed and armoured, some not, bustling to and from a seemingly endless line of buildings that sprawled out to form a ragged boundary around the outside of the city. The rasps of their forked tongues filled the air, and Azral was glad of the inferior hearing her Tok Govor provided.

Fixing her gaze on the back of Brima's scaly head so as not to stare at the extraordinary sights around her, the two moved towards a cluster of Tok Govor they had spotted entering the citadel moments earlier. Other groups were mustering around them, and while such numbers would usually have Azral readying for combat, in these circumstances the more there were, the smaller the chance of them being recognised as infiltrators.

Brima slowed and signed behind his back for Azral to follow her towards a huge, heavily fortified structure close to the sea, the same building the great majority of the assembling Tok Govor seemed to be heading for. Brima kept just enough distance from the knots of enemy to give them a reasonable chance of escape lest they were somehow revealed, and Azral felt a reluctant admiration build for him. The bravery required of Brima to make this perilous journey repeatedly was impressive, and thanks to his knowledge of the citadel, Brima skilfully weaved his way through the broad throughfare between the rows of buildings.

While they closed on the massive structure however, the sheer number of Govor and Tok Govor made for difficult progress, but Azral followed where Brima pushed through, making it look as if they had a vital mission to fulfil which, indeed, they had.

Brima suddenly looked upward and pulled Azral into a narrow gap between two houses. Pointing upwards, Azral tilted her head as best she could to peer above the jagged tops of dwellings and waited for her vision to slowly adjust to the inky night sky. At first, she could not understand what she was looking at. The stars kept disappearing and then appearing, as if covered by an unseen, fast-moving cloud. Then again, and again.

Following the tracks of the holes in the sky, she watched them move towards a towering cylindrical frame connected to the structure all the Tok Govor were congregating upon. Carefully peering around the corner of the alleyway into the main thoroughfare, she could see a series of illuminated wide wooden platforms forming a flat circle at the top of the tower, by far the tallest structure in the citadel. A row of *uphanii* strung around its circular mouth illuminated several forms reaching upwards into the sky and waving their arms.

The star-stealing shadows glided over the figures and into the unseen opening, their bat-like undersides briefly picked out by the lights arranged around the platform, before disappearing from view. They flew like no creatures she had ever witnessed; no wings fluttered or beat, they just drifted on the air. Azral's throat tightened inside her suit, and she struggled to fight the dread building within her.

Brima tapped Azral on her scaly arm and pulled her back into the gloom of the passageway. This, he signed with urgency, was a new perversion the Govor had created. He had seen the tower's slow construction over the last few alternations but had not witnessed these... Brima seemed to struggle in his description of what they had seen because their language did not readily have the words. The closest he could think of was *unnatural flying devices,* but that did not suitably define what they had witnessed.

If the Govor could somehow travel in the sky, that was beyond even Azral's once-fervent imagination. It begged the question why, if they had this ability, they had not used it on the battlefield, but she forced herself to stop her wild conjecture and concentrated back on Brima's signs.

The huge cylindrical tower had been built next to a structure that Brima recognised, so he felt convinced the answers they sought to the enemy's sudden ability to best them in battle would be discovered within its mighty timber walls. Azral's thoughts were spinning so fast inside her claustrophobic head, she did not know what to say – other than agreeing they had to press on and discover as much as they could.

As she finished signing, a large contingent of Tok Govor marched past them, heading directly for the tower. Despite the thoroughfare being crowded, all parted to allow the group's progress so Brima and Azral fell in behind, quickly progressing through a huge set of wooden doors that had swung open at the base of the tower to greet them. A few strides later, and they were inside.

The interior of the cylindrical tower revealed it to be a marvel of construction. Bound end to end with thick metal collars, huge tree trunks ran vertically upwards to form a circle framing the night sky high above Azral's head. *Uphanii* lanterns were everywhere, bathing a spider-web network of ladders and stairways spiralling up the interior in a warm orange glow. Forming a rough square around the centre of the cylinder, four huge winches supporting thick wooden platforms ascended and descended to a receiving area on the floor before her.

Dozens of Govor scurried around the wide, flat wing-shaped objects sitting on the platforms when they rested at floor level, and as a team dragged one off the closest wooden slab, Azral could see they were made of some animal hide Azral couldn't identify. It had been stretched tight over reed-like frames into a diamond shape, and appeared light enough for unarmoured Govor to lift then place next to a line of benches.

Yet more Govor bustled around the contraptions, carefully removing sets of large spheres containing a darkened fluid from the front and back of the wings. Azral was astonished to see the orbs floating into the air, pulling the ropes that had once connected them to the hides upwards as they drifted away. The Govor tugged at them, yanking them down and towards a large opening on the far side of the enormous tower's curved wall.

Brima and Azral followed the Tok Govor as they streamed towards the same exit. A gaggle of workers scurried past the two carrying smaller glass orbs set within thick rope cages retrieved from the rear of the contraptions. The way in which the lizard creatures cradled the spheres suggested to Azral they contained something of great value, but hindered by the inferior sight of her living armour, she could not make out the contents.

Despite the doorway being wide, the crush of bodies entering it slowed their pace and allowed Azral to peer down at one of the spheres. She glimpsed a faint blue glow between the protective hemp, but that gave her no better idea of what they might contain. Brima deliberately stepped in front of Azral, barging one of the Govor workers out of his way, and began to frantically sign behind his back for her to stay close and follow his lead.

So far, their disguises had allowed them to proceed unchallenged, but this was unknown territory to him. The confusion he had deliberately caused with the attack on the tower looked to have galvanised the enemy, and while it had protected them up to this point, he suspected they had ridden their luck to its breaking point.

Sure enough, as they came to the end of the corridor through which they had been squeezed, two Tok Govor stood forwards and stopped Brima with an outstretched claw while the teams of sphere carriers scurried past their towering scaly forms into a chamber beyond. To Azral's astonishment, Brima began to converse with the two in a series of clacks and clicks, the same foul tongue Azral had heard used by the enemy on the battlefield.

While Brima attempted to talk his way past the guards, Azral stared past them into the room beyond. A single huge metal vat supported by tree trunk stanchions dominated its centre, with ladders and platforms allowing Govor to pour in a variety of potions and liquids from around its circumference. Azral noticed they were using the same spheres as those being ferried from the flying devices, but the liquid they poured into its huge open top was green rather than blue.

Dozens of pipes ran from the undersides of the vat, radiating out to connect with cocoon-shaped cylinders lined upright across the walls of the room. Each sarcophagus had a rough wooden table next to it, from which Govor hurried to and fro, employing various devices and objects in their checks and adjustments. Even though the contents were hidden from view by roughly hewn stone covers, Azral recognised the shape and scale of the sarcophagi from Brima's feeding room, along with some of the equipment as like that she'd seen in his workshop. Looking back to the fluids being poured into the vat from above and the violent reactions spitting and bubbling into the air, she realised the facility's purpose.

It was the nursery for the Tok Govor.

For a moment, Azral considered pushing her way past the two guards talking animatedly with Brima to attack the unarmoured Govor workers. If she could somehow ignite the vat's contents, the whole thing would burn before it decanted its foul concoctions to grow yet more of the living armour within the cocoons. As yet more Tok Govor streamed in from various entrances set in the timber-clad walls, she came to her senses. She might inflict some damage and several casualties, but her actions would be futile, reveal both her and Brima's true nature and come no closer to solving the riddle of why the enemy had the sudden ability to fight so well.

Swallowing down her rage, Azral instead returned her focus to Brima's access attempts. Were he to fail, he would need all the help he could get, and being distracted by flights of fancy would not aid the situation.

Brima's conversation with the Tok Govor guards ended as abruptly as it began, and he strode off with purpose towards a smaller opening in the room's far wall. Azral received a perfunctory nod as she passed the two guards, fixing her stare on the back of Brima's scaly neck to stop herself gawping at the strangeness of it all. Even so, she noticed the *uphanii* were fewer the closer they got to the doorless opening, so the orange glow was less prominent in this part of the nursery. However, it wasn't without illumination – there was a distinct blue light seeping from the area they were approaching. Despite the utterly alien environment in which Azral found herself, there was something familiar about the colour.

Brima turned just before they crossed the threshold into the strange corridor and held his position. Azral took his cue and did the same, the two effectively presenting themselves as guards to the unknown area behind them. They allowed Govor workers clutching the blue glowing spheres past them, and Azral turned to watch a handful of the scurrying creatures disappear into a series of antechambers down a long, narrow corridor. Turning back, she beheld yet more Tok Govor entering the maturation chamber and, directed by the two guards they had successfully avoided on the far side of the room, some of the creatures began to file towards the cocoons positioned around the outer four walls.

Her eye was drawn to her shadow suddenly jumping before her as a series of brilliant blue flashes came from the corridor behind her, and she looked over to Brima who, having clearly seen the same thing, signed for her to wait until more Tok Govor assembled in front of them to mask their movement. Within moments, a line following the square shape of the room began to form, creating a barrier between the vat and the sarcophagi arranged around the walls.

Whether it was an honour guard or additional security measure, Azral could not tell. All she knew was she and Brima were now effectively hidden from the frenzied activity within the nursery, allowing them to step back into the corridor unseen.

As they crept backwards into the soft blue glow, Azral passed a series of open pens, all of which had a collection of spheres lined up on benches. Each had a tube connecting it to the next, allowing fluids to decant from left to right. Released from their rope protective webbing, the now exposed glass orbs revealed their contents, a bright blue liquid that, with each new orb to its left, changed colour in stages until the final orb on the right.

This was the same green as the fluid she saw poured into the top of the huge vat in the maturation chamber, so it was obvious the orb's original blue contents taken from the flying contraptions were undergoing some kind of slow transformational process, but from what to what? Azral threw Brima a glance. He stared at the pen transfixed, and it took Azral several nudges to get him to break his attention.

A single Govor worker squeezed past, breaking Brima's concentration. Throwing the two a curious look, the creature busied itself checking the spheres, muttering low incantations as it did so. When it began chanting, Brima stiffened. Azral signed to ask what significance the words had, and Brima angrily silenced her with a flick of his talons. Only when the Govor had left its ministrations of the orbs, thrown them another glance with a flick of its forked tongue did Brima turn to her, ensuring the creature had squeezed through the line of Tok Govor now standing with their backs to the two at the entrance to the corridor.

His signing was hesitant, as if he was struggling to express his thoughts. What he had to say would not be easy to comprehend. Azral looked to the movement beyond the steadily deepening line of enemy gathering within the nursery and turned back to Brima. There was no time to hesitate. If he knew what was happening, he had to tell her. Now. Brima signed slowly, deliberately.

The blue orbs contained the souls of their fallen brothers and sisters.

Azral stared at Brima's talons. Had she heard the words spoken, she would not have believed them. To see it literally spelled out before her did not make it any more believable.

Her own signing was an angry denial that the Mighty Keeper of Eternity would allow such a thing to happen. Brima waited for her to finish, and then continued quickly, watching the backs of the Tok Govor being pushed back perilously close to the entrance of the corridor. He had seen so much of what the Govor were capable of, even his faith in the Mighty Keeper had been shaken. But the puzzle pieces now all fitted together.

The floating devices in the cylindrical chamber beyond had been used to intercept the souls of their fellow warriors as they had ascended to The World Above, capturing them somehow in the orbs resting on the shelf before them. Through some dreadful alchemy, they were corrupting the spirits of their fallen comrades then adding them to the potion that created the Tok Govor. That was why the enemy she faced were so skilled in combat, and why they moved so differently to the living armour that had come before.

They were effectively fighting their own.

Azral stared into Brima's sunken eye slits and shook her head. No. That was absurd. It couldn't possibly be true. They are stealing our souls and using them against us? Impossible.

Brima looked to the floor, the scales of his Tok Govor reflecting the blue-green glow from the room opposite. Resuming his signing, he agreed it sounded ridiculous, but everything made sense. They must have known of some tribe's ritual sites and stealthily began capturing the souls from those warriors who had perished of old age or from minor skirmishes, experimenting and refining their witchcraft over unknown alternations until they had isolated the fighting spirit and removed the personal identity. That must have been what was hidden from Brima, what he had been looking to discover.

Azral's stomach lurched. To defile the body of an enemy was unacceptable, but to corrupt their very essence was unthinkable. The whole suggestion was beyond comprehension, but everything the two had seen since they approached the huge tower did, indeed, begin to make sense. Looking to the bright blue globe on the left of the room, there was no denying the colour was identical to that of the spirits she had witnessed leaving the bodies of her fellow warriors so many times.

The thought of Govor lying in wait, unseen, above their most hallowed places to steal what remained of her people on their journey to The World Above made her blood rage.

Brima stared at the orbs then shook his head. Stepping back, he turned and walked further down the corridor, claws balling into fists then extending again in a display of silent fury. Azral followed him further into the corridor of pens, blue light intensifying then dying back as the Govor process continued to strip the souls of warriors past into nothing but servants for the enemy. Azral looked behind to the corridor's exit into the nursery to the still-expanding gathering of Tok Govor then caught up to Brima and urged him to stop lest he drew attention to themselves. Brima whirled around and responded with angry, frantic signs.

He couldn't understand how he had missed the flying wings before, particularly when he had been so convinced the Govor were developing something, but under cover of darkness they would have been impossible to spot. How should he have known to look to the sky? Who could have imagined such a thing?

That might be excusable, but he had known of the Tok Govor maturation chamber for an age. It was the very same place, much smaller in its early days, from where he had stolen two discarded suits many alternations ago, nurturing and changing them into the disguises they now wore. There were so many more sarcophagi now, so many more new and deadlier Tok Govor to be born. The scale was terrifying, and there was no other way of looking at it - he had allowed it to happen.

Azral forced Brima to slow down, to calm himself as best he could, and distracted him with more silent questions. If the enemy had this advantage, why did they abandon the initial battle in which Timku was killed so quickly when they were winning, and why did they raid the Council with so few numbers? Brima looked back to the maturation chamber, past the unmoving backs of the Tok Govor waiting patiently for whatever it was they had assembled and paused to think.

Yes, he signed. It was all so obvious to him now.

The small but devastating force Azral and The Tribe Nubar had met on the borders of the Vale of Grey had left so many of their people dying because they knew they would be gathered together and taken to the ceremonial ascension sites as a concentrated group, making it far easier for them to collect many new souls from a single aerial location once they had been released to The World Above. And the raid on the Council – or, more specifically, the Repository - was clearly an attempt to learn the whereabouts of all their tribal ascension sites, thus allowing them to harvest an increasing amount of life essence and create yet more improved Tok Govor – like those undoubtedly reaching imminent maturity outside.

Brima's signing again became erratic, the realisation proving too much for him to take. How could he have been so blind? His fury mounted as Azral suddenly felt drained of all strength and emotion. She had been fighting so many different battles, in her head, her heart, her body against this alien thing that surrounded her, and it was overwhelming. Suddenly aware of just how vulnerable the two of them were, Azral pulled herself together.

The time for introspection was over. If this perversion visited upon them by the enemy was, indeed, the truth of the situation, their annihilation as a race was assured. The more the enemy killed of her people, the greater the number of lethal Tok Govor they could grow and the stronger they would become. It would be a cycle impossible to break. So, in this dreadful place at this nightmarish time, there was but a single question left to answer.

How could they fight back?

Brima stared at the orbs in the pen then back to the maturation chamber and its assembled hordes before signing to Azral. The sheer volume of Tok Govor suggested virtually all their armoured warriors were here, now, in this location to protect this new brood triggered by his attack on the tower. That showed how vital these unborn atrocities were. Having visited other Govor settlements over the alternations, he was confident this was the only maturation chamber the Govor had created. They could fight back, yes, but she had to escape this place and tell the Council of their discoveries lest his plan failed.

Azral shook her head. What plan could possibly succeed with him acting alone? He would die within a heartbeat. It would surely be better for them both to slip out unnoticed and flee, then make plans to attack the citadel with the combined might of their tribes. Brima would have none of it. Judging by the reaction of the liquids in the vat and the urgency with which the enemy had assembled to protect this place, by the time they mobilised their forces, they would be facing scores of new Tok Govor.

A handful had wreaked havoc upon their best warriors. Could she imagine what hundreds might be able to do? Besides, his time in the shadows had ended. He would die a warrior and might even be able to turn the tide of this conflict and save his people – much as he had tried to do in the past. If it didn't, he may be able to buy enough time for them to have a better chance of survival.

Reaching out to him, Azral touched his arm with an unfamiliar hand. She could not read his colours or see his face, but she could tell he was intent on carrying out whatever scheme his brilliant mind had concocted. Brima nodded in the direction past the ranks of Tok Govor over to where they had entered the maturation chamber. She needed to make her way behind the guard, past the rows of sarcophagi waiting to spew forth their dreadful contents and escape the complex through the cylindrical tower.

Azral signed one last time. She promised to tell their people Brima was a hero, that he had never turned his back on The World Beneath and should be celebrated with all the great warriors of old. Then, she wished the Mighty Keeper of Eternity would receive Brima with open arms in his upcoming battle. Brima's answer was brief and loaded with hope and determination.

So did he.

Azral stole back into the maturation chamber. Slowly, she made her way between the solitary abominations waiting besides their assigned cocoons, taking care not to trip over the thick tubes connecting the sarcophagi to the central vat. Looking between the majority of Tok Govor lined three-deep to her other side, she could see they were facing a smaller group that had assembled at the elevated base of the massive central vat containing the bastardised essence of her people.

Unarmoured Govor worked feverishly around the feeding tank, scurrying up and down its stairs, adding more green contents, checking connections at its base which shook with the violence of the reaction within the huge, elevated drum. She had no real idea of what she was witnessing, but it looked as if the process was nearing some critical, final stage, just as Brima had predicted. Despite the enormous danger surrounding her, she slowed her pace as she reached the two guards at the doorway through which they had entered, their attention also focused on the commanders orchestrating the events.

On the far side of the nursery, Azral spotted Brima squeezing through to join the front rank facing the vat. She heard a muffled command bellowed and, as one, the Tok Govor turned to face the sarcophagi on their closest wall. Thinking fast, Azral stepped into line, forcing her way in with a grunt directly opposite the last sarcophagus before the exit. Another command was shouted, and the single Tok Govor standing next to the cocoons reached clawed hands around the backs of their necks and pulled outwards.

The living armour began to part from behind, folding outwards then falling to the floor and curling inwards like a giant scaly reptile, as if it were attempting to protect itself while sleeping. Naked, the exposed Govor hosts shoved them roughly to one side with their broad webbed feet, presumably for them to die without sustenance now the more lethal versions were nearing maturity within the feeding chambers. Azral felt a tension in the air, an expectation of something terrible about to happen. For the Govor, it marked a turning point in their history. For

Azral, it forecast the destruction of her people. Panic turned to fury. Looking to the exit, she abandoned any thoughts of flight. She was here, now, and she had to do something to stop –

A roar went up behind her from the centre of the room. The exposed Govor next to the cocoons began pointing and shouting to their Tok Govor compatriots, who turned back towards the vat to see what was going on. Azral did the same and was astonished to see Brima stepping out of his Tok Govor in front of the half-dozen armoured enemy in front of the vat. Naked and defenceless, Brima launched himself at the group who, clearly shocked to see their enemy reveal themselves before them, stood in astonishment as he collided with their scaly forms.

Recovering their composure, the largest of the commanders grabbed a hold of Brima by his neck and lifted him up, staring into his eyes as he tightened his grip, then reached up and smashed his fist down onto Brima's skull plates. They shattered into fragments, and the creature discarded Brima's body to the floor behind him before barking out orders to the ranks, clearly stunned at this breach in their security.

As the Tok Govor looked to each other in confusion, Azral spotted the fatally wounded Brima dragging himself past the thick supporting pillars to the underside of the vat. What kind of plan was this of his? How could giving his life so easily help their cause? More shouts and cries went up, the rank suddenly reforming and regaining composure. One by one, they began to remove their armour, revealing themselves to the world and proving they were not another infiltrator. It was exactly the thing Azral would have done in such circumstances and, when it came to her turn, knew she was about to be revealed an imposter.

With the de-robing of the Tok Govor advancing relentlessly towards her, Azral tried to formulate a plan as she watched the outline of Brima crawling into the shadows, arrogantly discounted as a threat by the commanders who now stood, unarmoured, in front of him at the base of the vat. If she waited until she was the last suited figure in the chamber, she could potentially cause merry havoc in her armour – but as they confirmed themselves to be Govor, the ranks were already stepping back into their suits. That left her with a final choice, to flee through the cylindrical chamber out into the citadel, but she doubted she would get very far once they had realised they had another traitor in their midst.

Closer and closer, the Tok Govor peeled off in the lines to her left and right. Azral did not know what to do, so looked to Brima, now lying in the shadows beneath the vat, and cursed his name for giving up his life in such a pointless way.

But then she looked to him again. Now lying on his back, Brima reached up with shaking hands to his shattered skull plates. Despite being little more than a silhouette and unable to see his colour change, Azral knew he was parting the plates above his eyes and readying himself for death. She spoke the words that needed to be said.

"We commit our brother Brima al Duhul to the Mighty Keeper of Eternity with joy, and in the safe knowledge we shall fight together in The World Above."

Unseen in the chaos, Azral alone saw the sphere of pulsing blue light drift upwards from Brima's skull and hover above his lifeless body.

"Go."

She urged the word inside her suit. Still, Brima's soul did not ascend.

"GO!"

The light drifted upwards, disappearing into the underside of the vat.

Azral was suddenly aware the Tok Govor on either side had turned to look at her. Slowly they stepped away,

238

breaking rank, with some moving to protect the panicking, naked Govor hosts standing next to the cocoons which had still not opened to reveal the new batch. Somehow, her shout had translated to a sound, but one the enemy had not heard before. Azral was discovered, and had moments to make a decision – stay, fight and die, or run, fight and die.

She decided to stay and fight.

Those Govor still unarmoured rushed to don their living suits, while the closest Tok Govor sprang into action. Azral lashed out at the closest, knocking one into the other with the ferocity of her blow and spilling them into the nearby sarcophagus. Govor workers panicked and rushed into the fray, desperate to protect their precious facility but only getting in the way of their armoured counterparts, giving Azral a fraction more time to engage with the creatures closest to her.

Another Tok Govor charged her, but such was its anger she despatched it with ease. Their clumsiness defined them as the enemy of old, so she pressed the advantage she suddenly enjoyed with her own protective scales and considerably enhanced power even though she knew, eventually, she would face the newer, lethal versions.

Several more headed to engage with her, but an even greater number held back in defence of the cocoons as directed by the animated commanders. The two guards who had eventually let them into the nursery advanced on her, claws lashing outwards in fury, and she countered them with ease. Beneath her, she could feel a violent thrumming in the ground and as she kicked and swiped and lunged, she caught glances of the feeding tubes on the underside of the vat shaking wildly, Govor minions were swarming over the structure like insects protecting a threatened nest.

One Tok Govor landed a direct blow on her chest, but the scales did not yield. Even so, the force of the blow unbalanced her. Falling to one knee, she put a clawed hand out onto one of the tubes feeding the closest sarcophagus and felt it pulsing violently. With a heave she pushed herself upright, now grateful for all the times she had fallen over on the way to the citadel, and kicked her attacker in the chest, hurling them backwards into the advancing group.

More cries went up around the chamber, and the cocoons began to vibrate on their wall mountings. The commanders looked around the room in confusion, then split into different directions, barking orders and pointing to the sarcophagi – and to Azral, who they clearly wanted dead.

Five Tok Govor closed on Azral, and she allowed them to back her out into the short corridor connecting to the cylindrical chamber beyond. Behind them, the cocoons were rattling and shaking as if in an earthquake, the enemy's best efforts to keep them secure failing miserably. The leading two monstrosities rushed Azral, but she ducked the blows of one, took the kick from the other, then spun and smashed her elbow into one face and claws under the chin of the other.

One staggered backwards, the other fell to the floor, and the remaining three looked to each other as they rethought their advance. Azral readied herself for their assault, and just as they made their mind up to mount a simultaneous attack, the floor shook with an even stronger force. The Tok Govor halted their attack and looked to the ground but, as suddenly as it began, the shaking stopped, and silence reigned.

Without fanfare or announcement, the sarcophagi cracked open along the walls of the maturation chamber, the protective covers falling away to reveal their dreadful contents. Azral looked to the scales glistening in the soft orange light, newly bred and newly born. Without hesitation, the Govor workers eased the scaly creatures out of their cocoons and offered them to their waiting hosts, who hastily stepped into their living armour, lighter in shade than the older Tok Govor, and were immediately consumed by their protective sleeves.

Then, as one, the room turned to face Azral.

Azral fled down the short connecting passage into the cavernous interior of the cylindrical chamber. Mercifully, it seemed devoid of Tok Govor. However, the huge entrance through which she and Brima had entered was now closed and secured with a heavy log, impossible for her to lift despite her enhanced strength. Several of the Govor working on a platform looked to her as she searched for an alternative means of escape, pausing in their attachment of floating globes to one of the flying wings tightly lashed to the heavy wooden dais. Curiosity turned to alarm as dozens of their armoured brethren thundered into the chamber in close pursuit of Azral.

Charging the bewildered group, Azral kicked the first out of her way, sending it sailing into the air, and swiped a second and third, slashing their soft green throats and leaving them to stagger back, snake-eyes wide and reptilian mouths gaping as green blood fountained over their light leather armour. Looking skywards, Azral spotted a huge boulder counterbalance at the top of the chamber's open ceiling and followed a series of ropes down to an anchoring post connected to the platform. Reaching for the release lever, she was just about to jump onto the heavy wooden structure and escape to the heavens when she was smashed to the ground.

Azral rolled and tumbled, crushed under the weight of several Tok Govor who, in their bloodlust, had fallen over each other to get to her. Luckily, her suit absorbed the impact; had she been in her normal fighting armour, she would surely have been crushed or her bones fractured. Scales clacked and slid over each other, claws lashed out blindly, but somehow Azral managed to wriggle her way from under the pile, dragging herself out only to be grabbed by more waiting enemy. She felt herself lifted up and spun around, blows raining down on her from all sides. It was a strange, disconnected sensation, as if she was in a thick leather sack being beaten by sticks, and she knew it would only be a matter of time until they found a weak spot in her armour and either the Tok Govor or she would be mortally wounded by the enemy's talons. Sure enough, Azral felt her living sleeve shudder under the vicious attack and the tendrils in her gills sliding from her body.

This, she realised, was how it felt to die within the armour.

Rage flashed through her, the need to somehow get away and warn her people steeling her resolve. It was her turn now to kick and gouge and punch, but the sheer volume of enemy and the effort with which she fought quickly had her panting for breath. She felt herself weakening, her Tok Govor shuddering again and whiting out her vision. The outer shell of her armour suddenly pressed down onto her skull plates and chest, the muscle barrier failing, along with the hopes of survival for her people.

She tried to fend off the blows but it became futile as the impacts hammered her into the ground. Gasping for air, strange sensations flooded through her, and she suddenly felt cool air on the back of her neck as the armour began to peel open. What remained of her vision consisted of shadowy, moving shapes. Her world was relentless pressure, not yet pain, but that was sure to come. That she could accept, embrace even. Failure, she could not.

Azral became aware of a gap in the wall of enemy filling her dimming vision, and then another. The impacts on her shattered armour receded as the spaces became wider and, her now fully exposed back flat to the ground, her Tok Govor's vision failed completely. Lying there panting like a fish out of the river, Azral felt the armour open further underneath her, a wounded, mindless creature trying to shrivel up and protect itself from an inevitable fate. Losing control over its actions, it split apart and rolled away from her body, leaving her naked and exposed to face her inevitable death.

But it did not come.

First, her hearing returned. The huge chamber was filled with the clashing of scales and the screams of the enemy. Then her touch. The ground below her was hard, and she shivered in the night's cold because of her unclothed state. Finally, her sight. She opened her eyes and, scrabbling to her feet and crouching in a defensive stance, she tried to make sense of the confusion and turmoil before her. Govor workers were being slaughtered by the newly born Tok Govor, their talons slicing and hacking their way with abandon through the unprotected green flesh.

Most of the black wings had been trampled or crushed, with only the one on the platform next to Azral still intact. Those not marauding their way through the terrified creatures were grappling with the darker coloured mature Tok Govor, some of which fought back with equal skill and force, but most succumbing to the new-born monstrosities whose speed and power was astounding to behold, even compared to those she had seen in the attack on the Vale of Grey. Unleashed upon her people, they would wreak havoc… but why were these newly birthed soul-stealers fighting their own?

Spotting Azral's vulnerability, an older Tok Govor ducked through the melee and made straight for her, talons out and ready to strike. Azral looked around desperately and grabbed a hold of a pole the Govor used to retrieve the pulley's ropes. Weighing it in her hands, she smashed the hook off its end to form a point and waited for her lumbering opponent to close in on her. If she was lucky, it would be one of the originals and incompetent in a fight. As it feinted to the left and drew her lunge then swept in from the right, Azral realised she wasn't going to be lucky at all.

The creature hit her with full force, and she felt its talons slide into her flank just above her thigh. More out of anger than pain, she screamed a curse and spun away, the claws exiting her body cleanly. Spinning, she brought her makeshift spear around in an arc and connected with the side of its domed head, but her blow was not powerful enough to stop it swiping out and catching her breast plates. Luckily it was over-extended, only grazing the tightly stretched flesh, but Azral knew she was losing blood rapidly from the wound in her side and if the abomination landed another of equal precision and force, that would be the end of it.

The Tok Govor moved forwards, forcing Azral back towards the platform and its still-intact flying device. Probing forwards with her spear, she stumbled over the high step of the wooden structure and the creature took its opportunity to rush at her, batting her spear out of the way and sending it flying towards the thick chamber wall. Azral ducked one mighty swing but the second connected cleanly, smashing into the side of her head and knocking her down onto the leathery wing.

Smashing one of the floating orbs off its connecting rope, the Tok Govor loomed over her, savouring its victory, and raised its right knee to stamp the life out of her. Azral screamed at the creature as its foot rushed down, but the blow crashed through the platform's wooden planks to the side of her head as a new-born Tok Govor hit her assailant from nowhere, sending the two rolling across the floor.

Bleeding heavily, Azral tried to get to her feet to continue the fight, but her legs buckled and she fell to her knees. She vainly tried to stop the blood pumping from her side with her slim fingers, but it was no use. She had no way to stem the flow. Her head was already spinning so she resigned herself to the fact the wound was fatal. Leaning back, she held onto one of the pulley ropes to keep her upright and watched in despondency and confusion as the new-born Tok Govor finished off dispatching the older creatures. The battle had been short but extraordinary in its brutality and, one by one, the lighter coloured Tok Govor stood back and regarded the pile of slain bodies surrounding them.

Through foggy vision, Azral watched her saviour approach and regard her. For long moments it stood, unmoving with no sign of aggression. Azral stared back as the creature looked to her wound, then craned its head upwards to the chamber's open roof and back down again. Slowly, its fellow new-borns assembled behind it until dozens surrounded Azral on all sides of the platform in a wall of Tok Govor. Somewhere outside the cavernous tower, she could hear a great clamour in the thoroughfare leading to the structure and furious banging on the secured door, but the creatures seemed unconcerned with everything but her. Finally, her rescuer stepped forward, extended its claws and began signing.

The Tok Govor are slain, our people saved.

Azral's mouth fell open. She must be hallucinating because of the blood loss. She signed a question with a shaking hand. How could this be? A second new-born stepped forward and pushed the brake rope lever forward as the creature continued to sign and the platform rose into the air.

Brima is within us. Brima is with you.

Azral shook her head and tried to make sense of what she was being told. Rising higher as the counterweight picked up speed, she saw the scale of the carnage within the huge cylindrical chamber. Hundreds of Govor workers and older Tok Govor littered the room, but many of the new-borns had also fallen. Brima is within us?

And then, despite her thoughts sounding like echoes in a cavern, Azral understood what had happened. Brima had sacrificed himself to release his pure, unaltered soul into the alchemic mix in the vat. The strength of his life essence must have overwhelmed the Govor changes and awoken the hundreds of souls they had stolen. With this realisation, these newly born Tok Govor had overcome their hosts and slain the others.

Azral clutched onto a guide rope to maintain her balance, sorrow descending upon her like a blanket of cold guilt. She wouldn't be able to honour her promise to Brima and tell her people he had once again defeated the enemy. Shaking the darkness from her eyes, Azral looked down over the assembly who, as one, raised their arms upwards and began signing in unison.

I commit my soul to The World Above. Receive me, Mighty Keeper.

All reached behind their heads and pulled apart the living armour at the base of the neck. Then, while one hand held the flap open, the other thrust its talons into the exposed gap, killing the Govor host – if they had not already died of fright or suffocation – then tore open the head of their armour. The Tok Govor collapsed to the ground, scores of blue orbs leaving their now-lifeless hosts, casting a brilliant blue glow around the inside of the chamber as they coalesced into a single brilliant glowing sphere.

Azral felt tears run down her cheeks and, mustering the last of her strength, she shouted down to the beautiful sight beneath her.

"Go... GO!"

Collapsing onto the wing, Azral's hand brushed against one of the floating orb ropes, making it sway above her. Looking upwards through the approaching opening at the top of the tower, she could see the sun was rising, and at first could not understand why her body was bathed in brilliant blue light. But then she realised she was dying, ascending to the Mighty Keeper of Eternity. Smiling to herself, she closed her eyes.

Azral blinked. The sky was clear and brilliant, the sun

low yet pleasantly warm on her naked body. Why this surprised her, that The World Above would be any different to The World Beneath, she did not know. But what was that sound, somewhere far below, of screaming and shouting and banging and crashing? Why would the Mighty Keeper allow such a cacophony to disturb the well-deserved rest of her warriors? Azral looked to her left and saw a wooden structure with beams and platforms. To the right, the same, except the sea stretched away to the horizon behind the scaffolding. Reaching down, she felt for the lethal punctures in her side.

They had healed.

Sitting up, Azral looked about her. She wasn't with the Mighty Keeper at all, but on the battered platform which had come to rest at the open top of the cylindrical tower. Outside, past the wide platforms around the enormous structure's circumference, she could see the Govor citadel, with hundreds of the enemy running around like ants in a ruptured colony.

The blue light that had enveloped her must have been the combined souls of the fallen trapped and tricked within the Tok Govor, brought back to the light by Brima's life essence. Somehow, they had passed through her body and cured her wound on their way to the Mighty Keeper. But how could this be? She had asked so many questions over the last couple of days that would never be answered. One more would make no difference, so she satisfied herself with being grateful.

Her gaze was drawn to the floating orbs on each corner of the wing on which she sat, watching them curiously as they bobbed about in the light morning breeze. Below her, she felt the device try to lift itself from the straps tethering it firmly to the platform and put her hands out to steady herself.

Shouts and screams drifted closer, and Azral carefully leaned over the side of the platform to see a stream of Govor dashing up the staircases lining the inside of the tower's curved walls, all intent on killing her for the damage that had been wrought on their terrible plans.

Azral had already died once that day. She had no intention of doing it again.

Her fingers worked swiftly, undoing the large buckles at the front and back of the platform and allowing it to drift into the air. Arrows and spears flashed past, some of them passing through the wing and one narrowly missing Azral's leg, but as an onshore breeze pushed her faster and faster away from the tower and over the citadel towards her own lands, she laughed.

However long this contraption might stay aloft was a bonus and brought her closer to home – and the chance to tell everyone that, for now at least, their people were safe and Brima al Duhul had died a warrior and a hero.

ABOUT THE AUTHOR

Chris Dows has been widely and internationally published for over twenty-five years. His credits include a variety of independent and licensed-character comic books, and presently writes for both the Star Trek and Warhammer 40K franchises. Gaining his PhD from the University of Lancaster in 2007, he currently teaches Creative Writing at the University of Lincoln at undergraduate and postgraduate level as Senior Lecturer and Programme Leader for the Creative Writing BA.

www.ingramcontent.com/pod-product-compliance
Lightning Source LLC
Chambersburg PA
CBHW031316170626
46807CB00001B/436